The Heat
of the Moon

Books by Sandra Parshall

The Rachel Goddard Mysteries
The Heat of the Moon
Disturbing the Dead
Broken Places
Under the Dog Star
Bleeding Through

The Heat of the Moon

A Rachel Goddard Mystery

Sandra Parshall

Poisoned Pen Press

Poisoned Pen Press
6962 E. First Ave., Ste. 103
Scottsdale, AZ 85251
www.poisonedpenpress.com
info@poisonedpenpress.com

Printed in the United States of America

For Jerry

Acknowledgments

I owe my gratitude to many people for their help in bringing this book to publication and for sustaining my spirit as a writer over the years:

My husband, Jerry, a fine writer and editor, for his input and his unwavering faith in me.

Cathrine Dubie for her perceptive critiques, and both Cat and Babs Whelton for their constant friendship and encouragement.

Mira Kolar Brown for critiquing the book.

Dr. Carole Fulton, house call vet extraordinaire, for correcting my veterinary medicine mistakes.

Linn Prentis for invaluable comments on the early concept of the story.

Nancy Love for always believing *The Heat of the Moon* would be published.

Judy Clemens and Lorraine Bartlett for reading the book and encouraging me to send it to Poisoned Pen Press.

Barbara Peters and Robert Rosenwald at Poisoned Pen for making my dream come true; and Monty Montee and Poisoned Pen's cadre of manuscript evaluators who brought the book to Barbara's attention.

My wonderful agent, Jacky Sach, for service above and beyond the call.

Additionally, I am grateful every day for the camaraderie of the Sisters in Crime Guppies Chapter, especially my good friends and critique partners Carol Baier, Janet Bolin, Cristina Ryplansky, and Daryl Wood Gerber.

Chapter One

I drive slowly past a familiar house where strangers now live. Staring up the driveway like a voyeur, I watch a mother and daughter go about the ordinary task of carrying groceries from their car.

I swore I'd never come onto this street again, wouldn't be drawn to Mother's house, and until now I've kept away. My belongings were packed long ago by Rosario, our housekeeper, and removed by hired men. I've never seen the new wallpaper that covered all evidence of what happened in the kitchen and bathroom.

My sister Michelle and I let a real estate agent make decisions relating to the sale, and we weren't present at the closing. But the agent told me when the new owners would move in, and this, finally, pulled me back. I wanted to see who took our places. When we were supplanted by a happy, ordinary family, maybe I'd be able to put the past to rest.

This family came from California, and the real estate agent said in answer to my blunt question that no, they don't know someone died in the house. A neighbor or acquaintance will tell them soon enough. Most people can't wait to share a shocking story.

I look at my left hand on the steering wheel, run a finger along the scar until it disappears below my blouse cuff. What's hidden by the sleeve is too ugly to expose to other people's eyes, but I've memorized every rough inch of it.

I realize I've stopped the car in the middle of the narrow street, inviting attention, but I don't move on. The woman and her daughter, a dark-haired girl of perhaps ten, are at the far end of the long driveway, and they haven't noticed me. They swing plastic grocery bags from the car's trunk, disappear around the back of the house with them, return empty-handed. I picture the blue bags accumulating on the smooth white surface of the kitchen counters.

Something is wrong with the sun-dappled scene before me, something other than the presence of strangers, and it takes a moment for me to realize what it is. The yews along the street, which Mother allowed to grow so high that they shielded the house from view, have been chopped to no more than four feet. She would be horrified by the row of raw stubs.

My gaze is drawn upward by the arching, blossom-laden branches of a tree in the front yard. When Mother had asked what I wanted for my thirteenth birthday, I'd promptly said a weeping cherry tree. I remember leaning back against Mother, one of her arms hugging me to her, her other hand stroking my hair, while we watched two nurserymen hoist the tree into a freshly dug hole.

Happy birthday, Rachel. She'd kissed my cheek when the planting was done.

The tree is losing its spring blossoms now. Gusts of wind tear the petals free and swirl them into the street, and they drift against my windshield like pink snow. My cherry tree is the one thing I regret leaving.

Mother's house, where I spent most of my life, is an Elizabethan Tudor of brick, stucco, and timbers, set well back from the street. Although it's just minutes from the busy George Washington Parkway, and beyond that the Potomac River and Washington, D.C., the neighborhood feels hidden away, with winding curbless streets, and houses tucked among mature trees. Behind our house, the lawn and Mother's garden slope down to a wooded stream valley where my sister and I used to explore, searching for wildflowers on the banks and frogs in the water of Dead Run.

I watch the memory reel out: Michelle with a blond braid dangling halfway down her back, me with my auburn hair in the same chin-length bob I have today; Michelle carefully keeping herself clean while I scramble along collecting grime on my hands, my legs, my face. Back at the house Mother would shake her head and murmur, "Rachel, go make yourself presentable," her voice and manner so patient that I could never feel justified in believing she disapproved of me.

On the driveway the woman slams the trunk lid and she and the girl carry two last bags inside. Now they'll put away the groceries in the big pantry off the kitchen.

It's time to go. I have a three o'clock appointment at the veterinary clinic. For a living I doctor cats and dogs, and sometimes injured wildlife brought in by people who can't bear to leave nature to its own devices.

With one last look at the house—this time I know it will be the last—I drive away. I'm thinking about my sister. In her need to blame an outside force for what happened to our lives, she fastened irrationally on Luke Campbell. I can still see the hatred working under her rigidly calm expression when our conversation shifts toward him.

But it didn't start with Luke. It started with a basset hound named Maude who chased a squirrel into the path of a car.

<> <> <>

Late on a raw April afternoon, I stood at the front desk of the McLean Animal Health Clinic, adding a note to my last patient's chart. Gray rain streamed past the windows. The red mat inside the front door was sodden, and a confusion of muddy footprints, human and canine, covered the white tile floor.

The whoosh of the glass door swinging open made me look up. Young Mrs. Coleman stood there panting, her jeans and sweatshirt wet through, her short blond hair plastered to her scalp. "Dr. Goddard," she gasped. Her hands flailed. "Maude—she got hit by a car—Her leg—the bone's sticking out—"

I bolted for the door, calling back to the desk clerks, "Get Carl out front, and tell Dr. Bonelli we've got one for him."

I clambered into the rear of the Colemans' Jeep Cherokee and leaned over the basset hound. Maude's left hind leg was cocked at a crazy angle, jagged bone ripping the skin. She was conscious, her sad eyes staring up at me. Thick blood coated half her face and one of her soft floppy ears. The sweet-rank smell filled my nostrils and brought a flood of saliva to my mouth.

Gently but firmly, I pulled open her mouth to check her gum color, but I couldn't see much in the gloomy interior of the vehicle.

Behind me, out in the rain, Mrs. Coleman cried and babbled. "She saw a squirrel—not on the leash—just getting in the car—It's my fault, God, it's my fault."

Carl leaned in, handed me a soft nylon muzzle. I snapped it over Maude's jaws to keep her from biting when we moved her, then scooted to one side so Carl could position the small stretcher he'd brought. Together we slid Maude onto it, and Carl covered her with a blanket.

Grasping one end of the stretcher, I backed out of the vehicle. Carl, a young aide built like a football player, took the other end. Maude was a silent, limp weight between us.

Mrs. Coleman, sobbing loudly, followed us to the clinic's side door, then we were all under the bright lights of the treatment room. Carl took away the wet blanket. Two young female techs set to work quickly and smoothly, positioned Maude on the steel table, found a front leg vein for an IV, swabbed the surprisingly minor facial laceration.

I was listening to Maude's heart and lungs when Tony Bonelli walked in, pulling on latex gloves. "Okay," he said, peering at the fractured leg, "what have we got here? Want me to take over?"

I stepped back, rattling off what I'd found in my quick check.

Mrs. Coleman sagged against a wall and squeezed her eyes shut. I gave her a second to calm down and catch her breath.

"Maude's probably going to be all right," I told her. "I didn't see any sign of internal bleeding. Dr. Bonelli's a bone specialist, a surgeon, and he's the best one to take care of her right now. Try not to worry, okay?"

"All right," she whispered. "Okay." Then her hands flew to her face. "Oh my God! Kristin!" She wheeled in a circle, searching. "Where's my daughter?"

I clutched her arm to make her stand still. "I'll find her, don't worry. Just answer a couple of questions for Dr. Bonelli, and I'll have Kristin waiting for you out front."

She swiped tears and rain from her cheeks with the flat of her hand, then bobbed her head. As I pushed open the door I heard Tony's calm, unhurried voice asking whether Maude had been able to stand up after she was struck.

I ran to the Cherokee. The child wasn't there. She must have gone in the front door when her mother did, although I didn't remember seeing her.

I found Mrs. Coleman's three-year-old daughter in the reception area, pressed against the front of the big desk with her tiny hands clenched at her sides, her face puckered. She was invisible to the four young women answering phones and working on computers behind the desk.

"Hi, Kristin," I said, leaning down. Rain dripped from my hair. "Your mom's in the other room with Maude. She'll be out in a minute."

Wet blond curls hugged her head. Her jeans and blue sweatshirt, miniature versions of her mother's, were soaked, and one sleeve had a smear of blood across it. "Mommy," she whimpered.

I knelt before her. "She'll be back just as soon as she finishes talking to the doctor about Maude."

Her face screwed up. Her blue eyes, wide and frightened, brimmed with tears. "I want Mommy now!" She drew in a gasping breath and began to wail. "Mommy…Mommy…"

Poor kid, terrified by seeing her dog broken and bloody, then the rush, and her mother's panic. "Everything's going to be okay," I told her. "Your mommy's coming back in just a minute."

"Mommy!" she screamed.

Her cries cut through me. A stab of distress made me reach out and clasp her in an embrace. She stiffened for a second, then wrapped her thin arms around my neck. Her hair smelled of baby shampoo and rain. She was so tiny and delicate. So much like my sister Michelle as a child. How many times had I hugged Michelle this way to chase away her fears?

As I knelt with Kristin, a door swung wide in my memory and through it I glimpsed an old, half-forgotten image of my little sister standing in the rain, crying. I stared inward, caught fast by the familiar strangeness of the vision. My surroundings receded, the ringing of the phone and the faces behind the desk faded away.

Michelle stood in a great open space, menacing in its bleak emptiness. Long golden hair clung wetly to her scalp, cheeks, neck. Her hands were balled into fists at her sides. Her plea was high and thin and tremulous. "Mommy! I want to go home!"

I was no longer in the clinic, I was out in the streaming rain, and I was a child again too with nothing to hold onto but my sister. "Please don't cry!" As if from outside myself I heard my voice rising, shrill and frantic. "She'll come back, she will, please don't cry!"

Someone was trying to pull us apart. A hand tightened on my shoulder, shook me hard. Dazed, I looked up at a tall sandy-haired man with a boyish face, and struggled to recognize him.

"Dr. Goddard? Rachel?" Narrowed eyes, creased brow. "Are you all right?"

Lucas Campbell. My boss.

Suddenly I was conscious of my crushing hold on the girl and her squirming and squeals of protest.

When I released her, she stumbled backward, her eyes swimmy with tears and huge with fearful wonderment. A bloodstain blotched the shoulder of her sweatshirt.

Mrs. Coleman reappeared and lifted the girl. Still on my knees, I reached up, seized by an urge to snatch the child back from the woman. Then I dropped my arms, baffled by my own impulse.

Dr. Campbell slid a hand under my elbow and helped me to my feet.

"I told Dr. Bonelli to do whatever's necessary," Mrs. Coleman said. "I'm going to take Kristin home now." She bounced the child gently and rubbed her back.

The sight of the little girl being comforted in her mother's arms brought a bewildering wave of sorrow and longing. All I could do was nod in response to what she'd said.

Mrs. Coleman sniffled and managed a brave smile. "Maude means so much to us. We always call her our first-born." She tried to laugh, but the sound strangled in her throat.

"We'll do our best for her," Dr. Campbell said.

Mrs. Coleman walked out into the rain with her daughter, who fussed and begged, wanting to know where Maudie was, why she wasn't coming home with them.

Dr. Campbell's hand still cupped my elbow. I met his solemn gaze briefly as I pulled my arm free. Now that the fog was clearing from my head, I realized with a jolt that I was the center of attention. People in the waiting area, a woman paying her bill at the desk, all were staring at me. I caught the eye of Alison, the young desk supervisor, and she quickly turned away, long brown curls swinging around her neck. At the same instant the other three clerks unfroze and resumed their work.

I shoved my wet bangs off my forehead and tugged at my drenched, dirty, bloody lab coat, trying to straighten it. God only knew what was going through Dr. Campbell's mind. What could I say to redeem myself?

He spoke first, his voice so quiet I was sure only I could hear it. "Are you okay? You're white as a ghost. What happened?"

"I'm fine." I tried for briskness and almost succeeded. "I'd better go clean up."

"Look, if you've still got patients, somebody else can take them—"

"No, I'm finished for the day, I was about to leave. I'm fine, Dr. Campbell, really." I spun on my heel and retreated.

He let me go, but when I reached the door to the rear corridor and glanced back, he hadn't moved or taken his eyes off me.

He might have been a boy standing there, tall and lanky and handsome, wearing jeans and athletic shoes, his hair grown shaggy between cuts. But he wasn't a boy. He was in his mid-thirties, a respected veterinary cardiologist, and he'd recently bought this big state-of-the-art clinic for a staggering amount of money. I was a junior associate whose contract he acquired along with the building. I wanted his good opinion. Until now I'd been sure I had it.

I stepped into the hallway and closed the door, glad to be out of his sight.

In the staff restroom I stripped off my lab coat, dropped it on the floor, then spread my hands and watched them tremble. Blood on my fingers. Good God, I'd grabbed that child with bloody hands. Leaning over the sink, hot water scalding my skin, I scrubbed furiously.

Mommy. Mommy! The plaintive cry dragged me back to that vast open space where my sister and I huddled in the rain, thunder rumbling through the sky above us, so alone, alone and scared.

I gripped the cold hard rim of the sink and watched pink-tinged water swirl down the drain.

It was starting again. So many years—how long? Years of peace when I didn't have to fear my own thoughts, and now it was starting again. Memories, visions, dreams. I'd never known what to call them. I'd never wanted to define them. I'd wanted only to be free of them.

I had to get out of here and pull myself together. After drying my hair as best I could with paper towels, I hurried to my locker in the staff lounge.

Maude. I should check on her before I went home.

No. I couldn't. Seeing her would bring it all back, I'd get swept up again.

"Oh, for God's sake," I muttered, jerking open my locker door. This was ridiculous. I was an adult, a professional, and I'd be damned if I'd let myself behave this way.

I was yanking a comb through my hair when Dr. Campbell walked in.

"Just checked on the basset," he said. "She's stabilizing already, she looks good. No sign of internal injuries."

"Oh, that's great," I said, momentarily forgetting my self-consciousness. "How bad's her leg?"

"Comminuted fracture, just the diaphysis involved. Tony thinks she'll be able to handle anesthesia by morning, then he'll go in and put a plate on it."

"Can I do anything to help?"

He shook his head. "It's under control. Go on home."

I covered my relief with activity, dropping my comb into my purse, swinging the bag out of the locker and over my shoulder.

Dr. Campbell took a couple of steps beyond me, headed toward the coffee maker in the corner. Then he stopped, backed up and openly studied my face. I met his gaze, annoyed by this scrutiny and equally irritated at myself for bringing it on.

Breaking eye contact, I banged the locker door shut. "Don't worry about me, Dr. Campbell. I'm fine."

"Okay. Good." He watched me turn the locker's key. "You know, I wish you'd call me Luke."

How many times had he asked me to use his first name? I wasn't sure why I hadn't been able to do it, why I drew this line between us and balked at crossing it.

I nodded, gave him a quick smile and said, "Well, good night." I forced myself to add, "Luke."

"Good night, Rachel."

I drove home at dusk, up Chain Bridge Road past the low buildings that made up McLean's Central Business District, then along narrow residential streets shadowed by tall trees. The rain had slacked to a drizzle. Dark pools of water glistened in the gutters. In every yard, masses of azaleas appeared as shapeless dripping mounds, their gaudy blossoms ravaged by rain and dulled by twilight.

Alone with my thoughts, I couldn't banish the image of my little sister, a child again, crying in the rain, and I couldn't fight off the unaccountable desolation that enveloped me. The press of hot tears against my eyelids surprised me. It had been a decade since I'd cried about anything.

Then something cold slithered through me, my throat constricted, and although it made no sense at all I was suddenly desperate to see my sister, I had to get home and make sure she was all right.

Chapter Two

I was hardly conscious of parking my car behind Michelle's in the driveway, flinging open the kitchen door, hurtling past Rosario where she stood plump in a white apron at the island counter.

"No snacking from the dinner platter," she said the moment she saw me. She held out a saucer with something on it, I didn't see what. "Here is for you, special."

"Not now, Rosie."

I was already in the hallway when I heard her exclaim, "You, not hungry? Call the record books!"

I sprinted up the stairs, my footfalls muffled by the thick carpet, calling out, "Michelle! Mish! Are you here?"

Second room on the left, the door standing open. I stumbled to a stop in the doorway, grasping the frame.

Michelle sat at the dresser wearing a pink silk robe, a blusher brush in one hand. Her blue eyes were wide with surprise when she turned to me. "What on earth? Is the house on fire?"

Laughing breathlessly, I crossed to the bed, sank onto it and lowered my face to my knees.

"Rachel?" Michelle prompted. "What's wrong?"

Straightening, I shook my head. I was amazed by my own behavior, and couldn't explain my enormous relief at seeing Michelle safe in her blue bedroom. "Nothing. Nothing's wrong."

Avoiding her skeptical eyes, I ran a hand over the cool surface of the blue satin bedspread and realized my palm was sweaty.

I took a deep breath and let it out slowly. "Are you going out somewhere—Oh, that's right. Kevin's coming over."

My odd entrance apparently forgotten, Michelle shifted her attention back to the mirror and dusted her cheeks with a blush of color. "It's ridiculous how excited I am about seeing him again. The boy I went to the senior prom with!" She laughed. "I feel like I'm back in high school, getting dolled up for a date."

I watched her apply rose-pink lipstick, then release her blond hair from a clip and shake it loose over her shoulders. My sister wasn't a school girl; she was twenty-three years old and a graduate student in psychology, following in our mother's footsteps.

When we were kids I was the one Michelle followed, padding after me through water and woods. She dutifully studied the birds I pointed out, she cringed when I handed her live frogs and snakes to examine but held them anyway, all the while emitting a faint high mewl from the back of her throat.

For years she was held fast by an inexplicable fear that I would leave her, that one day I wouldn't come home from school, that every separation was permanent. "Promise you'll come back" was always her parting plea. I would have done anything to make her feel secure.

If she was coddled and indulged, allowed to become demanding and temperamental, it was my fault as much as Mother's. I wasn't jealous of Mother's special tenderness toward my sister. Michelle was the fragile child we both doted on.

Her dependence on me lessened as we grew up, but the bond didn't go slack until I went away to vet college in upstate New York. Michelle, nineteen and already a student at George Washington University, bawled like a heartbroken baby when I got in my crammed-full car and backed out of the driveway for the trip to Cornell that first year. The sight of her sobbing in Mother's arms stayed with me for weeks and made me sick with guilt.

Her resentment over my desertion solidified like a clear sheet of ice between us. I couldn't break through it. Michelle grew closer to Mother, and gave up any pretense of sharing my interests. My summer breaks at home didn't restore our attachment.

I worked at the clinic as a tech, she took supplementary courses and worked at a school for autistic children, and we didn't see a lot of each other.

Then came my long final absence. After graduation I stayed on for a six-month internship in internal medicine, and for a year and a half I saw Michelle and Mother only briefly, at Christmas and when they traveled to Cornell to watch me receive my doctorate.

Returning to McLean for good, moving back to Mother's house, I hoped Michelle and I could form a new kind of friendship, as adults, equals. But here we were four months later, and I still had the odd sensation that we were simultaneously close and distant, intimate strangers.

I wanted her to have what would make her happy, and at the moment that seemed to be a reunion with Kevin Watters.

He'd grown up on this street, two houses down from us, but his family moved to Chicago while he was in college and we hadn't seen him since. Now he was back to take an associate position in one of the big D.C. law firms.

I'd always liked Kevin, a big handsome jock who was a lot smarter than he looked, but the last thing I wanted was to spend an evening listening to him and Michelle catch up. Sighing, I lay back on the bed and closed my eyes.

The scene arose in my mind, complete with the sounds of thunder and my sister's terrified wail, the cold wet feel of rain plastering my tee shirt to my back. I sat up.

"Mish, do you remember—" I wasn't sure how to phrase it. "Do you remember ever being left out in the rain when you were small, maybe two or three?"

She gave me a quizzical look. "Well, I remember leaving my bike out in the rain once. Does that count?"

"I'm serious. Do you remember anything like that? Stranded outdoors in a thunderstorm? You used to be afraid of storms—"

"Mother got me over that."

"But do you—"

"No, I don't, because it never happened. Mother wouldn't have let it. What brought this on?"

I shrugged. "Oh, just a dream I had."

"Dreams aren't usually a replay of reality." Michelle peered in the mirror, turning her face this way and that. "I'm so pale. I just fade away next to you and Mother. But I look like a clown when I put on a lot of makeup." Her gaze shifted to meet the reflection of my eyes. "You're beautiful with or without makeup. And you know, you ought to have a man in your life. Time's passing, Rachel. Remember your biological clock."

I laughed, startled by the abrupt change of subject. "Can it wait till after dinner? You know, I figure at twenty-six I've still got a few good years left. What do you want me to do, anyway, prowl the singles bars?"

"Don't be ridiculous." She rose and moved to her closet, shrugging off the robe on the way. "Don't a couple of single men work at the clinic?"

"Uh huh, and neither one is the least bit interested in women." But there was also Luke Campbell. He was well into his thirties and not married, yet somehow I knew beyond doubt that he wasn't gay.

"Oh, for God's sake!" Michelle cried. I looked up. She stood at the closet in her slip, holding a blue dress. "I told Rosario to take this to the cleaners. What's wrong with her?"

"I imagine she's been busy cooking this special dinner you wanted."

She yanked the dress off the padded hanger, threw the hanger on the carpet, and marched to the door. "Rosario!" she shouted. "Come up here. I want to talk to you."

"Michelle." I stood. "For heaven's sake. You've got a closet full of clean dresses."

Michelle glared at me. In a moment Rosario was at the door, wiping her hands on a kitchen towel.

"Didn't I tell you to take this to the cleaners?" Michelle demanded.

She shook the dress in Rosario's face. With calm dignity Rosario took the dress, raised her chin, and said, "I will take it to the cleaners on my way home. You will have it back tomorrow, Friday."

"If you remember to pick it up," Michelle said.

"I will remember. Good night." With the dress over her arm, Rosario walked away.

I followed her to the top of the stairs. "Rosie, I'm sorry," I said helplessly.

"You have not one thing to say sorry for." She glanced back in the direction of Michelle's room and muttered, "*La princesa.*"

I walked back to my sister. "You know," I said, "sometimes I think two different people live in there." I tapped her forehead, making her flinch. "One of them is a perfectly nice grown woman. The other one's about two years old and needs a spanking."

She tried to stare me down but couldn't. Cheeks flaming under the pink blusher, she ducked her head and said nothing.

I raked back my bangs and let out a long breath. "I'd better go down and feed my animals, then take a shower. I smell like a wet dog."

Michelle was silent until I reached the stairs, then she called after me from her door, "Put on a dress for dinner, will you?"

"*Si, princesa,*" I muttered.

❬ ❭❬❭

Company was a rarity for us, and Rosie had overreacted, filling six big vases with spring flowers and setting them about the living room. The air was sick-sweet with the clashing fragrances of hyacinth and freesia. I knew Mother would think it was all too much, so I removed four of the vases and tossed the scented flowers in the trash, leaving two arrangements of white and yellow tulips.

Mother's living room, rich and elegant, needed no embellishment. The walls were creamy yellow, the carpet was a carved Oriental, the furniture was upholstered in a Chinese design of flowers and birds on a Mandarin red background. Every little jade figurine, every porcelain bird, every candlestick and ginger jar had its place, and if Rosario shifted something when she cleaned, Mother soon moved it back where it belonged. She did this unobtrusively and without comment, maintaining the order she desired while she avoided hurting Rosie's feelings.

I'd long ago stopped wondering why Mother cared so much about the appearance of the house when hardly anyone except the three of us and the housekeeper ever saw it.

Mother arrived home ten minutes before Kevin was due, yet she managed to change and be at the front door, cool and unrushed, to greet him. She'd traded her navy business suit for an emerald silk sheath that accentuated her willowy figure and brought out the high color of her complexion. I was sorry she hadn't taken the time to loosen her hair. It was a glorious auburn, darker than mine, and gleamed when it spread over her shoulders, but for work she twisted it in a knot at the nape of her neck and it was still that way now.

"It's wonderful to have you back," she told Kevin, pressing his hand in both of hers.

Her smile was warm, her voice welcoming, but when she turned to close the door behind him I thought I caught a flicker of something in her eyes—what? dislike? displeasure? It was gone almost before I had time to register it.

Kevin, brought up to be a gentleman, gave Mother his full attention for a moment of pleasantries. I was next. "Rachel! Look at you!" he said. He threw his arms around me in a bear hug and lifted me off my feet, making me laugh. "You look fantastic!"

"I wore a dress just for you," I said, and grinned past his shoulder at Michelle.

She rolled her eyes but gave in and grinned back.

Having done his duty to Mother and me, Kevin focused on the real object of his interest. He caught Michelle's hand and they stood smiling wordlessly at each other. A good-looking couple, the delicate blond and the tall muscular young man with wavy brown hair.

I glanced at Mother. Her face was expressionless as she watched them.

All through the pre-dinner chat, then the meal itself, Michelle was absorbed in Kevin and I was absorbed in the study of our mother. After a lifetime of observing every nuance of Mother's behavior, I still couldn't figure out what she was thinking half the time. I knew something was wrong now, I knew I was the only one picking up the vibrations, but I couldn't pin it down.

Mother asked after Kevin's parents, who now lived in Chicago. She showed a flattering interest in his new position as an associate in a D.C. law firm. He asked Mother about her work, and she replied that yes, she still specialized in treating people with phobias. Kevin followed wherever Mother took the conversation, but his eyes kept straying to Michelle. Mother's gaze also slipped toward her again and again, lingering for a second each time, assessing.

Seated next to Michelle on the living room sofa after dinner, Kevin grinned and said, "Just look at the three of us, all grown up. A veterinarian, a soon-to-be doctor of psychology, and a lawyer. I could swear it was only yesterday I was picking up Michelle for the senior prom."

He smiled at her. She beamed.

"Hey," he said, "have you still got those pictures Rachel took on prom night?"

"Sure we do," Michelle said, already rising, walking to a chest in a corner. She pulled open a door and slid out a thick blue album. "We'll probably be embarrassed to look at them now."

She dropped the album into Kevin's hands and sat close as he leafed through it.

Mother's mouth tightened faintly, a shadow seemed to pass over her eyes. I remembered prom night. Mother told them to be home at the ridiculously early hour of midnight. Midnight came and went. Mother paced, fretted, and snapped at me when I said I was sure they were fine, just caught up in the fun. At a quarter to one they burst through the front door, Kevin babbling his apologies, Michelle in tears because they'd witnessed an accident in which a classmate was hurt. Mother enclosed Michelle in her embrace and said a curt good night to Kevin. She was cool to him after that, as if she blamed him for the anxiety she'd suffered while he and Michelle were giving statements to the police at the accident scene.

When they found the prom photos, Kevin hooted with laughter. "Oh, man," he said, "look at me, all puffed up in my rented tux. I really thought I was something. King of the penguins."

"God, my hair," Michelle groaned.

"Your Princess Diana phase," I said. "Short and stiff."

"Well, our kids'll get a kick out of these pictures someday," Kevin said.

I shot a glance at Mother, her frozen smile, the unsmiling dark eyes.

Kevin thumbed toward the front of the scrapbook, past photos in which Michelle and I, and sometimes Mother along with us, grew progressively younger. On the album's first page was a picture of us when we were about three and six, both gap-toothed, both with our hair in braids. Whenever I looked at that picture I was suffused with a longing that had no name or object, and I felt it now, even though I was seeing the photo upside down from several feet away.

"Hey, where are your baby pictures?" Kevin said. He grinned at Michelle. "Don't I get to see you on a bearskin rug?"

Mother stood so abruptly that all three of us looked at her. "Would anybody like more coffee?" she said. "Kevin, wouldn't you like another slice of Rosario's apple cake?"

"Oh, boy, I shouldn't," he said, a hand on his flat stomach.

Mother smiled. "Just a small piece."

He laughed. "You talked me into it, Dr. Goddard."

"I'll help you," I said, rising to follow her.

While Mother cut the cake for Kevin, I placed the silver coffee pot, still half-full, on a tray with fresh cups and saucers.

"Mother," I said, "where are our baby pictures? I'll get them out, if Kevin really wants to see them."

She turned on me a look so raw, so wounded, that I almost sputtered an apology. I'd violated an invisible boundary, and I'd done it knowingly, intentionally.

Before I could speak, Mother composed her expression around a tight smile. Her voice was flat and cold. "I'm sure he's not the

least bit interested in our old family pictures, and I'd appreciate
it if you didn't bring it up again."

I felt as if I'd been slapped. A spoon clattered to the tile floor
and I realized I had dropped it.

When I stood after retrieving it, Mother touched my arm and
said, "I didn't mean to snap at you. Let's talk later. You haven't seemed
yourself this evening. I can see something's bothering you."

Of course she could. She always could.

When we walked into the living room with the trays, Michelle
and Kevin broke off an animated conversation. "We're going
sailing on the river this weekend," Michelle said. "Kevin's parents
gave him a sailboat when he passed the bar exam."

For a second Mother's hand hesitated as she held the coffee
pot over a cup. "We have the conference on Saturday," she said,
pouring the coffee, not looking up.

"Oh, we're going sailing on Sunday."

Michelle had forgotten something, but I hadn't, and I didn't
miss the flash of hurt in Mother's eyes.

"That sounds like fun," she said. She passed a cup to Kevin.
A pause. "It's too bad you'll have to miss the Picasso exhibit
though."

Michelle's mouth rounded. "Oh. Oh no." Her eyes flitted
from Mother to Kevin. "We've got tickets," she told him. "We've
been planning—"

"You go with Kevin and enjoy yourself," Mother said, smiling, her voice pleasantly insistent. "This weather's perfect for
boating."

"Oh, Mother," Michelle said, "I'm sorry. You've been looking
forward to it so much—I mean, we all have."

"Don't make a fuss over it." Mother was still smiling. "It's
not important."

"Kevin," Michelle said, "could we do it weekend after next
instead?"

"Don't be silly," Mother said, firmly now. "I don't want to
hear another word about it. The two of you will go sailing and
have a wonderful time, and Rachel and I will go to the National

Gallery to see the Picasso exhibit. Kevin, can I wrap a slice of cake for you to take home?"

He fumbled for words, then smiled too broadly and thanked her too energetically. His eyes met mine for a second, and he looked like what he was, an outsider caught in an undercurrent that he felt but didn't quite comprehend.

Michelle slumped back on the couch, eyes downcast.

Silent, furious, I demanded of Mother, *Why won't you let us make it right when we disappoint you?* I couldn't believe she deliberately made us feel guilty, I knew that as a psychologist she would scoff at that as the cheapest kind of emotional blackmail, yet her sacrifices and generosity could turn the smallest incident into a major betrayal in our minds. I saw it when it was happening to Michelle, but seldom saw it happening to me until it was too late and I already hated myself for being a thoughtless daughter.

I hoped she'd forget about our talk, so I could go to bed and wipe out this day. After helping Michelle load the dishwasher, I retreated to my room. This space, with deep coral walls and white woodwork, with paintings of outdoor scenes, and a wide bookcase crammed full, was completely mine, and when I was in it alone I felt free. I could stack books and magazines on the floor beside the bed. I could play the music I liked, as long as it wasn't loud enough to disturb Mother across the hall.

I called the clinic to ask Tony about Maude—she'd stabilized and he would go ahead with surgery in the morning—then got ready for bed. I was turning down the covers and listening to a new Mary Chapin Carpenter album when Mother's soft knock sounded on the door. I sighed and switched off the CD player. Mother never forgot anything.

She waited until I responded before she entered.

"Let's sit down," she said, crossing to the love seat that sat against a wall. She wore a long robe of a fleecy white material, which she smoothed over her knees. Her shining hair fell loose around her face.

I sat beside her, hands clenched in my lap.

"You've been so quiet all evening," Mother said. Her fingertips brushed my wrist. "Is something wrong?"

Without warning my mind was flooded with the Coleman girl's inconsolable cries, and I felt an answering wrench in my heart.

"Something happened at the clin—" I stopped, literally, in the middle of a word, but I couldn't have said why I stopped.

"What, Rachel?" she coaxed. "What happened?"

I hesitated. What would she make of my actions that afternoon, the sensation I'd had of being transported to another place, my inability to get the crying girl out of my mind, my panicky flight home to make sure Michelle was all right?

Part of me wanted to tell her. Maybe she could reach into her psychologist's bag of explanations and pull out a neat, reassuring label for my experience, tell me how it all tied together. But for some reason I didn't understand, I was reluctant—no, afraid—to tell her about it. I knew with absolute certainty it was something I could never discuss with Mother.

I shrugged, at the same time looking away, avoiding those dark eyes that always seemed to see and understand everything. I gave her part of the truth. "A dog, a patient of mine, was hit by a car. It really got to me."

"Oh, sweetheart."

She slipped an arm around my shoulders, and like a child seeking comfort I leaned into her gratefully, let myself be hugged by my mother.

"You know," she said, "I worry sometimes that your work might be too stressful for you. You love animals so much, and you have to see all that illness and pain and death. It must take a toll."

A prick of irritation made me sit straight, pulling away from her. "Most days all I do is give vaccines and examine perfectly healthy animals. But illness and death are part of the job. If I couldn't handle it, I wouldn't be doing it."

She removed her arm from my shoulders. "Of course you can handle it."

The image of little Kristin in her mother's arms swam up before my eyes, and a deep sadness washed through me. My mind lurched away from the remembered scene, toward a patch of equally treacherous ground. Before I could check myself I blurted, "Mother, don't we have any pictures of Daddy? Kevin started me wondering."

I couldn't look her in the face. Now I'd mentioned my dead father twice in one evening, and I couldn't claim Kevin's ignorance of the unspoken rules. My pulse tapped in my temples as I waited for her answer.

She sat perfectly still, staring down at her loosely folded hands in her lap.

Unable to bear the silence, I jumped to my feet and said, "I just wondered. I can't remember ever seeing any pictures of him except the one in your room."

"I—" She stopped, cleared her throat. "It's still so hard to talk about him, even after all these years."

She paused, pressed a hand to her mouth, and I saw the glimmer of tears before she squeezed her eyes shut. The hook of guilt caught at my heart. I sat beside her, slipped an arm through hers. "I don't mean to bring up bad memories—"

She squeezed my hand. "It's only natural you'd want to know about your father. And I feel like such a fraud sometimes, a psychologist who can't talk about the painful things in her past." She gave another self-deprecating laugh, this one choked with tears.

I said quietly, "I remember his death."

I felt her tense. She looked at me, eyes wide. Her grip tightened on my hand. "You do?"

I reached back in time, but came up with little more than vague images and impressions. "I mean, I think I remember you telling us he'd had an accident and we wouldn't see him again. I remember—I remember crying. You holding me. It was hard on us all, I guess."

She drew in a sharp breath and looked away as tears came to her eyes again. "It was the worst time of my life." She paused. "I didn't think I'd survive it."

A terrible pity filled me at the sight of my proud, strong mother brought to tears by an old grief. "I shouldn't have brought it up."

"No, no, you have a right to wonder about your father." She let go of my hand, sat straighter. "And we'll talk about him sometime soon, I promise. Right now I want you to get some rest. You've had a rough day."

She'd reoriented her concern, turned it outward to me again, and I would get nowhere by pushing her with more questions. But she'd promised that soon we'd talk about my father, at long last.

"Would you like me to take you through some relaxation exercises?" she said, entirely herself again. "It'll help you sleep."

"No, thank you," I said. "I'll be fine."

"All right then." She stood and walked to the door, where she hesitated for just a second, as if she wanted to say more. But all she said was, "Good night." She closed the door as she always did, silently.

I removed my robe, turned out the lights, slipped between the sheets. Lying rigid in the dark, I closed my eyes and tried without success to shut down my mind.

The pictures. I was sure our baby pictures were around here somewhere, in an album we hadn't opened in years. I remembered looking at them, although I wasn't sure when. We must have pictures of our father holding us.

But the only mental image I had of my father came from the photo on Mother's dresser. Young, impossibly handsome, with blond hair brushing his ears in the style of the mid-seventies. Michelle, hardly more than a baby, sat on his lap. They were laughing. I couldn't remember his laugh. I couldn't remember his voice, what his body looked like in motion. I'd been five years old when he died. Surely memories of him were buried in my head, waiting to be coaxed forth.

Turning onto my side, I pressed my cheek into the pillow and again tried to empty my mind. I was too exhausted to think about these things anymore.

Taking deep breaths, letting them out slowly, I gradually relaxed into drowsiness.

I heard her crying. A high thin wail, a keening. My tiny sister stood alone in a vast open space, stood in the pouring rain and cried. A woman's sad defeated face turned toward me then faded away before I could make out its features clearly. An angry man slashed the air with his hand.

I jerked upright, hauled myself out of the dream.

I stumbled from the bed and over to a window. I pushed it open, leaned my face to a cool breeze and waited for my thudding heart to slow. The night air vibrated with the songs of frogs down along the stream, a chorus that rose to a crescendo, dropped to a murmur, swelled again. It was mating season on Dead Run.

I'd thought I was rid of them, those phantoms in my dreams. Even in wakefulness they floated through my head like tendrils of fog, impossible to catch and give meaning.

They'd left me for years, left me in peace. I'd thought they were gone forever.

I slumped onto the bed, massaging my suddenly throbbing temples. What was I thinking about before I went to sleep? The pictures. My father. What brought on the dream?

Mother was right, I was stressed. My mind was jumping from one thing to another without logic.

I needed rest. But I sat on the edge of my bed for a long time before I was willing to lie down in the dark again.

Chapter Three

I walked into the clinic shortly before nine the next morning to find half a dozen staff members, including Dr. Campbell, clustered in front of the reception desk. Alison saw me, gestured with a flourish of her arm and exclaimed, "Dr. Goddard—our bat doctor!"

For a second I thought she'd said "our batty doctor." Then I saw that the short man at the center of the group held a bird cage containing, yes, a bat. A tiny red one with a crinkled forehead, big shell-like ears, an upturned nose.

"You the doctor for wild animals?" the man asked. He raised the cage for me to see. "My cat brought it in last night."

I sighed inwardly at this variation on a tale I heard too often. Somebody's free-roaming cat was always dragging in something. I peered into the cage. The bat blinked.

"Okay, come with me and I'll look it over," I said.

"Can I watch?" Dr. Campbell asked.

"Well, sure, if you want to." A half-formed thought: was he checking me out because of what happened yesterday?

I led the way through the waiting area and across the hall to an exam room. The man with the bat chattered, telling me he'd taken time off work and driven in from Herndon after the county animal shelter gave him my name. He was young, with a brown crewcut, and wore some kind of uniform, denim pants and a gray work shirt with the name Pete embroidered in blue on the pocket.

While Luke Campbell held the cage in place on the exam table, I opened the door just wide enough to snake in a hand. Alarmed by the touch of my fingers, the bat scrabbled around on the cage bottom, tearing the newspaper lining, and began to unfold its wings. I caught both its thumbs to stop that, and removed the animal from the cage. The little body was warm in my palm and vibrated with the frantic pulsing of its heart.

Acutely aware of Dr. Campbell watching me, I riffled through the rusty-red fur looking for blood or bite wounds. I found none. Next I gently extended the leathery membrane of each wing.

The man talked nonstop and with high good humor about his cat running in the back door with the flapping bat in its mouth, about the hour-long effort by both cat and man to recapture the bat after it got loose in the house, about the damage done while this was going on. He didn't seem to notice that neither Dr. Campbell nor I was the least bit amused. My boss had developed a pronounced scowl.

"I think this little girl's just shaken up from being caught," I said. When I released the left wing it snapped back against the bat's body with a small *whap*. "If you've had her since last night, she's probably weak from hunger and dehydration by now."

He drew back, looking offended. "Well, I don't know what to feed a bat. You tell me what to give him, I'll see he gets fed."

"You won't have to worry about it. We'll take care of it."

"Hey, wait a minute. I'm gonna keep it. Just tell me what to feed it."

I glanced at Dr. Campbell, who seemed about to speak but decided against it.

"You want to keep a bat as a pet?" I asked the man.

"Well, yeah, why not? Don't worry about my cat getting it. I'll keep it in a cage all the time."

If I wasn't careful, I was going to say something truly memorable. "Mister—" I didn't know his last name. "Pete," I began again. "You can't keep a bat as a pet. It's illegal, for one thing, because you're not a licensed wildlife rehabilitator. And you couldn't take care of it properly."

He was getting impatient. "Yeah, I can."

He put out a hand for the bat but I held it out of reach. Red-faced, he dropped his arm.

Time for the heavy weaponry. "Bats carry rabies. You'd never know when it might bite you. And after you're bitten, you'd have to undergo a long series of very painful injections, which still might not prevent onset of the disease. If you developed rabies, you'd die. There's no cure."

His face had gone from red to white.

"By the way," I added, "is your cat up to date on its rabies vaccine?"

His head bobbed. "Oh, yeah, I get him his shots on time."

"Good. But you'd better examine him for bites, and watch him for any signs of illness." I opened the door with my free hand. "We'll take care of the bat. And, you know, you really should keep your cat indoors, for its own safety."

He started to protest that, but shut his mouth again. He grabbed the cage Dr. Campbell held out and left with a backward glance at the bat, a look that mixed longing and fear.

"Good grief," I muttered when he was gone.

Dr. Campbell, to my relief, burst out laughing.

"Did I overdo it?" I said, starting to laugh myself. "Somebody's bound to tell him I lied about the rabies shots. If he knew it's only two injections now, he'd probably be willing to risk it."

"You got rid of the jerk, that's the main thing. You were a hell of a lot nicer to him than I would've been." He stroked the bat's head with his index finger. The animal's eyes were squeezed shut against the glaring overhead light.

Alison's high clear voice came over the intercom. "Dr. Campbell, your first appointment is here. Dr. Goddard, your first appointment just drove into the parking lot."

He opened the door to leave, casually throwing his words back over his shoulder as he went. "Let's find some time to sit down together later. I want to talk over something with you."

The little breeze my sigh created made the bat flex her big ears and open her dark eyes. "You know what he wants to talk about, don't you?" I said. She closed her eyes again.

I turned the bat over to a technician with instructions to feed her meal worms and water, then find a rehabber who could take her back to Herndon and release her that night.

So the day began, with an animal saved and a seed of worry planted.

That morning, for the first time I could remember, I'd dreaded coming to work. All through a restless night I was plagued by dreams, some old and familiar, others new and brought on by my encounter with the Coleman child. Morning sunshine couldn't dispel the dark images. I was afraid they'd stay with me and I'd be fighting all day to keep my mind anchored in the here-and-now. I was sure everybody I worked with was still wondering what had come over me, clinging to a little girl, scaring her with my tight grip and hysterical cries.

But as I worked through the hours, the dreams faded to the back of my mind, I settled into routine and camaraderie, and I felt a little foolish for expecting my co-workers to dwell on my behavior.

Only Lucas Campbell gave any sign of remembering that I'd come unhinged in the middle of the reception area the day before.

In and out of exam rooms, passing through the corridors, returning charts to the front desk, I ran into him everywhere, and he caught my eye each time. His look was speculative, and I didn't want to consider what it meant.

The hospital room reeked of disinfectant when I went in to see Maude in mid-afternoon. Carl, on his knees cleaning one of the lower dog cages, smiled up at me and said, "The little hound dog's surgery went off real well, I heard."

Dr. Campbell stood at the far end of the room, leaning into a cage, his stethoscope on the chest of a big orange tabby cat. If I'd known he was there I would have checked on Maude later.

"Yes," I said, turning my attention back to Carl. "I'm so glad she's okay. She's one of my favorites."

"Hey, now, Dr. Rachel, you're not supposed to have favorites." Carl hauled himself to his feet, wet rags in his hands.

I laughed. "Don't tell anybody."

Luke Campbell was closing the cat's cage.

I unlatched the door of Maude's cage and swung it open. She lay motionless on her nest of blankets, her eyes closed. A thick bandage encased her fractured leg. Earlier that day Tony Bonelli had installed a permanent plate to support the damaged bone, and Maude was still groggy from the anesthesia and painkiller.

"Hi, Maude, it's me," I whispered, stroking her ear. Most of the blood had been cleaned off, but I felt tiny bumps of it, hard and dry, under the hair.

Her eyes half-opened. Slowly the white tip of her tail lifted in salute then dropped again.

"Ah, sweet girl," I said. Behind me I heard Dr. Campbell's footfalls, rubber soles on vinyl tile, coming closer. Why hadn't I turned around and left when I saw him in here? "You're going to be fine."

"She's got a good attitude," Dr. Campbell said. He'd come up on my right.

"Yeah," I said. "She's a plucky little pooch. How's the cat?"

"Better than I thought she'd be at this point. She came in this morning in bad shape. Pulmonary edema."

I motioned at Maude. "Would you mind having a listen? I was about to check her over, but since I've got a cardiologist right here I might as well make use of you."

He laughed. "Sure."

I moved aside, and he leaned over Maude, murmuring reassuringly when she stirred. With one hand he positioned the stethoscope bell on her chest; with the other he stroked her muzzle. His rolled-up sleeves exposed the ropy muscles of his forearms. I watched his eyes lose focus and his face go still as he concentrated on Maude's heartbeat throbbing in his ears.

He straightened and dropped the stethoscope earpieces around his neck. "Sounds good. Her lungs are clear, her heart's strong, respirations normal."

"Thanks. I appreciate it."

"Anytime." He was smiling, but his eyes were reflective, considering, as if he had something to say and was weighing his words.

Carl had left the room, I realized. "Well, good luck with the cat." I closed Maude's cage and started for the door.

"Rachel?" he said. "Could you stay a second?"

Reluctantly, I faced him again. *Yes, he's going to have a little talk with me.*

He raked back his sandy blond hair, then jammed his hands into his jeans pockets. His eyes met mine briefly before sliding away. "I've got a little free time and I was wondering if, uh, you'd like to walk over to that coffee place with me." He gave a short laugh. "I've never had a café latte, or whatever it's called. I'd like to expand my experience."

I was flummoxed. He wanted to go to Starbucks? And why was he suddenly acting like an awkward boy? It dawned on me that he wasn't looking forward to our talk, and he wanted to get me on neutral ground for it. Resigned, I said, "Sure." I glanced at my watch. "But I've got a patient in—"

"Forty-five minutes. I checked your schedule."

I was too surprised to say anything but, "Oh."

We walked around the corner, under flowering crab apple trees, on a sidewalk dotted white with fallen blossoms. He moved with a long-legged lope, hands in his pockets. He'd pulled on a denim jacket over his faded blue shirt. It occurred to me I'd never seen him in one of the white lab coats the other vets wore.

He asked, startling me, "Why does everybody get so dressed up for work?"

I'd have to remember that he could read minds. "Old habits. Dr. McCutcheon was fussy about the staff's appearance. Ties for the men, no jeans, but he did let the women wear slacks. Lab coats for the doctors, always."

He pulled a face as if he'd been caught at something. "I must look like a fish out of water."

"Dr. Campbell, you own the place now. You can come to work in a dress if you want to."

He laughed, a warm deep laugh, and I had to smile at the image I'd called up.

"I can promise I'll never show up in a dress, but I don't think you'll see me in a tie either. And call me Luke, okay?"

"Oh, sorry. Sure."

This was all very friendly so far.

Starbucks, a tan stucco building with green trim and awnings, was on Chain Bridge Road next to a 7-Eleven and across from an auto tire store. Despite the poverty of the view, two couples drinking coffee at sidewalk tables seemed to be enjoying the bright brisk day. A dark-haired young man raised his face to the sunshine with that goofy can-you-believe-winter's-over expression people get in spring. Inside, half a dozen customers stood in line at the service counter.

Although I'd eaten my sandwich lunch less than an hour before, my mouth watered when I breathed in the aromas of coffee, nuts, mint, chocolate. Luke's face took on a comically bewildered expression as he studied the list of coffees posted behind the service counter. "Mocha, mocha almond, hazelnut," he read aloud. "Whew. I'm just a country boy. I'm dazzled."

I smiled. "Dazzled by coffee. You've led a sheltered life."

"You choose for me," he said. "I trust you."

"Okay, let's keep it basic."

I ordered two short lattes, wondering if all this geniality was supposed to make me more receptive to criticism. I decided to beat him to it. As soon as we sat down with our coffee at one of the little round tables, I said, "If this is about my behavior yesterday, I'd like to apologize. You don't have to tell me it was pretty strange—"

"Good God," he said, sitting back. "Did you think I brought you over here to talk about that? It's the last thing on my mind. Forget it."

"Oh." What were we doing here then, drinking coffee at Starbucks in the middle of the work day?

He wasn't ready to tell me. He said, "I think Dr. McCutcheon might come storming back from Florida and kick me out in the street if he heard I wasn't being nice to you. You're pretty special to him."

"Dr. Mac's taught me a lot. He let me start working at the clinic as an aide part-time when I was sixteen."

Luke nodded, but seemed distracted. I wished he'd get on with it, whatever it was.

Instead, he asked, "Have you heard from him since he retired?"

"He called me last week, actually. He wanted to know how you were working out."

Luke laughed. "I hope you gave me a good report."

"Glowing."

"Right answer."

This time we both laughed. Then we fell silent, and the silence stretched out long enough to be uncomfortable. I didn't want to keep up the chat, though. I wanted to know what was really on his mind.

"Look," he said. That disarming awkwardness reappeared, and once he started his words tumbled out in a rush. "This is my clumsy way of trying to get to know you better. Personally, not professionally. Now, if you think this is politically incorrect, or you're involved with somebody, or you just think I'm a creep and you want me to buzz off, say so now and that'll be the end of it, no hard feelings."

I stared at him. Then I burst out laughing.

His embarrassment was too naked to miss, but he hid it quickly behind a self-deprecatory grin. "I guess that's better than a slap in the face."

"Oh, God, I'm sorry. It's not you—" I tried to suppress it, but laughter kept bubbling out. I couldn't meet his eyes. Outside the window, a young couple in business clothes held hands across a sidewalk table.

"Don't tell me you had no idea I was interested," Luke said.

Now I looked at him, and sobered. My relief at what he hadn't said gave way to astonishment at what he had said. "No. My gosh, no. I never expected—" I shook my head. "Why don't you try your coffee before it gets cold?"

He seemed glad to have something to do. He grabbed his cup, took a gulp, and coughed. "Strong," he choked out.

I resisted the urge to smile. "It's loaded with caffeine. You'll be wired all afternoon if you drink too much."

"No danger of that." He set down the cup and pushed it aside. Then he leaned on his arms, studying me. "So, have I just made a total fool of myself, or is there some remote chance we could get to know each other away from work? I feel like I have to come right out with it like this because of our professional situation. I can't exactly—" He searched for a word and came up with one I found charmingly old-fashioned. "—court you at the clinic. And the last thing I want to do is pressure you. This doesn't have any bearing on your job, now or ever."

I sipped my coffee, giving myself time to think. His whole body seemed to be straining toward me, and the intensity of his gaze weighed on me like a demand.

Why me? A useless question. Who could explain the spark between two people? Why not me?

And why not him? The truth was I'd been fighting a sneaking attraction to him since the day we met. Intellect and skill plus rangy, boyish good looks—an irresistible combination.

I yanked myself back to reality. Why not him? One very good reason: he was my boss. I was used to casual relationships that were fun for a while and ended with no bothersome consequences. A relationship with my boss could never end cleanly.

Setting down my cup, I said, "This is flattering, but—"

When I broke off, he waited a second, then prompted, "But?"

"It's not that I don't—It's just—It can get messy, seeing somebody you work with. Not that I know firsthand. I just imagine it could be. Don't you?" Good grief. I was babbling. "I mean, after they break up they still have to work together—"

He threw up his hands with a laugh. "You haven't gone out with me yet, and you're already planning the breakup."

"Well—" I shrugged. "You have to look ahead."

He leaned toward me again. "I am looking ahead, Rachel."

For a moment he did nothing but smile at me, and everything he imagined for us was clear in his eyes. All trace of the awkward boy was gone. I held his gaze. His eyes were deep blue. Heat bloomed inside me and rose to warm my skin. He slid a hand across the small table, next to mine, an inch away. I wanted him to touch me, and was afraid he would.

I drew back.

"Let me think about it," I said, and I heard the huskiness in my voice. I'd think about it, all right. I'd go wild thinking about it.

He sat back too. "Good enough."

He sipped his coffee again, winced, and we both laughed too much.

A moment passed in silence, then he said, "Will I be pushing my luck if I invite myself over to see your hawk? How's the wing doing, by the way?"

"The bird seems to think it's ready to go." Did I dare let Luke come to the house? My young, single, handsome boss—Mother would jump to conclusions and be full of questions. "I removed the binding last weekend, and he's been exercising it. He'll fly again, I'm sure."

"You did a neat job placing that pin," Luke said. "What's your rehab setup like?"

"I've got outdoor space for several large animals and some smaller cages I can set up indoors if I need them. The hawk's outdoors."

"This is in your yard?"

"Yeah. Well, my mother's yard. It's her house."

"Ah." His eyebrows shot up, and for a second he seemed to consider. "You live with your mother."

It occurred to me that it might seem odd, a woman my age still living at home. Normally I never gave it a second thought, but for some reason I wanted to justify it to him. "Yes," I said.

"It's convenient, it's near work. And my mother has a big beauti-ful house. I couldn't afford comfort like that on my salary."

"You mean your boss doesn't pay you enough?"

"Oh, I'm not angling for a raise. He has a big loan to pay off."

"You're very understanding." We grinned at each other like flirting kids. "Your father, does he live in that big beautiful house too?"

"No, he doesn't." Last night's black dreams ambushed me, made my breath catch in my throat. I lifted my cup, put it down again because my hand was trembling. With an effort I shoved the invad-ing phantoms out of my head and slammed the door. "My sister lives at home, though," I added, surprised my voice was steady.

"So, tell me," he said, "what do you do when you, uh, have a visitor and you want privacy?"

I watched his long fingers lightly stroke the side of his cup and let myself imagine his touch on my cheek, my neck. What would he be like, avid or gentle? Both, I thought. Yes, both.

"Privacy's out of the question," I said, mock serious. "We sit in the parlor and make conversation with my mother and sister."

"Very proper."

He was leaning forward, and I'd almost unconsciously moved closer. I had a quick and vivid fantasy of him ravishing me, or me ravishing him, in the middle of Starbucks on that little green table, with clerks and customers cheering us on.

"So," he said, "can I come and see your hawk?"

"Sure." I mentally ran through the possibilities. Tomorrow was Friday. On Saturday Mother and Michelle would be gone from early to late. I alternated Saturday duty with another young vet, and this was my week to be off. Rosario didn't work on the weekend. We'd have the house to ourselves.

Crazy. What was I thinking? I barely knew him. And he was my boss.

But I said, "How about Saturday? Come at noon. I'll feed you."

"Sounds great. Your mother won't mind?"

"Not at all." I'd let him think my family would be home, so he wouldn't come expecting anything to happen between us. Nothing would. Not in Mother's house, the first time Luke and I were alone. If anything happened, it would be much farther down the road, when I knew him better.

But oh, how I loved this feeling. The rush of excitement. The newness of it. The look in his eyes made the air crackle between us.

In my car on the way home that night, I pushed a Mary Chapin Carpenter tape into the player and sang *I want to be your girlfriend* along with her, jubilant, silly as a teenager, tapping time with my palm against the steering wheel.

‹›‹›‹›

Mother and Michelle were in the kitchen, putting the final touches on the dinner Rosario had left for us.

"Hey, Mish," I said, swinging an arm around my sister's shoulders. "How'd it go at the dentist?"

She looked startled by the hug. I released her quickly, feeling obscurely foolish.

"It was okay," she said. "You're in a good mood."

"It's nice to see," Mother said. She smiled at me but her slender fingers went on mincing basil leaves in a saucer. The strong minty aroma filled the kitchen. "You went out of here this morning with a cloud over your head."

"I had a good day." I stood at the sink to wash my hands and hide my smile.

When I turned back, Mother was still watching me, her expression quizzical. She dropped her gaze and sprinkled bits of basil over a bowl of cold pasta salad. "Rachel," she said, "would you bring in the iced tea?"

She carried the pasta through the doorway to the dining room.

Michelle poked at her jaw. "I'm still a little numb," she muttered. "I hope I don't bite myself." She picked up a basket of rolls from the island counter.

As I was following her out of the kitchen the wall phone sounded its soft burbling ring. I answered. It was Kevin, returning Michelle's earlier call, he said.

I handed the receiver to her.

Her voice was cool and she didn't bother with a greeting. "I wanted to let you know I won't be able to go sailing with you Sunday."

I'd started for the dining room, but this made me stop and turn around in the doorway.

Michelle said, "I've changed my mind, that's all. I just don't want to go."

A pause, then an exasperated sigh. "No, Kevin, I don't want to discuss it. I don't want to go, that's all. I'm sorry you don't understand. We're just sitting down to dinner. Good night."

She dropped the receiver into its cradle with a clink.

I stood gaping at her. She brushed past me into the dining room, sat down and spooned pasta salad onto her plate.

"Mish," I said. "What's up? What was that all about?"

"You heard what I said to him." Her clear blue eyes were wide, expressionless. "May I have some tea?"

I realized I was still holding the glass pitcher, and I put it into her reaching hands. I didn't know what to make of the way she was acting. "For heaven's sake. You were looking forward to going boating with Kevin. What happened? Why did you speak to him that way? It was downright mean, Mish."

"Rachel," Mother said, "why don't you sit down?"

I dropped into my chair. "Mish?"

"It was a mistake to accept the invitation in the first place. I shouldn't let him think I'm interested in a—a relationship." She spat out the word as if it felt slimy on her tongue.

I could have sworn a relationship was exactly what she was interested in. I glanced at Mother, who was carefully slicing a tiny section from an asparagus stalk. Turning back to my sister, I chose my words more carefully and kept my voice even. "It's just that you seemed so happy to see him."

"I was happy to see him," Michelle said. "But that doesn't mean I want to have a romance with him. It's unfair to let him believe I do."

Dumbfounded, I sat back and watched her slice her asparagus exactly as Mother did hers. I glanced from one to the other. Mother didn't seem at all surprised by any of this.

She caught my eye and smiled. "Have you made any plans for Saturday? While Michelle and I are at the conference."

I hesitated. Hiding boyfriends from Mother's analysis was an old habit for me, but I'd never before felt such an urgent need for secrecy.

I spoke down at my plate, avoiding her gaze. "I have a lot of reading I need to catch up on."

"Well, you deserve a rest," she said, "after a stressful week."

She reached to squeeze my hand, and her touch stirred guilt and a desire to be honest with her, to repay the solicitude she lavished on me. But at the same time I felt an almost overpowering impulse to draw away. The same old push and pull, as familiar to me as my own breathing in and out.

I left my hand where it was, allowed her to break the contact.

They began talking about the professional conference they would attend the next day, and terms like interpersonal press and dissociative fugue and depersonalization made me tune out. When they discussed psychology, my mother and sister were in a world I couldn't enter.

I ate my dinner, lifting my head only once to listen to the raspy bark of a fox somewhere outside.

Chapter Four

I stood at the door of Mother's bedroom. I had a few minutes, but only a few.

It was early Friday evening. Down in the kitchen Rosario made occasional clinking sounds as she prepared dinner. Michelle wasn't home yet and Mother had a late session at the home of a woman she was treating for agoraphobia.

I just wanted to look at the picture of Michelle and our father. In and out, it wouldn't take a minute.

Yet I hesitated, time slipping away, as I tried to put down the paralyzing sense of wrong that kept my hand from the doorknob. Privacy was sacred to Mother. Not even her daughters could walk into her room without permission.

"Do it," I whispered. I grabbed the knob, twisted it, pushed the door open. The room was in shadow, the deep peach color of the walls and bedcovers robbed of vibrancy.

Leaving the door ajar so I could hear anyone coming along the hall, I tiptoed across a strip of polished floor and stepped onto the big blue Chinese rug. Silently, as if someone lay sleeping in the bed, I crept to the dresser and switched on the lamp.

The photo stood beside the lamp on the otherwise bare dresser top. Leaning close, I examined the image, a moment from the past caught in a silver frame: my father holding Michelle, the daughter who was named for him. He was so young, happily unaware that his life was almost over. I pitied him in the way I might have pitied an unfortunate stranger.

He was a handsome man, with the same high cheekbones I saw every time I looked at my sister. Blond hair fell across his forehead in a bright fan. I couldn't see the color of his eyes because he was gazing down at Michelle. She beamed up at him.

How old was she? Two, perhaps. A little younger than she was in my strange memory, dream, vision, whatever it was.

I carried the picture to the bed, sat and turned on the bedside lamp. My father leaned against a tree. Sunlight dappled the grass around him and Michelle. He wore a blue knit shirt with a little alligator on the pocket, she was in a pink romper suit with short sleeves and legs. Summer. Sun and heat and the buzz of cicadas in the air. Where were they? In our yard in Minnesota, at the home I couldn't remember?

And where was I? Standing off to the side? Next to Mother as she snapped the picture? Why wasn't I in it too?

We must have other pictures of our father that included me. I'd seen them, hadn't I? Suddenly I was unsure. They certainly weren't kept in any part of the house where I would come across them. Where would they be if not in Mother's room? Her study downstairs was a possibility, but I doubted that she kept anything personal among her work-related papers. Besides, every drawer and file cabinet in that room was probably locked.

I glanced at my watch—6:25. If Mother finished her appointment at 6:30, she'd be home by 6:40.

Careful not to make a noise that would catch Rosie's attention, I pulled out the night stand drawer. It held only a box of tissues and a yellow leather bookmark. I crossed to the closet and slid open one of the louvered doors, wincing when it rumbled in its track. The scent of floral sachet enveloped me. Mother's garments were arranged by type and length: blouses, skirts, jackets, dresses, all further divided by color. I scanned the shelves to one side of the clothes racks and found nothing but shoes and purses.

Back at the dresser, I opened the top drawer on the left. It contained Mother's brush and comb, her mirror and a small cache of cosmetics.

Quickly I explored the rest of the drawers, running my hand under nightgowns and underwear. As my fingers brushed the cool silky fabrics I was reminded of movies in which people furtively searched places where they had no right to be. I stopped, repelled by what I was doing. Going through my mother's underwear. Good God.

But after a moment I was back at it. I wanted to see those pictures, the ones of me with my father. If I discovered where they were, I could come back to them tomorrow, when I'd be alone in the house for a while.

Among folded sweaters in a bottom drawer of the chest, I found a brown packet tied with string, bulging. My fingers shook as I fumbled with the knot. It came loose and shiny papers slid out of the packet, fluttered to the rug. Travel brochures. Palm trees, a white cruise ship, impossibly bright blue water.

Just then I was startled by the lilt of Rosario's voice from downstairs, the words indistinguishable but the cadence familiar: she was giving Mother a run-down of things she'd done that day, before leaving for home.

"Damn," I muttered, and knelt to scoop up the brochures. I shoved the half-tied packet among the sweaters, shut the drawer. I switched off the lamps on my way out.

I was in my room with the door closed when Mother came upstairs.

All through dinner Mother and Michelle talked about the paper on phobias that Mother would deliver at the conference the next day, the passages she still wasn't happy with, the case histories she'd used. A businessman terrified of elevators. A woman so afraid of heights that she couldn't go above the first floor in a building. People who'd been unable to leave their homes for years. All were success stories, emotional cripples now leading normal lives because of Dr. Judith Goddard. Mother seldom had a failure.

How ironic it was, I thought, that this masterful psychologist who had helped so many fearful people couldn't face her own grief for a husband dead more than twenty years. She'd told me we would talk about my father, and I believed she meant it when she said it. But would we ever have that talk, would she ever be able to answer the questions that roiled in my mind?

After dinner I went to my room expecting to spend the evening with my feet up on my little sofa, reading a veterinary medicine journal. The journal lay unopened on my lap when Mother's knock interrupted my thoughts.

The instant she walked in I realized what I'd done. In her hand she held the silver-framed photo. I'd left it in the middle of her bed.

With a sigh, I swung my feet to the floor. Why couldn't I have waited for a time when I wouldn't be rushed?

After she closed the door she stood over me, clasping the picture frame with both hands.

"Rachel?" she said, not sharply, not angrily, but in a gentle inquiring tone. "Were you in my room earlier?"

Guilt and shame robbed me of any defense. I rolled the journal into a tight tube between my hands. Peripherally I saw her sit on my bed with the photo in her lap. "Mother—"

"If you wanted to look at this picture, why didn't you just tell me? I wish you hadn't gone into my room when I wasn't here. I thought we respected each other's privacy as adults."

Just the slightest stress on the words, mixing surprise and disappointment, enough to open a wide hollow space inside me. "I'm sorry," I said, feeling ten years old.

"Thank you." She held out the picture. "Here. Why don't you keep it for a while? Look at it all you want to."

I dropped the journal onto the couch beside me but I didn't reach for the photo. "It's the other ones I'd like to see. Pictures of me with him, all of us together. They might help me remember him."

She withdrew the photo and laid it in her lap again, then began massaging her left temple. I wondered if I'd given her a headache.

"I suppose we'll have to talk about it," she murmured.

I squelched the automatic instinct to back off from anything that distressed her. "It's only natural I'd want to remember him." It sounded like an apology.

The look she gave me was odd, impersonal and assessing. "Why has this become so important to you? Now, at your age? Is this Kevin's doing?"

"Kevin? No. I've always wondered about my father."

"Always?" A dark eyebrow lifted. "You didn't come to me with your questions."

How could I have gone to her? The subject of our father was forbidden territory. Michelle and I saw the glint of pain in her eyes, her withdrawal into cool formality, when other people blundered onto the topic. We were afraid she'd withdraw from us as well if we asked about him.

But now I took the small opening she offered, although I expected the door to close quietly in my face at any second. "Maybe I'm just ready, I've reached a stage where I need to remember," I said. "I do want you to tell me things, but what I really want is to remember."

"And Michelle? Have the two of you have been discussing this?"

I shook my head. "Not lately. But maybe all three of us could talk about it together."

She rose from the bed and came to sit beside me on the couch. The photo was face-down in her lap. "You know, you were very young when your father died. Your lack of memories isn't unusual. I don't remember much about my early childhood either. Not with any guarantee of accuracy."

Her voice was soothing and reasonable, a therapist's voice, and I could imagine her speaking to a patient in that tone. I shifted slightly away from her.

"Maybe if we talk about him and I see some other pictures, I might get back a few memories, at least. You must have more pictures. That one can't be the only one ever taken."

I saw the resistance in her eyes, the tension in her jaw, and wanted to back down. But hadn't she invited this? Hadn't she just said *I suppose we'll have to talk about it?*

Twisting toward me, she grasped both my hands in her warm, strong fingers. "Rachel, I wish you'd just let it be. Please. Believe me when I tell you it's for the best."

I tried to wriggle my fingers free of hers but she wouldn't let go. "How could forgetting my father be a good thing?"

For a long moment she sat motionless, then she withdrew her hands from mine. Her gaze had turned inward, she was in the grip of some thought or emotion that washed ripples of pain over her features.

"I could never be sure how much damage was done," she said at last, quiet and slow. "Maybe you're right. Maybe you are ready to remember. But, oh, Rachel, I wish you didn't have to."

Her solemn face, her brimming eyes, the deep weary sadness in her voice suggested something terrible, and I couldn't imagine what it was. I opened my mouth, wanting to stop her from saying what I'd begged to hear. But I didn't speak, because equally strong was the need to know what she would tell me.

"When your father died in that horrifying accident—" Her voice broke on a husky note. She cleared her throat, then met my eyes. Still, she hesitated.

I ran my tongue over dry lips. "Mother, what?"

"You were devastated by it."

"But—" I faltered. "It's normal for a child to grieve over a parent's death." Somewhere far back in my mind a memory stirred, little more than a feeling, a welling sorrow. "I told you I remember crying about it. Vaguely."

She shook her head. "I'm not talking about ordinary grief. There was nothing ordinary about it." Her dark eyes peered into mine, so intently that I drew back. "You really don't remember what you did?"

I managed barely a whisper. "What I did?"

She raised her chin and went on. "It's not an exaggeration to say you were traumatized by the loss of your father. It almost destroyed you. I'll be honest, I was afraid you'd never recover. More than once I thought I'd be forced to hospitalize you, but I couldn't bring myself to do it."

I sat in stunned silence. My mind went blank, my memory offered nothing.

She squeezed her eyes shut for a second. Tears seeped through her dark lashes and ran down her cheeks. "The suddenness of it, and not being allowed to see his body, not being able to really say goodbye to him. He was so mangled—" She raised a trembling hand to her mouth. "I couldn't imagine letting you see him. I thought I was doing the right thing at the time."

She turned to me, imploring. "You have to understand, I was torn apart myself, I wasn't capable of making decisions. Now I think I might have been wrong. Maybe if you'd seen him—" She paused, took a deep shuddering breath. "It's so hard to judge what to do when a child's emotions are involved. Everything has lifelong consequences."

She hugged the photo tight against her, but when I grasped one edge of the frame she allowed me to take it. With a fingertip I traced the lines of my father's face, his shoulders, the arms that held Michelle. My father, my dead father. *Mangled.* Why couldn't I feel anything for him beyond a vague sense of loss?

Mother gently removed the picture from my hands and laid it beside her on the couch, out of my reach. "You were so angry at your father for leaving you. Anger's a normal part of grieving, but with you it was extreme. You'd fly into rages and destroy things that belonged to him."

"Rages?" I said in confusion.

"One day I left you alone for just a few minutes, I thought you were reading and I went out in the yard for a few minutes, and you tore all the pictures of your father out of the scrapbooks and burned them in the fireplace. But this one—" She glanced at the silver-framed photo. "It was in a desk drawer and you overlooked it."

My hands formed tight fists in my lap. My nails dug into my palms, but I noted the pain abstractly and did nothing to lessen it. I could imagine the auburn-haired little girl feeding photos to the flames. I could almost feel the heat on my hands. But something in me resisted, wouldn't allow me to put myself in that child's skin, to make her me.

"Don't dwell on it," Mother said. "Please. You're a grown woman now, you've made a wonderful success of your life, there's no reason to relive old heartaches."

I jumped up, stumbled a few steps on stiff legs, jerked around to face her. "How could I do something like that and not remember? How could I be so grief-stricken it made me—sick, and not even remember him now?"

She stood. I saw her composing herself, setting her pain aside to focus on mine. "Forgetting is a blessing sometimes, Rachel. Maybe you should be grateful for it."

"How can you say that?" I cried. "You spend your life helping people remember, and you're telling me to be grateful I've got this big hole in my memory—"

"Rachel." She stepped over to me, her shoes whispering on the carpet. She held me by the shoulders. "Calm down. Listen to me. If you want to remember, if you're absolutely sure it's what you really want, then I'll hypnotize you. I'll help you remember."

She studied my face for a moment, and I felt her analyzing me, assessing my state of mind. I met her gaze, determined to show the confident strength I knew she was looking for.

But I couldn't summon that strength. I didn't know what I wanted.

Sick and dizzy, I spun away from her. I had to get out of this room, this house, into the fresh air. "I'm going outside," I said. "You still have work to do on your paper—"

"Rachel. You know you're more important to me than any paper."

I was already out the door.

I walked down the back lawn, away from the circle of light on the patio, and turned my eyes to the northwest sky. It was the spring of the comet with the funny name, Hale-Bopp. This apparition in the heavens fascinated me, and on most clear nights I went out to look at it. A glowing ball with a fuzzy plume of a tail, the comet seemed to hang motionless, yet it was hurtling through space, moving, changing, shedding its essence behind it.

I shivered, already chilled. I'd come out without a sweater.

How could I forget a cataclysmic event in my life, however young I'd been? Could I trust my own mind, if it was capable of blotting out my father and my grief for him?

Thank God I hadn't told Mother about my vision of Michelle crying in the rain. Surely it wasn't a memory. Mother would never have allowed her children to be out alone and terrified in a storm. It made no sense, and I didn't want Mother to find out about it.

What would she make of the other dark images in my head? All through my teens they'd haunted me, hovering on the edge of my consciousness, inhabiting my dreams. I'd fought them, not knowing why they scared me. I'd wondered, when I dared to wonder, if something was wrong with my mind. I couldn't talk about them with anyone, least of all my mother. During those turbulent years when I was trying to pull free of her calm understanding, when I wanted to be somebody she couldn't understand, I'd hugged my secret terrors close and never allowed her to suspect them.

When they faded, I'd been enormously relieved to have them safely locked into a back room of my memory. Little Kristin Coleman, an innocent child, had somehow opened the door, and now my phantoms were roaming free again. Staring into the dark woods that loomed beyond the lawn, listening to the spring frogs along Dead Run, alternately shrill and throaty, I sensed the shadowy presence of the sad-faced woman, the angry man. And I had a clear vision of my little sister crying in the rain, wet strands of blond hair clinging to her cheeks, her blue flowered dress soaked through.

Blue flowered dress? Oh, dear God. Now my imagination was filling in details.

I forced myself to make the connection between what Mother had told me and what I alone knew. Grief had unbalanced me at a critical point in my childhood. It left a wound that had never healed. It made me do things I couldn't remember, and remember things that had never happened.

I turned toward the house and saw Mother in the rear window of her study, the room bright behind her as she peered into the dark. She couldn't see me, I knew. After a moment she moved out of sight.

I wasn't surprised that she'd wanted to protect me from memories of a ravaging grief. She'd always tried to shelter Michelle and me from the worst in life.

But I sensed that something more, something far worse, that she couldn't or wouldn't talk about, still lurked behind her words. What was she holding back? What else was she protecting me from?

Chapter Five

With a tin plate of raw rabbit meat in one hand, I walked down the driveway to the front of the house, wondering what had happened to Luke after I heard his Range Rover pull in. He was in the front yard, contemplating the blossom-heavy weeping cherry.

I watched him from the driveway. He looked different, dressed in gray slacks and a navy sports jacket over a white tieless shirt, with polished loafers on his feet. All this, no doubt, because he expected to meet my mother and sister. Today I was the one in jeans.

He turned with a smile. "That tree's a knockout," he said.

And so are you, I thought. "My mother had it planted on my thirteenth birthday. I got it in my head that I couldn't live without one."

He nodded, seeming to approve the sentiment. "Someday I'd like to have a house with one of these in the yard."

For a moment we stood smiling at each other. More than once that morning I'd almost called and told him not to come. I couldn't shake off the things Mother had said to me the night before; her words trailed through my head like smoke, poisonous and smothering. I couldn't find the lightness of spirit to play flirtatious games with Luke. But now that he was here, all slicked up and making the same general impression as a gust of fresh air, I was ridiculously happy I'd let him come.

He nodded at the plate of rabbit meat. "Lunch?"

I laughed. "For the hawk. Let's go down and see him."

The back lawn sloped away from the house, with Mother's perennial beds on either side and her roses in the sunny center. Tulips and late daffodils dotted the borders with pink and red and yellow. The rosebushes bristled with thorns and tiny new leaves.

Luke turned and walked backward for a few steps, looking up at the house, then around at the trees that ringed the yard. "How much belongs to your mother?"

"An acre and a half," I said. "All the trees on either side, and down to the stream in back. We've got our own private little woods."

"Sure beats apartment living. Now I see why you don't want to leave home."

I let that go without an answer, unwilling to start a discussion of my living arrangements.

At the bottom of the yard, we followed a path through a shield of evergreen shrubs and came into a streamside clearing. The four large rehab cages, which I'd built myself with lumber and chicken wire, were mounted on platforms four feet off the ground.

Luke peered into the cages. His thick sandy hair had been neatly combed back but now drifted across his forehead again, and the inevitability of it made me smile.

At the moment the only animal I had besides the hawk was a small raccoon with a serious bite wound on her flank. She slept out of sight in a nest box. Sunlight striped one side of the hawk's cage, but the bird perched on a pine branch at the shaded end. He cocked his head, keen dark eyes focused on the dish of meat.

I unlatched the feeding door at the bottom of the cage and slid the dish in, next to the wide shallow pan I'd filled earlier with fresh water. When I stepped back, the hawk crab-walked along the branch, talons scraping bark, and emerged into the sun. He swiveled his head to eye the food, then us.

"Hey, handsome," I said to the bird, "show us what a good job I did on your wing."

To my astonishment he lifted both wings, and in slow motion unfolded them, spread them wide. I caught my breath, waiting to see if he'd fully extend the injured one. He did.

For a moment he posed in the sunshine, displaying his reddish brown underwings and chest and his dramatic black and white barred flight feathers.

"Wow," Luke said. "Talk about having a way with animals. Does he do everything you ask him to?"

"I wish. I took the binding off a week ago and I've been waiting ever since to see him open that wing. You know, I don't think he wants company. He won't eat while we're watching. Let's go have our own lunch."

Luke straightened his jacket and brushed the hair off his forehead. "Okay. Do I look neat enough to meet your family?"

I suppressed a smile. "Actually, they're not here. They're both at a professional conference downtown."

His eyes went wide. Then the corners of his mouth tugged upward as he realized I'd invited him knowing we'd be alone. "Well, then," he said, "if we're not keeping anybody waiting, how about taking me on a walk in your woods? I haven't spent any time outdoors in so long, I've got a raging case of cabin fever."

"You should ease up on those sixteen-hour work days."

"All I need is a good reason."

When we turned I felt his hand on my back, a light touch, the briefest contact. Behind us, I heard the silky whisper of feathers and the thump of the hawk's feet on the cage floor.

The path along the stream bank was dense and cushiony with generations of fallen leaves, and so narrow that our bodies couldn't stay separated as we walked. Our arms brushed, our hands touched. Above us a fuzz of new green colored the massive oaks and maples.

"I put myself through a drill getting ready to meet your mother," Luke said. "I had a lot of small talk rehearsed."

I stopped and faced him. "Really? Why'd you think you had to do that?"

He shrugged. "I'm not great at socializing to begin with, and a psychologist—I'm sure your mother's a very nice woman, but I'd probably feel like everything I did was being analyzed."

Oh, I thought, *you have no idea.*

He was so close I could feel his heat. I took a step back and said lightly, "Then it's just as well she's not here. How'd you know she's a psychologist?"

"I asked around. Grilled a couple of the other vets."

This made me laugh, but at the same time it stirred a faint apprehension. "They must wonder why you're so interested in my family."

"Well, they didn't tell me much." He grinned. "Am I being too pushy?"

"I can't decide whether you're pushy or cute."

"Whatever I am, it got me this far."

"Just watch your step," I said.

"I'll consider myself warned."

A half-smile on his lips, he followed a downy woodpecker's jerky ascent of a maple on the far side of the stream. A cardinal's rich throaty song rose above the happy racket of other birds. "I really like this," he said. "Have you lived here all your life?"

"Not quite. We moved here when I was five, from Minneapolis." Was that true? I wondered suddenly. It was what I'd always believed, but my memory couldn't provide any proof.

"My family's farm has a creek and a patch of woods like this," Luke said.

I pulled myself back to the conversation. "Oh, right, a country boy, you said. Where is this farm?"

"Pennsylvania. And I've never milked a cow, if that's what you're thinking. It's a horse farm. Palominos and Shetlands. I'm the only one in the family who's not part of the operation."

He told me about his mother, who was financial manager for the business, his younger sisters, Janet, Emily, and Margaret, all married with kids and all expert horse trainers, and his father, who loved a good joke as much as a fine Palomino.

I could picture them: tall, lanky, sandy-haired, wholesome as wheat. Easy-going people who were exactly what they seemed. I imagined Luke laughing at the dinner table with his family.

"Rachel?"

Neither of us had spoken for a couple of minutes.

His fingers brushed my shoulder, trailed down my arm. His hand closed around mine.

A tremor went through me, delicious and alarming. I disengaged my hand from his, smiling so the action wouldn't seem abrupt. "Ready for lunch?"

He stopped in the kitchen doorway. "Whoa," he said. "I think I could fit my whole apartment in here."

I glanced around, trying to see it as he did: walls lined with pale oak cabinets, center island, breakfast table in one corner. Bigger than many kitchens, I supposed. The spotless uncluttered surfaces, the white tile floor and white walls made it seem even more spacious.

"Can I have the ten-cent tour of the house?" he asked.

Leading him through the downstairs rooms, I had the acute sensation that Mother was somehow looking on as this stranger invaded her sanctuary.

"It's perfect," he said in the living room. "I'd be afraid to touch anything."

Just as well, I thought.

When he stepped into the den, a cozy space with plump blue-striped chairs and sofa, Luke exclaimed, "A proud mother wall!"

"A what?"

He waved a hand at a collection of framed photos. "My mom's got a wall just like this in the den back home. All the high points in her kids' lives. I call it her proud mother wall. She's got one of these hanging up too." He tapped a framed letter: my acceptance at Cornell University College of Veterinary Medicine. Luke had attended Cornell ten years before me.

"Our mother lets no milestone go unrecorded," I said.

Here we were, smiling through the years: me with my prize-winning science fair exhibits, Michelle in a filmy costume for

a small role with the Washington Ballet, me in cap and gown
between Mother and Michelle, Mish in cap and gown between
Mother and me. Birthdays, Christmases, beginnings, endings.
But no photos of our father, no pictures at all from our early
childhoods.

"Your sister?" Luke studied a shot of Michelle blowing out
candles on her twenty-first birthday. "Older, younger?"

"Three years younger. She's a graduate student at GW, getting
a doctorate in psychology."

"Ah. Any special interest?"

"Autistic children."

"Whew. She must like a challenge."

"She has an incredible empathy with them. Maybe that's what
it takes to break through. I think she'll be great at it."

"You two must be good friends. Not many adult siblings
could live together in peace. And with their mother, to boot."

"Well," I said, "there are different kinds of peace."

His eyebrows lifted quizzically. "What does that mean? Or
shouldn't I ask?"

I shook my head. "Nothing. Never mind."

His gaze lingered on my face a second before he turned back
to the pictures. "Are these your grandparents?"

In my high school graduation picture I was flanked by
Michelle and Mother on one side and a white-haired couple
on the other.

"No," I said. "They're old friends of my mother's. Theodore
and Renee Antanopoulos. But I guess they've always seemed a
little like grandparents. Renee died not long after that picture
was taken, but Theo's still very much alive."

A thought struck me: How much did Theo know about my
father? He was the one person Mother might confide in. He
wouldn't repeat those confidences to me, but surely he could
give me a few scraps of information. If I dared to ask him.

"Are your grandparents back in Minnesota?" Luke asked.

The question brought me up short at the edge of a gulf.

"No," I said after a moment. "My grandparents are dead. All of them." People whose faces I wouldn't recognize, couldn't recall ever seeing. I murmured, "It's always been just the three of us. As long as I can remember."

"Are your parents divorced, or—"

"My father's dead." Suddenly I wanted to talk about him, speak of him smoothly and without reluctance, prove to myself that I could, even here in Mother's house. "He died in a car accident when I was five. He was young—" I realized with a small shock that I didn't know exactly what his age had been. I added, making a guess based on Mother's age, "A little younger than you are now."

"That's rough," Luke said. "Your mother never remarried?"

"No." Mother with a husband—impossible to imagine.

As abruptly as the urge to talk had come over me, it vanished, and I couldn't bear to speak or hear another word about my parents. I turned to the door. "Why don't we eat now?"

Luke shed his jacket and helped me carry our sliced chicken salads and iced tea to the breakfast table by the sun-brightened kitchen window. Sitting three feet across from him, unable to move away or escape his gaze, I was momentarily gripped by panic. All the reasons why this was a bad idea chattered in my head.

What on earth was I thinking when I asked him to lunch? He'd wanted to see the hawk—no, he wanted more than that, he wanted the proper beginning of something, but I hadn't been obliged to give it. An invitation for a quick visit would have been polite but noncommittal. Now I was alone in the house with him, the afternoon stretching ahead of us, no interruptions in sight.

But he was easy to talk to, and didn't resist when I nudged him away from personal questions. We compared our experiences at Cornell and swapped tales about a classic absentminded professor we'd both had. As long as I avoided looking into his intense blue eyes for more than a second, I could almost persuade myself that I wasn't actually in the middle of a first date with my boss.

We'd been talking for half an hour when he said, as if it were just another turn in the conversation, "I want to ask you about something."

"Mmm?" I said, forking a bite of chicken into my mouth.

He twisted his sweat-beaded glass round and round on its coaster. "But I'm not sure you'll want to talk about it."

I looked at him, suddenly wary. His face was serious. I swallowed the meat without chewing.

"Exactly what happened the other day," he said, "after the basset was brought in? I can't get it out of my mind, that expression on your face. Like you'd seen a ghost."

I stared at the remains of my lunch, chicken slices and sugar snap peas and carrot slivers nestled in lettuce. I'd thought he'd forgotten, but all along he'd been puzzling over my crazy behavior.

"What was it that rattled you like that?" he said. "I'm not asking as your employer. I'm asking as your friend."

I made myself meet his gaze. Warm eyes, full of honest concern. My heart lurched. What would this supremely sane man think of the turmoil inside my head? With a shrug I told him, "It reminded me of something, that's all. An old dream."

He sat forward, interested. "A nightmare? About what?" He waited, patient and receptive.

I shook my head. "It wouldn't make any sense to you."

"Try me."

I was silent, scraping my fork back and forth across my plate until the *screek screek* of silver on china got through to me and I stopped. I didn't want to offend him with a rebuff, but I had no intention of spilling out a story of dreams and strange faces and the father I couldn't remember.

When I didn't answer, Luke sat back and said, "Do you ever ask your mother to analyze your dreams?"

My head snapped up. "My mother?"

"Don't psychologists analyze dreams?"

"I don't want to have my dreams analyzed. To tell you the truth, the very thought of therapy of any kind gives me the creeps."

"Oh, that's a great endorsement for your mother's business."

That struck us both as funny, and we laughed together.

"I apologize for what happened at the clinic," I said. "You know I don't usually go around scaring little children. Let's not talk about it anymore, do you mind?"

I rose and carried my plate to the sink, silently pleading for an end to the subject. He followed with his own plate and I scraped our leftovers down the garbage disposal. The machine's growl stopped talk and allowed me to regain my balance.

When I switched off the disposal I changed gears. "I had a dream last night that I'd defy anybody to analyze. You'll be interested in this, it's the kind of thing only a vet could appreciate."

"Tell me." Hands in his pockets, he leaned against the counter next to the sink.

I paused to recall details of the dream that awakened me with giggles during the night. It had been such a blessed change from the dark questions crowding my head before I fell asleep.

"I dreamed that a horde of basset hounds showed up at the clinic. They walked in by themselves, they didn't have people with them. They filled up the reception area and overflowed into the cat waiting area, with some pretty lively consequences."

Luke smiled. "And?"

"They were all suffering from terrible halitosis, which I diagnosed as bassetosis."

I loved the sound of his laughter, so I kept going, embroidering the silly dream.

"Pretty soon the place was carpeted with dozens of bassets standing around on their stubby little club chair legs, all looking mournful and very embarrassed by the whole situation. The smell they gave off was so overpowering, and the atmosphere got so dense with it, the staff was running around opening all the doors and windows and fogging the place with air freshener."

"You're making this up."

"Absolutely not. You know how crazy things are in dreams. I remember that my biggest problem was classifying the disorder. I had to examine every dog carefully to determine whether it had smallmouth bassetosis or largemouth bassetosis—"

Luke burst out laughing, and I laughed with him, and somehow by the time we subsided to crinkle-eyed amusement he had an arm around my waist and I was leaning into his shoulder.

He sighed, brushed a finger across my cheek, and murmured, "God, Rachel, you're so beautiful."

His hand slid under my hair to caress the back of my neck, sending a shiver through me. I hadn't planned on this. Had I? He was assuming too much. I'd allowed him to.

I let him pull me closer, but I kept my arms up between us, hands splayed on his chest. His heart thudded under my palm.

"You know something I've wanted to do since the first time I saw you?" he asked, his voice husky against my ear. His cheek, slightly rough, brushed mine.

My fingers curled, clutching the fabric of his shirt.

"The first time I came to see the clinic, you were standing by the desk with your back to me, I guess you were leaving, you didn't have your lab coat on. I saw this beautiful long sexy back, and I wanted to go up and do this—"

Slowly, with a gentle pressure, both his hands traveled down my back and up again, while he kissed my neck, my cheek, my forehead, my temples. Heat rose in my skin where his lips touched.

Why not? One kiss. What was the harm in a kiss? I raised my arms, circled his neck, and met his mouth with mine. He drew me closer, locked me tight against him from shoulders to knees. His fingers were in my hair, cradling the back of my head.

Suddenly I felt once again the sharp sense of Mother's presence hovering and watching. I broke the kiss, breathless. At first I thought he wouldn't let me go, then he reluctantly withdrew his arms so I could take a step back.

A flush of color rode his cheekbones. "Zero to sixty in thirty seconds or less," he said, then scrubbed a hand across his mouth and gave a short laugh. "I didn't mean to come on so strong. It's just that—" With his thumb he traced my moist lower lip. "In my imagination, we've already…"

A shock of pleasure surged through me and heat flooded my face. I almost moved back into his arms.

Instead, I managed a smile, smoothed down my hair with shaky hands, and said, "Maybe it'd be a good idea if we took this conversation out to the patio."

For a moment he stood with one hand braced on the counter, staring down at the floor. He looked up with a slow rueful grin, all his thoughts and desires playing across his face.

"Okay," he said. "Out to the patio."

We stayed on the patio into the afternoon, sitting in the sun and talking with the safety zone of the patio table between us. His visit stretched on so long that I began to worry about Mother and Michelle returning and finding him still there.

When he said he had to check on a post-surgical patient, and rose to leave, the pang of disappointment I felt was mixed with relief.

At the front door, his jacket slung over his arm, he said, "Have dinner with me tonight. I'll come back in a while and pick you up."

"Oh, I can't, I'm sorry," I said automatically.

"Tomorrow? We can spend the day together."

"I promised Mother I'd go somewhere with her."

He sighed. "Okay. Soon, though?" He stroked his thumb across my lips. "Real soon. Maybe next time you can come visit me."

He slipped an arm around my waist and gave me a lingering goodbye kiss, but I held myself back, kept a slice of space between our bodies.

I watched him drive away, then closed the front door and sagged against it, releasing a long breath. If we hadn't been in Mother's house, we might have ended up in bed. If I'd had dinner with him, we would have gone to his apartment afterward and ended up in bed. I imagined us in a tangle of sheets, bodies naked and moist.

It would be wonderful. But he wanted far more than sex. He deserved more. I was tempted to take a chance, surrender to his openness and warmth and see where it led, but the stronger part of me was already in full retreat. Not only because he was my boss. He didn't know me. We could talk forever about books and music and work, and he still wouldn't know me. I was beginning to doubt that I knew myself.

Silence hung over the house, as it often did even when Mother, Michelle and I were all at home. A house of secrets, of unspoken things.

In Luke's eyes my life here probably seemed a comfortable convenience that nevertheless robbed me of independence and privacy. But it had been unimaginable for me to live anywhere else after I came back to McLean. Mother would have been wounded and bewildered if I'd chosen to be alone in some tiny apartment, and I wouldn't have been able to bear her stoic show of pretended understanding.

I walked down the hall, intending to tidy what little mess was left from lunch. Erase any evidence of Luke's visit.

I stopped outside Mother's study, across from the kitchen. Normally the door stood open, but she'd closed it the night before and left it closed. This was her way, I assumed, of letting me know she was still displeased by my invasion of her personal space. The thought made me feel like a punished child, ashamed and resentful.

I doubted the room contained anything I would want to see, among the old case histories Mother consulted when writing papers.

But while I had the chance I might as well take a quick look just to be sure. I'd already committed the worst offense, searching Mother's closet and dresser drawers. This would be minor by comparison.

I grasped the knob, tried to turn it. The door was locked.

I jerked my hand back. She'd never locked her study before. Did she distrust me so much that she thought I'd rifle through confidential patient records?

Or was she hiding something that she didn't want me to find?

I stared at the closed door. The clock on the living room mantel chimed five times. The psychology conference was ending about now.

I was at the kitchen sink scrubbing tiny red potatoes for dinner when my mother and sister walked through the back door.

Michelle, deep into research and composition, spent evenings at her computer with a do-not-disturb expression hung on her face. Mother was always just across the hall or downstairs. How could I get my sister alone and in a mood to talk?

In a fit of impatience, after waiting a couple of days for an opening, I walked into Michelle's room one night and closed the door. She sat at her desk in a corner, inclined toward the computer monitor, long fingers busy on the keyboard. The screen was filled with words.

"I need to talk to you," I said.

Tap tap tap. "In a minute," she murmured.

I sat on the bed, watching her. She'd tucked her hair behind her ears, but a stray strand fell across her right cheekbone. Chewing her lower lip, an old habit of concentration, she looked so young that it was hard to believe we were both adults and everything had changed between us.

I walked to the window. Beyond it lay the side yard, but I saw only my ghostly reflection in the glass. Michelle typed, engrossed in her task.

"Mish," I said, turning, "could I interrupt you for just a few minutes?"

Her hands lifted and clamped into fists above the keys. When she swiveled in her chair, her long blue cotton skirt twisted around her legs. "All right, what's so important, Rachel?"

The second the harsh words were out of her mouth, her expression softened. Sighing, she said, "I'm so wound up, all this work to finish." She pushed the tendril of hair off her face. "God, graduate school's a grind. I should've stayed home Sunday and worked on this paper, instead of going off to the gallery to look at those ugly paintings."

I sat on the bed again. "Or maybe you should have gone sailing with Kevin and relaxed a little."

I hoped this would prompt her to tell me she'd seen Kevin only a few hours earlier. An accidental meeting, she was meant to think. Since she broke their boating date Kevin had called me a couple of times, wanting advice on how to win her over. I'd given him her seminar schedule and suggested he bump into her on the street and invite her to lunch. Today was the day he'd planned to do it. During the afternoon he'd called the clinic and left a message, conveyed to me by Alison: "It worked."

But Michelle wasn't going to confide in me. At the mention of Kevin's name a furtive look came into her eyes, like a curtain closing, before her gaze flicked downward. Like me, she wanted to protect her secrets.

She tugged her skirt, straightening it. "What did you want to talk about?"

I leaned forward, elbows on my knees and hands together prayer-like. How could I get into this? Questions, a dozen of them, swirled in my head. "You're studying childhood memory, aren't you? What people remember from different ages and so on?"

Looking faintly incredulous, she glanced at the computer screen. I'd interrupted her work for this? Then she folded her hands in her lap and assumed a patient, knowing expression that she might have copied from Mother and practiced in a mirror. I was on my guard before she spoke.

"I don't remember you burning the pictures," she said. "If that's what you're about to ask me."

My mouth fell open. My suspicion was right: Mother and Michelle had been discussing me. Since Friday night I'd been keenly aware of Mother's watchful gaze, keeping tabs on my psychic balance, but when it seemed that Michelle also looked at me that way, I told myself I was imagining things, going paranoid. I couldn't stand the thought of them murmuring together over my emotional wounds.

"When did she tell you about it?" I asked. "Saturday?"

"That doesn't matter." Michelle leaned into the space between us. The strand of hair loosened and brushed her cheek again. "I understand why it upset you. Mother's sorry she told you now.

If you were able to deal with it you would've remembered it on your own. Sometimes forgetting is a blessing—"

Parroting Mother, her very words.

I sprang to my feet, wanting to run out. But need kept me where I was. "All right, since you two have been analyzing the whole thing, analyzing me, tell me something. If I was such a mess, why did Mother leave me alone? How long did it take, burning all those pictures? And where were you when I was doing it? You were practically a baby. Did she leave you in the house with your mixed-up sister—"

"Rachel, Rachel." She rose and crossed to me with three quick steps. "Mother wasn't at home when it happened. It was the nanny, she wasn't careful—"

"Mother said she left me alone—"

"Well, you must have misunderstood her. It was the nanny. Mother fired her for it."

I gaped, hardly knowing what to think. The Mother-like mask faded and in her face I saw my sister again, just Michelle, beseeching, anxious.

"Why are you bringing all this up?" she said. "Can't you see how much it hurts Mother? It tears her apart, having it all dredged up. Can't you see that?"

"Of course I can, it makes me feel awful. But we're talking about something major that happened to me. Don't I have a right to know about it? And don't we both have a right to know more about our—"

Michelle's hand slipped into mine, and I was silenced by a sudden disorienting memory of her as a tiny child, little hands reaching for me, fingers clutching.

"Please don't dwell on it," she said. "Please, Rachel. Don't torment yourself."

I backed away, freed my hand. "I'm sorry I bothered you."

As I opened the door to leave I heard her sigh, softly.

‹›‹›‹›

I paced my room, propelled by the questions that slammed around inside my head. Every answer created another doubt. Why hadn't

Mother told me about a nanny? I was positive she'd said she was the one who left me alone. Could I have misunderstood because I was upset when she told me about it? If it was a careless nanny who allowed me to destroy the pictures, could the same person have let Michelle and me get caught out in a storm? But why would our careful mother hire somebody like that?

It was such a long time ago. Maybe she'd been a different person then, not as watchful and thorough. Or was she so grief-stricken herself that she hadn't been thinking normally, had taken risks with her children? I could imagine what would happen if I went to her and tried to probe this subject. She would turn sad, reproachful eyes on me and the words would freeze in my throat.

I flopped onto my back across the bed. She was downstairs in her study, the room she now locked because I couldn't be trusted to stay out of it, the room whose closed door I casually ignored.

I was exhausted by the effort of pretending nothing was wrong.

Sitting up, I reached for the cell phone on my night stand. I had the next day, Wednesday, off work, and I would put the free time to good use. Theo Antanopoulos, Mother's old friend and former professor, might have the answers to some of my questions. I flipped open the phone and punched in his number.

"What a treat!"

Theo stood in the morning sunshine outside his red brick townhouse, one arm flung wide and waiting to hug me. His other hand leaned on a four-footed metal cane. I walked into his hug and kissed his cheek just above the white beard.

"What a pleasure to see you," he said, patting my back. "Did you have to park far away?"

That was always his first question of visitors to his Georgetown home. Parked cars lined the narrow streets, and finding a space near your destination was a wildly unlikely stroke of luck. "Not too far," I told him. "Over on N Street."

"Oh, excellent, excellent. Your young legs can handle that quite nicely."

He shifted toward his door, the pain of the movement producing a wince. Theo's barrel-chested body didn't look frail, but the brisk stride I remembered from years ago had given way to a slow shuffle. I didn't ask about the state of his knee and hip joints because I knew he considered his arthritis the single most boring topic under the sun.

When he pushed open the bright red front door, two Siamese cats jumped back with a duet of unholy screeches. "Oh, now, now," Theo chided. "Here she is, just as I promised."

When I leaned to pet them, Helen leapt onto my shoulder, where she dug in her claws for purchase and ecstatically rubbed her chocolate-brown face in my hair. Sophia shrieked and started climbing my slacks.

"Good grief." Laughing, I tried to extract Helen's claws from my skin and the silk fabric of my blouse without doing further damage. "I think it's time I gave these girls another pedicure."

"I'd be grateful, if you wouldn't mind." Theo waved a gnarled hand, scowling at it in disgust. He couldn't manage the nail clippers anymore.

"No problem." I hoisted Sophia onto my free shoulder, and with Helen balanced on the other I followed Theo into the living room.

I plopped, cats and all, onto an overstuffed green velvet sofa with shredded arms. The antique wedding ring quilt thrown over the seat cushions also had a few rips, I noticed. It was one of many quilts Theo's late wife Renee had collected, and it still carried a faint scent of the lavender sachet that always called up her smiling image.

Theo stood his cane to one side of a deep plump chair, then grasped the chair arms and lowered himself slowly to a sitting position.

"You let these animals run wild," I said, fingering a rent in the quilt's delicate old cotton. Helen stood on the sofa back and licked my hair while Sophia circled in my lap preparatory to settling.

"Oh, I know, I know," Theo said. We'd had this exchange before. "But aren't they charming little anarchists?"

Sophia answered with an ear-splitting yowl. Theo and I laughed.

"Now," he said, "tell me how things are with you."

For nearly an hour, as I made coffee for us, trimmed the cats' claws and brushed their creamy fur, I answered his questions. Theo—Dr. Theodore Antanopoulos, professor emeritus at George Washington University, semi-retired private practice psychiatrist—had known me since I was five and was acquainted with all the surface details of my life. I hoped he knew more, and would be willing to tell me. But before I could work back to the past, I had to satisfy his curiosity about the present.

Eventually, as I knew he would, as he always did, he asked, "And do you have a man in your life these days?"

Usually I gave him a quick no, or shrugged and said I'd seen some guy a few times but it didn't amount to anything. This time I hesitated, grinning in spite of my effort not to.

Theo's eyes widened. "There is someone," he said. "At last! Who is he? He must be special to put that sparkle in your eyes."

"I'm not sure what's going to happen. It's just—" I stroked Sophia, curled on my lap, then gave equal treatment to Helen, whose hot little body pressed against my right leg. "It's too soon to talk about it. I doubt anything will come of it." I glanced up. "Don't mention it to Mother, okay?"

"Of course not. A true relationship takes time, you know. You mustn't rush and make a mistake. But do give it a chance to grow. Promise me that?"

I nodded. "I'll try." Luke and Theo, I thought, would be crazy about each other. Maybe I'd introduce them someday.

Only after giving me his whole attention for so long did Theo ask about Mother and Michelle. Although he seemed fond of Michelle, the two of them had never been strongly attached, and his questions now seemed more politeness than genuine interest.

His feelings for Mother were a different matter. He loved her the way I imagined a father might love a daughter. His wife Renee had felt the same. They had no children, and I sensed that Mother filled that gap in their lives, if only partially. The one time I'd seen my mother break down and sob was the moment Renee's coffin was lowered into its grave.

I tried to talk about Mother as if everything were fine between us. "She's getting all her fear-of-flying patients together for a chartered flight in a couple of weeks," I said. "Low altitude, and not too far from the airport. She's got one person who might freak out, so she wants to stay near a runway. She doesn't want a repeat of the Washington Monument experience."

Theo threw back his head and roared. "I have to take credit for that, I'm afraid," he said when his laughter subsided. "I referred that poor man to her. But I swear I thought his only problem was a fear of heights. I had no idea he was harboring a latent claustrophobia."

"Well, it's not latent anymore. She's treating him for it now." I glanced at my watch. It was almost 11:30, and I knew he had afternoon patients to see in his K Street office. I'd better get to the point.

"Theo, did you ever know my father?"

He laughed. "Please signal the next time you're about to change directions. You've given me whiplash."

"Sorry. It's just that talking about Mother made me wonder. Actually, I've been thinking about him lately. Wondering what he was like. I guess they weren't married when she was here getting her doctorate. Her maiden name's on her degree."

He gave me an odd look, surprised and puzzled. "Good heavens, no. They weren't married until she returned to Minnesota. Rachel, don't you know when your parents got married?"

"Not really." Here was my opening, and I tried to sound as if it were all occurring to me on the spot. "Now that I think about it, I don't know much of anything about their marriage. Mother won't talk about him, you know."

Theo shifted in his chair and seemed to be scanning the books on the shelves behind me. "Well, of course, it's still painful for her. Losing him when they were both so young was a terrible blow. Terrible. She was very much in love with him."

Why was it hard for me to imagine my mother as a young woman deeply in love?

"Did you know them while they were married?" I asked.

"Oh, no. I completely lost touch with Judith after she earned her doctorate and went back to Minnesota. I had no contact with her until she called, out of the blue, to tell me her husband had been killed in an accident and she wanted to get away from home and all the reminders."

"So she came back here with Michelle and me. Just the three of us."

Theo nodded. "Yes. Well, you know about that. Renee and I helped her get set up in practice, but she didn't require a great deal of help. She's always been a superb therapist, and her reputation spread quickly."

"Did you ever meet my father?" I asked again.

"Oh, yes. He came to visit her once when she was my student. Actually, I seem to recall he was here because he had business in Washington. In any case, she brought him to one of our little buffets, you know the kind of party Renee liked to give for students and faculty. He made quite a stir among the women, as I recall."

"Really? How do you mean?"

"Oh, his looks, of course, to begin with. You know how handsome he was. It was extraordinary the effect he had when he walked into a room. But that was only part of it."

"I don't remember any of that." How had Mother felt about other women being attracted to her husband on sight?

"Well, look at his pictures and add to his handsome face a charming personality, very smooth, very self-confident, a talent for witticisms—"

He went on, but I'd frozen on one phrase: look at his pictures. Theo should know the pictures were gone, that I had destroyed them. Had he simply forgotten?

"I have to admit," he said, "I was a bit worried about Judith marrying someone so different from herself. Not just the personalities, but the backgrounds."

"How were their backgrounds different?"

He cocked his head, frowning. "Rachel, that's a very strange question."

"Why? I don't know the answer."

He studied me, his frown deepening. At last he sighed and said, a statement rather than a question, "Judith has never told you about the trouble in her family."

I went still and cold inside. "No."

He averted his head, staring into the empty grate of the fireplace. "I thought surely she would have told you by now."

I waited for him to go on, but he didn't. Bursting with frustration, I demanded, "Tell me what you mean. What kind of trouble in her family?"

"Rachel, if your mother wanted you to know—"

I jumped up, dropping Sophia off my lap and startling both cats into resentful screeches. "Why is it up to Mother? This is my family we're talking about too, my flesh and blood. What's the big secret? You obviously know. Why shouldn't I?"

He was silent for so long I thought I'd scream. But I could see him thinking. I stood with my hands clenched at my sides and made myself wait for him to speak.

"Rachel, dear girl," he said, "please sit down."

When I was on the couch again, facing him, he said, "It's not so much a secret as something your mother simply doesn't like to revisit. I've certainly never felt it was my place to talk to you about it. And since you've never asked before—"

"Theo!"

He raised a hand, asking for patience. "Judith's parents, their home life, it was a dreadful situation. Devastation and chaos. It's a testament to her strength of character that she made such a success of herself. She's an admirable woman. If you want to know more than that, you'll have to ask your mother."

I rubbed at the tiny fierce pain between my eyes. *Devastation and chaos.* I couldn't remember Mother ever talking about her family. It was one more subject that wasn't discussed in our home. But what astounded me was the realization that I'd never given them more than a passing thought. Surely it wasn't natural to have no curiosity about my grandparents, aunts, uncles—Good God, I didn't even know if I had any aunts or uncles.

I felt as if some part of me was waking from a long sleep.

Theo watched me with a kind, steady gaze. "Is this why you came to see me? To ask me these questions?"

Helen and Sophia crowded onto my lap, jostling each other and muttering resentfully. I stroked them and tried to speak in a calm and reasonable tone. "I want answers. About my family, my childhood. I don't think Mother's ever going to tell me any more than she already has. Theo, I can't remember my father at all. Or our lives before he died. I want to remember what happened to me right after he died."

I saw him flinch and draw back, his fingers tightening on the chair arms. I hurried on, before he had a chance to deflect my questions. "Was I really in such a bad state that Mother thought about putting me in a mental hospital?"

"Oh—" He hesitated, a crease cut between his full white brows. "She would never have done it, Rachel. She knew the three of you needed to be together."

"Then it's true?" My voice wavered. "I had some kind of breakdown?"

"Not a breakdown. I wouldn't use that term at all. You were very hard-hit by the loss of your father. But you were perfectly functional. You did well in school. Your mother made certain the headmistress and teachers understood the situation. They went out of their way to help you."

The faces and names came up on cue, the wonderful staff at McLean Country Day School, where I'd attended classes in a sheltered, privileged atmosphere. I remembered the headmistress and teachers, and I recalled myself in the later grades, but the first couple of grades were a blank.

"Was I difficult? Did I—fly into rages, or what?"

Theo laughed gently and shook his head. "Rages? That's a very harsh word. You had occasional outbursts, yes, early on. Completely understandable. But for the most part, whenever I saw you during that time, you were withdrawn, very quiet. Grieving, as I said. But eventually you healed, as much as any child can heal from such a loss. You have your mother's patience and love to thank for that. It turned out she knew what was best."

"How—What—" My lips felt numb, and I stumbled over my words. "What was that? What was best? Did I see a doctor? A child psychiatrist?" Somebody who might still have records.

"No. I urged her to place you in therapy with a specialist, but Judith was determined to get you through it by herself. Frankly, at the time I thought it was a bad idea, not only because you're her daughter, but because she was in a terrible state of grief herself. She believed it would be a healing process for both of you. And she was right, I must admit."

"What did she do? Did we talk, have therapy sessions?"

"Talk, yes. Hypnosis, also, on occasion. You were always receptive to hypnosis, but of course you know that."

I nodded. Mother had hypnotized me, and Michelle, many times. To calm pre-exam jitters, to cure Michelle of her fear of thunderstorms, to relieve anxiety about any big upcoming event. I'd been a willing subject until the nightmares and inexplicable visions started when I was fifteen. After that I'd refused Mother's help, however much I wanted or needed it, for fear that I would inadvertently allow her a glimpse of the crazy things going on in my head.

I sat silent for a moment, sifting through Theo's words, Mother's words, layer on layer. "Why don't I remember grieving over my father's death?"

"I don't know, Rachel."

"I'm blocking it out—I'm blocking him out—for some reason."

Theo's voice was quiet. "There's a reason for everything the mind does."

I was sitting but I felt like I was falling, tumbling through empty space. I gripped the sofa cushion on either side of me. Unsure what I was asking of him, I asked anyway. "Theo, will you help me?"

He leaned forward and stretched out a hand. His twisted fingers had little strength, but they were warm and gentle.

"Of course I will," he said. "If I can."

Chapter Six

During dinner that night my gaze stole toward Mother again and again, furtively studying her, seeing her anew. What did I know about her, really? She was the parent who'd raised me, but in many ways she was as much of a mystery as my dead father.

My head ached. I couldn't eat. I was grateful for the excuse to escape when my rehabber friend Damian Rausch arrived to pick up both me and the red-shouldered hawk.

The bird was less than thrilled about being grabbed just as he was settling down for the night, then stuck in a cat carrier and taken for a ride, and ultimately pinned on a cold steel table at the vet clinic. He protested the only way he could: he opened his beak and hissed. If Damian and I hadn't been wearing falconers' gauntlets, we might have lost a finger or two.

"Ungrateful little bastard," Damian said affably. He restrained the bird's body while I extended its wing under the tube head of the x-ray machine. Damian, who looked a little like a hawk himself with his beaky nose and hooded dark eyes, had been rehabbing raptors for twenty years, and showed none of the tension I felt at handling such a dangerous yet exquisitely delicate creature.

The clinic, closed for the night, was eerily quiet around us. From inside the cubicle housing the x-ray controls, Luke called out, "Ready. Hold it."

The machine hummed. The hawk's body vibrated with rapid breaths and racing heartbeats.

"Okay, now," Damian said. "Let him up real easy."

We synchronized our movements, slowly allowing the hawk to get to its feet and fold its wing. The bird was back in the carrier and glaring at us from behind the grilled door when Luke came out with the developed radiograph. He slapped it onto the lighted view box. We studied the white-on-black image of a hollow bone healed around a tiny metal rod.

"Looks great," Luke said, beaming at me as if he took a personal pride in my achievement.

"Not too shabby, if I do say so myself." It was the first surgery of this type I'd ever done. "When I see him flying free, I'm going to pop the cork on a bottle of champagne."

"I want to go with you when you release him," Luke said. "I'll supply the bubbly."

"Won't be long," Damian said. He hoisted the carrier off the table. "Okay, pal, let's get you to your new accommodations." He had a big flight cage where the bird could get back into hunting condition before being freed. "You ready to go?" he asked me.

"I'll give you a ride home, Rachel," Luke put in quickly. "It's right on my way."

My house wasn't even close to his route home. I hesitated, reading the question in his eyes. For the last two days I'd avoided being alone with him for a second, and it had felt like a form of self-torture. The so-near-and-yet-so-far method. Doubts clamored in my head, but suddenly I wanted him so much I thought I couldn't get through another hour without him.

"Okay, thanks," I said, trying to sound casual.

Damian glanced between us, then nodded with the same knowing expression I'd been seeing on my coworkers' faces. Luke and I hadn't so much as touched since his visit to the house, but we must be giving off some kind of signals. Alison, the desk manager, had even taken to wiggling her dark eyebrows at me when Luke walked by.

When Damian was gone, we were alone on the darkened main floor of the clinic. Under the pale security light in the reception area, Luke put his arms around me and said, "I missed you today. The place seems kind of empty when I know I'm not going to see you coming around a corner." His lips skimmed mine. "You know I'll take you straight back to your house if you want me to, but—" His smile was nervous, boyish. "Will you come home with me for a while first?"

The uncertainty and longing in his voice brought a rush of warmth that dissolved my doubts. "Yes," I said, and put my arms around his neck and kissed him. I was going to do this, and I wouldn't let myself think about anything else.

〉〉〉

He lived in a highrise off Leesburg Pike, in a congested area ten minutes from the clinic and a world away from the quiet streets of McLean.

Going up in the elevator, Luke pulled me into his arms for a kiss that lasted to the eighth floor. The door opened on a white-haired woman carrying a small plastic basket of laundry. When we separated quickly, she smiled and said, "Don't stop on my account. It looks like fun."

Laughing, his arm around my shoulders and mine around his waist, we walked down the long hallway to his door.

It was hard to believe he'd lived in this apartment for weeks. An open carton of books sat beside a half-filled bookcase. No pictures on the white walls. Venetian blinds, no curtains, on the wide window. Half a dozen cardboard boxes formed a ragged pyramid in a corner. The beige-striped couch and two chairs seemed marooned on the forest green area rug, trying their best to look cozy.

"Not exactly what you're used to, I know," Luke said. He stood beside me, hands in his pockets, as I surveyed the room.

"Well," I said. "It's very…clean."

He laughed. "I can't get real excited about decorating when I'm the only one who ever sees the place." He slid a hand under my hair and caressed the back of my neck. "Now, if I could count on regular company, I'd make it more inviting."

I turned into his arms, letting my shoulderbag slide to the floor. We kissed, then I said, my voice muffled against his shoulder, "I should call home and tell them I'll be a while getting back."

"Ah, I like the sound of that. The phone's right there." He pointed to a desk that also held a computer.

If Mother's Caller I.D. registered Luke's number I would be barraged with questions. "I'll use my cell phone," I said, reaching for my shoulderbag.

While I talked to Mother, Luke's arms circled my waist from behind and he trailed kisses down the side of my neck. Somehow I managed to keep my voice cool and even.

After I snapped the phone shut, Luke asked, "Want something to drink?"

"Not a thing." I dropped the phone into my purse and faced him.

"How about a snack? I've got a bag of cookies that might still be fresh."

I laughed. "Very tempting, but no, thanks."

"I'm just trying to be a polite host," he murmured against my ear.

"Oh, Miss Manners would give you an A-plus." Nuzzling his neck, I drew in the wonderful smell of his skin, like grass and wheat and clean air on a hot day.

The top buttons of his blue shirt were open, showing a pale gray tee shirt with some sort of picture on it. With a fingertip I traced the outline of a canine ear. "What species are you wearing?"

He grinned down at me as I undid the rest of the buttons to his waistline and pulled his shirt open. A gray wolf looked back at me with a disarmingly friendly expression. "A wolf fancier, huh?" I said. "I like wolves myself."

"Is that right?"

He smoothly freed my shirt from my jeans waist and slipped a hand beneath it, onto my bare skin. His hand felt hot, but his touch made me shiver.

"I went to the Wolf Sanctuary once," I said, "and did the twilight howl thing." I kissed his neck and ran my fingers up through his hair. It looked coarse but it felt silky. "You know, when they get the people and wolves howling together."

His tongue flicked my earlobe. "I've got a tape of wolf howls," he said. "Want to hear it?"

"Well, I had my heart set on seeing your etchings—"

"The tape's in the bedroom."

"What luck."

His bedroom looked as unfinished as the living room. The bed was made with white sheets and a couple of pillows. We removed our shoes and stretched out, propped on our elbows, the tape player between us. The glow from the lamp behind him turned Luke's hair a soft gold.

From the recording a single wolf's voice lifted in a long deep-throated undulating howl. One by one other voices joined in, rising and falling in an ecstatic chorus, like a gospel choir at Sunday service, carried away by the joy of being alive.

I began to howl with them, and so did Luke, both of us lying back and baying at the ceiling until we burst out laughing.

"The neighbors are going to call the cops," he sputtered. "God only knows what they think we're doing in here."

He clicked the tape player off and laid it on the bedside table, his laughter settling to a smile. He drew his thumb across my lips and looked into my eyes for a long time. "Are you sure about this?" he said at last.

Was I? A stab of fear made me hesitate. But then I said, "Yes. Yes, I'm sure."

We undressed each other slowly, fabric slipping over skin, hands exploring. No one had ever touched me the way Luke did, lingering, savoring the fullness of my breast in his palm, the curve of my hips, tasting the hollow at the base of my throat.

I moaned shamelessly as he kissed my nipples, my stomach, my thighs, and I cried out when he touched his tongue to the ache between my legs.

When he slid inside me a sharp flash of alarm froze me and I jerked my head aside so he wouldn't see my face.

"What's wrong?" he asked hoarsely. "Look at me, Rachel. What is it?"

I turned my head, focused for a moment on his chin before raising my eyes. His gaze mixed tenderness and desire. The moment of anxiety melted away, and without answering him I drew his head down and covered his mouth with mine.

He began to move inside me. I locked my legs around him and buried my face against his shoulder as he made love to me.

Afterward I lay in his arms, knowing that everything had changed.

He brushed a damp strand of hair from my cheek and kissed my forehead. "Are you okay?" he asked softly.

I skimmed my fingertips over the scratchy blond stubble on his cheek, my voice stolen by a clutch of unnameable dread. How easily he had become precious to me. How easily he might wound me, even unwittingly.

For a moment he rubbed my back, his hand moving up and down in a gentle caress, then he said in a quiet voice, "What are you afraid of, Rachel? I can tell you're afraid of something."

I pulled away and sat up.

"You're not still worried about this affecting your job, are you?" Luke said.

I shook my head, but said nothing because I didn't know what to say.

"I wonder," he murmured, almost to himself.

His fingers traced the bumps of my spine. Suddenly wanting to cover myself, I tried to draw the sheet around me, but it was caught underneath us.

He sat up beside me. His hand massaged my shoulder. "Have you been involved with somebody who hurt you?"

I shook my head. No one had ever hurt me because no one had ever gotten close enough. I thought fleetingly of the other men I'd been with, two of them, guys my own age, totally wrapped up in working toward their futures, as self-absorbed as I was. A lot of fun, no demands, easy partings. We hadn't made love; we'd had sex. No other man had touched my heart the way Luke did.

"Whatever's bothering you, I want you to tell me," he said. He cupped my chin in his hand and turned my head toward him. "I'm falling in love with you, Rachel."

I stiffened. "How can you be sure of that? It's too soon—"

"It's about time, I'd say. I'm thirty-six years old and I've never found anybody I wanted to be with, till now. I don't jump into things like this. I'm sure about how I feel."

"But you hardly know me. Maybe I'm not the person you think I am."

"I doubt that. And we've got all the time in the world to fill in the blanks. I want to know everything about you, nothing left out."

Oh, do you? I could tell him a few things that might break his fall and send him off to find some nice uncomplicated girl with a normal family. If he recoiled—well, better now than later, when it would hurt me more.

But I said nothing. I swung my legs off the bed. Where was my underwear? I scooped panties and bra from the floor, then sat still for a moment before I shifted to face him. "I've never been seriously involved with anybody before. I'm just feeling a little overwhelmed."

"Okay. I understand." He touched my hair. "I'm not scaring you off, am I?"

He laughed a little, but his eyes were filled with an apprehension that wrenched my heart. I put my arms around him.

"Let's take it one step at a time," I said. "Please. For now. And just see how it goes."

He smiled with obvious relief and kissed my bare shoulder. "Sounds good to me."

Then his hand was on my breast, gently rubbing the nipple erect before gliding over my stomach and urging my legs apart.

<>‹›‹›

It was so late. I had to get home. I cleaned up as best I could in the bathroom, then pulled on my clothes.

Luke was coming into the living room from the kitchen, two glasses in his hands. I took one, sipped cold tingly ginger ale, washing the taste of him out of my mouth.

"Come on, sit down while you finish that," Luke said. He gestured at the couch.

"I've really got to go."

He frowned and smiled at the same time. "Your mother got you on a curfew, or what?" he said, then laughed as if to soften the question.

I shrugged, dropping my gaze to conceal my embarrassment. "She's a real worrier, that's all."

I set the ginger ale on the coffee table and turned away from him, looking for my purse. My gaze fell on the cardboard cartons against the wall, big brown boxes with thick black words on the sides: clothes, sheets & towels, dishes.

I stared at the boxes, the writing, as the image of another room struggled to take form in my mind. An unfamiliar room filled with boxes, taped shut and labeled and stacked, boxes everywhere, looming, higher than my head, a prison of boxes.

A flood of panic nearly knocked me off my feet. I spun around, stumbled a few steps, and leaned on the windowsill to steady myself. One thought drummed in my head: *I don't want to remember. I don't want to.*

I forced myself to focus on what was in front of me, what was real. Down on Leesburg Pike traffic had thinned to a few widely spaced cars; the nearby office towers had emptied, the sprawling shopping centers a few intersections to the west had closed.

Luke gripped my shoulder. "Rachel! Are you all right?"

"It's late." I sidestepped away from him. "Please take me home."

The front door swung open before I got my key into the lock. "I was beginning to worry about you," Mother said.

I brushed past her into the foyer. "I called you."

"But I didn't think you were going to be this late."

"You could've called my cell phone number if you were worried."

"I don't like to bother you."

I wanted to get upstairs and take a shower. Luke's delicious odor clung to me, I could smell it, and I was certain she could too. I started up the steps.

"That wasn't Damian who brought you home," she said.

I stopped on the third stair. "No, it wasn't."

Michelle appeared, coming up the hall from the kitchen, a half-eaten yellow apple in one hand. "So where'd you lose Damian?"

Sighing, I turned to face them. "Damian took the hawk home with him. Luke Campbell was at the clinic, and he operated the x-ray machine for us. We went out for coffee afterward, then Luke gave me a ride home."

Michelle crunched into her apple, eyes sliding toward Mother.

"Coffee?" Mother said. "All evening?"

"Coffee and conversation," I said. "Why the inquisition?"

"Inquisition?" Mother exclaimed. "Can't I take an interest in my own daughter?" Without waiting for a response, she added, "You went out with Dr. Campbell?"

Oh God, there'd be no stopping her now. "Don't jump to conclusions," I said.

"What's he like?" Michelle asked.

"He's okay. Look, I'm tired. I'm going to bed."

I ran up the stairs and raced along the hall to my room.

I couldn't turn off my churning thoughts. Lying in the dark, I listened to showers running, watched the hallway light blink out under my door. My stomach rumbled. Maybe a glass of milk would help.

When the house was silent, I crept out and down the stairs.

Moonlight lay in silver bands across the living room and Mother's study. I was in the kitchen before I realized what I'd just seen. I turned back. The door to the study stood open.

I stepped across the threshold, a little breathless with the thrill of it. This was the third time in my life that I'd been inside this room. When Michelle and I were little girls, Mother had brought us to the door and given us instructions: never come in here without permission, never go near Mother's private papers.

The empty expanse of the desktop gleamed amid the shadows. Three oak filing cabinets lined up, tall dark rectangles, along the wall to my right. Close enough to touch. I trailed a hand down the smooth cool face of a drawer, looped my fingers over a handle, tried to persuade myself the motion was casual and meaningless.

I tugged. Locked.

Privileged information inside, the case files of former patients.

Did she keep a file about me, about my "case"? Had Mother been professional and methodical in recording her own daughter's emotional trauma? I'd bet on it. Maybe that file had been here, but she'd removed it in the last few days, taken it to her office, and now felt safe in leaving the door unlocked again.

Or maybe she was using reverse psychology, leaving the door open again to make me think the room contained nothing I'd want to see.

But no, my mother wouldn't go to such lengths to hide things from me. Would she? Something deep inside me, below the layers of respect and confidence and love, answered my suspicion with immediate belief.

I backed out. I'd look for the file when I was alone in the house. When I'd figured out a way to defeat the locks. When I'd worked up the courage to read what I found.

In the kitchen I poured a glass of milk with shaking hands and stood at the glass patio doors, watching the fox family sniff around on the moonlit lawn. Two adults with four young ones trailing. One adult raised its head and jumped back when it saw me. All six animals disappeared into the shadows beneath the trees.

Chapter Seven

Theo looked stunned. He stared at me across the wrought iron patio table. His cats, Helen and Sophia, lay limp on the sun-warmed bricks at our feet, enjoying one of the first summery days of the year.

"How did you arrive at such an idea?" he asked.

"It makes sense." I'd thought so, anyway, until I'd said it aloud.

"Is it what you want to believe?"

"What I want to believe is beside the point! God, Theo, if you only knew how hard it is for me to even think about such a thing. But it fits, doesn't it?"

I pushed my iced tea glass aside and leaned forward, elbows on the tabletop. "Look, you never really knew him. You didn't see what their marriage was like or what kind of father he was. Isn't it possible he—" A wave of revulsion stopped me for a moment. "—he did something to me, and I've repressed the memories? Plenty of people say it's happened to them."

Theo's gaze roamed distractedly over the pyracantha espaliered to the high brick garden walls. The intense perfume of the plant's tiny white flowers drifted on the air.

"Tell me this," he said at last. "Do you have sexual problems? Are you frigid? Afraid of sex? Do you dislike it?"

Surprised by the intimate questions and his challenging tone, I drew back and folded my arms. "No. I don't have any problems with the physical side of it."

His thick white eyebrows jumped, his eyes widened. "Do you have problems with the emotional side? Forming attachments, making commitments?"

"I didn't mean that." It came out too sharp and loud.

Theo's voice was gentle. "I'm trying to help you sort this out. I'm not trying to hurt you or embarrass you or trick you into saying things you don't mean."

I took a deep breath and released it. "I know." He was waiting for an answer to his question, and I had to give one. I'd started this, after all. "If I met somebody I could trust—and love, of course—I could make a commitment."

He studied me for a moment, making me distinctly uncomfortable. "I notice you mentioned trust first," he said. "Have you never been involved with a man you felt you could trust?"

I shrugged, trying to appear casual, trying hard to keep Luke out of my thoughts. "I haven't had any long-term relationships. When have I had time? Besides—" I laughed. "It's not easy finding somebody who'd live up to Mother's standards."

I instantly regretted saying that, and expected Theo to pounce on it. But he said, "The last time I saw you, you told me you had a new man in your life. How is that working out?"

I shifted in my seat and watched a sparrow hop along the top of the brick wall. "It's just a casual thing."

"And you want to keep it that way?"

"Yes," I said firmly. "For a lot of reasons."

"I see." Again he paused to give me an appraising look. "Have you had a great many sexual partners? Would you consider yourself promiscuous?"

"No, Theo. For heaven's sake."

Relief showed in his quick smile. "I didn't think so. Of course these things can be quite complicated, and I'm wary of oversimplifying, but sexual abuse—incest—leaves a mark, Rachel. One doesn't come out of it unscarred."

"Look at me," I cried, throwing out my arms and laughing helplessly. "I *am* scarred. If losing a chunk of my memory isn't a sign of trouble, I don't know what is."

He frowned, and took a moment to answer. "Still," he said, "other explanations are far more reasonable, in my opinion."

Despite his words, I detected a strong undertone of doubt in his voice. He did believe it was possible that my father had sexually abused me. A sudden rush of bile to my throat made me cover my mouth and swallow hard. Both the cats had raised their heads, and two pairs of bright blue eyes were fastened on me, waiting for another exclamation or expansive gesture.

If this awful thing was true, I thought, Mother had carried the burden of it alone for two decades.

"Perhaps the real explanation," Theo went on, "is simply that your mother is a complex woman who has found it easier to bury all of the past, good and bad, rather than be constantly reminded of the bad along with the good. I saw her do exactly that when she was my student. She made her family into objects of study, distanced herself emotionally. Then she put them out of her life."

Excited, I grabbed this slender thread of information. "What made her do that? What was so terrible about her family?"

Theo sighed. "I've already said too much. I must ask you again not to put me in the position of betraying Judith's confidence."

Frustration almost got the better of me and I was on the verge of lashing out at him when Helen, with a fluid leap, landed on my lap. She plastered her purring body to my chest. Stroking her, I silently reminded myself that I couldn't push Theo. If I made him betray Mother's confidence, he might feel compelled to betray mine.

His voice became cajoling. "You're not in a terribly unusual position," he said. "Very few people are well acquainted with the facts of their parents' lives. You should hear my patients trying to patch together coherent portraits of their parents. I myself have often regretted not learning more about my parents while I had the chance—"

"Theo, I'm trying to learn about mine," I said quietly.

He sighed, his shoulders slumping. "I said I would help you, but instead I only seem to be putting roadblocks in your path.

I suppose I'm reluctant to see you become obsessed with these questions. With the past."

"You're trying to protect me, just like Mother is. I know that. But now that I've started wondering about these things, I feel like I'll go crazy if I don't get some answers." I hesitated, then added, "Would you hypnotize me, to see if I can pull out some memories?"

My mother's face rose in my mind, her sad reproachful eyes making me feel furtive and deceitful. But I had to do it this way. I didn't believe Mother would ever tell me more about my father. I couldn't press her; I was afraid the slightest touch on a tender area would make her withdraw from me completely. She didn't have to know what I uncovered. She need never know.

"Do you believe you can accept whatever memories you bring forth?"

"Yes," I said, hoping I sounded confident. I didn't feel that way. I was less certain with every second that passed. I wanted this. I didn't want it. Eager but frightened. What if I'd guessed right, and something unspeakable had happened, something I'd buried because it would destroy me if I faced it? The clutching pressure in my chest warned me to stop now.

"You realize," Theo said, "that what you recall may not be the literal truth? And you must take into account the fragmentary nature of early memory."

I shook my head. I had no early memories, fragmentary or otherwise. "What do you mean?"

"Few people can remember very much, if anything, before the age of two and a half to three. And childhood memory after that is seldom crystal clear or complete. It's selective, and frequently confused. And sometimes highly inventive."

"Inventive?"

"Children don't see the world the same way adults do. They naturally give events a different interpretation, colored by their limited experience. That flawed and totally subjective view becomes cemented in place as memory."

"That sounds like we shouldn't trust any childhood memories."

"No, not really. It's our emotional perceptions that shape us, more than the literal truth. And emotions don't arise without cause. They are certainly linked to reality at some level."

A woman's sad tears, a man's angry shouts, a child's fearful cries. Were these my emotional perceptions of early childhood? Would I ever know what reality they were tied to? Before I lost my courage, I said, "I understand. But I want to do it."

"I'm going to insist that we wait a bit," Theo said. "Two or three weeks, perhaps, then we'll talk again. If you still want to try hypnosis, we'll discuss it then."

I didn't want to prolong this. I wanted answers now, I wanted to know what my father had meant to me, to my mother, my sister, and why he'd been erased from our lives and memories. But I had no choice; I had to wait. Theo was behaving ethically, the only way I could reasonably expect him to behave.

This was the best I could get, and I took it gratefully.

Mother must have guessed that I spent my evenings out with Luke, at dinner, at the movies, at his apartment, in his bed. But to my surprise she watched me coming and going and said nothing. Two weeks went by before she brought it up.

I came home one night and found Mother and Michelle in the kitchen, emptying the dishwasher and deep into a discussion that had probably been going on for an hour. They seemed not to notice me when I walked through the back door, or when I opened the fridge and took out a bottle of spring water. Pouring water into a glass, I listened to them talk about the delicate maneuvers required to communicate with borderline autistic children. Apparently Michelle had some hope of getting through to a girl at the institution where she worked part-time.

Mother had never taken this kind of interest in my work. Why should she? Healing sick cats and dogs wasn't exactly her thing. What I couldn't get used to was Mother treating Michelle like a colleague.

"You're home late, Rachel," Mother said.

I turned. "Mmm."

She removed the last serving bowl from the dishwasher and closed the door. "Have you had dinner?"

"Yes, I have."

She placed the serving bowl in a cabinet. "You know, I can't help wondering about you and Dr. Campbell."

I paused with my glass halfway to my mouth. "Wondering?"

"I admit I'm a little concerned."

I glanced at Michelle. She was watching me with bright-eyed interest. "Concerned about what, Mother?" I said.

A faint shrug of one shoulder. "He's your employer. A relationship with him would put you in a vulnerable position."

"I can take care of myself."

"Then there is a relationship."

Damn. I sighed.

"Why don't you invite him over for dinner? I'd love to meet him."

Meet him. Inspect him. Grill him mercilessly in that soothing therapist's voice. Find him lacking, in the end, not good enough for her daughter.

I gulped from my glass to give myself a second to think.

"Yeah," Michelle said. She rinsed her hands under running water and tore off a sheet of paper toweling to dry them. "I'm dying to get a look at this guy."

"That's rushing things a little," I said.

"Well, whenever you're ready," Mother said. "But I hope it'll be soon."

I watched her move around the room, pick up a hand towel and hang it on the rack behind the sink, push the salt and pepper shakers into perfect alignment on the counter next to the stove.

Then I looked more closely at her slightly slumped shoulders, a lapse of her perfect posture, and the hint of dark circles under her eyes. Sharp concern drove out all other thoughts. "Mother, do you feel all right?"

"Oh, I'm just a little tired," she said with a quick dismissive smile. "I seem to be getting into a pattern of insomnia."

Something was bothering her. She hadn't been the same, really, since the night she told me I'd destroyed my father's pictures. Michelle's words came back to me: *It tears her apart, having it all dredged up.*

Mother swayed on her feet and fumbled at the edge of the counter, trying to grab hold. Two steps and I was at her side, an arm around her waist.

"Mother? Mother, what is it?" She was deathly pale. I gripped her wrist, feeling for her pulse.

"Oh, don't, Rachel." She twisted her arm free. "Don't make a fuss. I just—" She seemed to run out of breath, and for a second she sagged against me.

Michelle, ashen-faced, was at her other side. "Come sit down."

"I think I'd just like to go up to bed." Mother seemed to be regaining strength now, and drew away from me.

"You shouldn't be climbing the stairs," I said. "Sit down and I'll call your doctor."

"It was just a passing dizzy spell. All I need is a good night's sleep."

"Let me help you," Michelle said. She slid an arm around Mother's waist, a hand under her elbow. I trailed them down the hall and watched them mount the stairs with their heads together, murmuring. I stood at the bottom of the steps, forgotten, unwanted, unneeded.

My throat constricted. I wheeled around and returned to the kitchen, where I yanked open a drawer and grabbed a flashlight.

The full moon drenched the back lawn in light, and I didn't have to switch on the flashlight until I passed under the trees and through the wall of shrubbery to the cages.

My only patient at the moment was a little opossum with an infected foot. When I trained the beam on him, he froze for a second, then scurried on three legs into his box shelter. He'd been eating the cat kibble and fruit I'd left for him when I'd stopped by the house on my lunch hour. The bit of pear with an antibiotic pill imbedded in it was gone. After two days of not eating, barely moving, he seemed on the mend.

"Rachel?"

I jumped at the sound of Michelle's voice. Pushing past the shrubs, I came out onto the lawn where she stood. The flashlight in my hand cast a bobbing light over her face, making her blink and avert her head.

"It's spooky out here," she said.

I switched off the flashlight. "Then why did you come out?"

She ignored the question and raised her eyes to the sky. In the moonlight her long hair had a silvery sheen. "Your comet's gone. I never understood why you liked watching that thing so much. You had to stand out here an hour just to see any proof it was moving."

"Is Mother all right?"

"She seems fine." After a second's pause, she added, "What's wrong between you two? Are you still upset because—"

"Don't worry about it."

"How can I help worrying about it? I feel this tension in the house—"

"Maybe I should think about getting a place of my own." The words came out of nowhere, and left me feeling mildly shocked.

"What?" Michelle stepped closer. "What on earth for?"

"I'm almost twenty-seven. I ought to be on my own by now."

"But you were gone so long, and it seems like you just came back—" Her voice was high and breathy. "Can't we keep the family together for a while before you leave again? Why do you want to be alone?"

"It's just something I might think about."

"So you'll have a place to bring Luke Campbell?" She made it into an accusation. "Where you can have privacy?"

"A little privacy might be nice. Mother still treats us both like children sometimes, Mish. She doesn't want us to have men in our lives."

"That's ridiculous. Didn't she just ask you to bring him home so she can meet him? She's willing to accept him."

"Oh, really? The same way she accepted Kevin? Right after he came to dinner, you broke that sailing date with him just to please her, didn't you?"

"What are you talking about? I told you why—"

"She sat you down and convinced you it'd be a bad idea to get involved with him, didn't she?"

"I have a mind of my own, you know." She folded her arms across her chest. "For your information, Mother and I never discussed it."

I didn't believe her, but the more I prodded, the more adamant her denial would become. "Oh, to hell with it," I muttered. I stared into the blackness under the tent of trees. Crickets sawed and frogs sang on the creek.

Michelle touched my arm. "Rachel." A soft plea. "I just hate this."

When I didn't answer, she dropped her hand and said, trying to sound upbeat, "Are you ever going to tell me about Luke? I want to hear all about him." She drifted into wistfulness as she added, "You used to tell me about the guys you dated."

Two sisters sharing confidences. I wanted to weep, for a closeness that seemed lost forever. I faced her. A breeze thrashed the branches above us and cast shifting shadows over the planes of her face.

"I'll talk to you about Luke if you'll talk to me about Kevin," I said. "I know you're seeing him. Why do you feel like you have to hide it from Mother? Can you answer that?"

I sensed rather than saw her body stiffen. She stepped back. "I'm going in."

She spun around and strode up the moonlit lawn, hurrying as if afraid I'd try to stop her. I waited until she was in the house before I followed.

‹›‹›‹›

Outside Mother's bedroom I stood for a moment with my hand raised before I made myself knock. "Mother, are you all right?"

I expected her to open the door. Instead she called out, "I'm fine, Rachel. Go on to bed. Good night."

I bit down on my disappointment, telling myself she wasn't rebuffing me, she was just tired and didn't want any more fuss.

In my room, I locked the door, then ran a hand under the mattress and slid out something I'd hidden: *The Complete Book of Locks and Locksmithing*. Settling on my little couch, I found the chapter titled "Decoding, Picking and Emergency Entry."

"All done." I eased the last stitch from Maude's shaved-bare forehead. "Pretty as ever. And what a good girl you are." I kissed the basset hound's muzzle and she caught me on the cheek with a wet swipe of her tongue.

Mrs. Coleman laughed. "You've gotta move fast to dodge Maude's kisses."

I tore a sheet from the paper towel roll by the sink and dried my face with it while I scratched Maude's neck with my other hand. She sat on the exam table panting happily, her still bandaged leg stuck out to the side. I was ashamed to think how much I'd dreaded the dog's visit, and how relieved I'd been when Mrs. Coleman showed up without her daughter.

The field next to Dulles Airport was a fast-food carryout for hawks, serving up a steady supply of mice and rabbits to swooping red-shoulders, red-tails and sharp-shins. Luke and I stood in the sun and watched the hunt as departing and incoming planes roared low above us. Damian would arrive any minute with the rehabbed red-shoulder. On the back seat of my car, champagne was chilling in a bucket of ice.

I hadn't intended to mention Mother to Luke, but it came out unexpectedly, abruptly. "My mother wants to meet you. She's started bugging me about it every day."

He jammed his hands into his jeans pockets and glanced up at a silver airliner climbing into the sky. He waited until the engines' thunder subsided before he said, "She wants to check me out, I guess."

I shrugged. "Well, she is my mother. I'm not asking you to do it. I'm just saying she's been after me to invite you. Don't feel obligated."

His gaze flicked over my face. "Why are you so nervous about it? Never mind, you don't have to answer that. Sure, I'll come. It's time I met your mother and sister."

A spurt of alarm made me want to protest, argue against his decision. Why had I done this? Inviting him to meet my family was a milestone, a signal of seriousness, and I wasn't sure I wanted either Luke or Mother to think the relationship had a future. I knew I didn't want to expose Luke to Mother's scrutiny.

I abandoned the subject with relief when I saw Damian's beat-up brown van pulling up behind my car.

"Hey, folks," Damian called as he hopped out. "Great weather for thermals." At the back of the van he swung open the door on the cat carrier containing the hawk.

I peered through the grille. The bird hunched and glared. "Don't look so mad at us," I said. "We're about to give you the thrill of your life."

I grabbed my falconer's gauntlets from the back seat of my car and Luke and I followed Damian into the middle of the field. Damian knelt and extracted the hissing bird from the carrier. He didn't let go until I had my gloved hands securely around the hawk's body.

I bent low to gain momentum, then threw my arms high and tossed the hawk into the air. His wings snapped open and pumped furiously, carrying him up and away from us, back into his own life.

Laughing with a mixture of joy and envy, I lifted my arms straight out like wings. *Fly away. Fly away free.*

"Here you go," Luke said, handing me the cold champagne bottle.

I forced the cork and yelped when the foam overflowed onto my hands.

Chapter Eight

An hour before Luke was due, I put on black jersey crepe slacks and a belted tunic of white silk. I thought I looked pretty good until I saw Michelle in a pink dress of some floaty material, her sheet of golden hair brushing her shoulders.

I went back to my room and changed into a dress: deep blue, sleeveless, scooped neck, not tight but fitted closely enough to show off my figure. With a swipe of a tissue I removed pink lipstick, then I slicked on a coppery red. I ran my fingers up under my hair to fluff it out. "That ought to do it," I murmured to my reflection.

Down in the living room I fussed over the sofa cushions, plumping and rearranging them, and tugged at a vase of white roses and baby's breath between glances out the window.

"The flowers are perfect," Mother said, coming up beside me. "But they won't be perfect much longer if you don't let them be." She smiled and gave my arm a light squeeze just above the wrist.

"Don't worry," Michelle said. She perched on the arm of the couch and grinned at me. "We'll try not to disgrace you."

My answering smile felt feeble on my lips. I reminded myself that Luke was no high school or college kid coming to pick me up for a date. They couldn't find fault with him. Anybody would like Luke. Anybody. And after overcoming his nervousness at being scrutinized by a shrink, he might get along perfectly well with Mother.

I hoped he wouldn't say anything to make her realize he'd been in the house before.

His tan Range Rover turned into the driveway.

"That must be him," Mother said. "I'll get the door."

I stayed where I was, although I wanted to rush forward and shield Luke.

"Relax, for heaven's sake," Michelle said with a laugh.

When Mother opened the front door the honeyed scent of spirea wafted in on the warm evening breeze.

"Dr. Campbell." She extended a hand as Luke stepped in. "I'm Judith Goddard. I'm glad to meet you at last."

She was warm and gracious, and I couldn't help thinking of Kevin, who'd walked through that door not long ago believing she welcomed him into our lives.

Luke was an ill-at-ease boy in a charcoal gray suit, white shirt and plain navy blue tie. He shook Mother's hand, exchanged pleasantries, asked her to call him Luke. He looked beyond her, searching for me, and only when he found me did he smile.

They stepped into the living room, Mother with a hand on Luke's elbow like an adult urging a child forward. He came to my side quickly, and I was afraid he'd kiss me or take my hand, but he just grinned and murmured, "You're gorgeous," so low that only I could hear.

Michelle was full of winsome charm, soft-voiced and big-eyed. A tiny spot of worry faded when I saw that Luke, while he was friendly to her, didn't seem bowled over by her pretty face and feminine manner.

"Rachel's been keeping you a deep, dark secret," Michelle said, almost impish.

He glanced at me, one eyebrow raised, amusement on his lips. He looked incredibly handsome.

Mother said, "Sit down, Luke, please. Let me get you something to drink. We have a bottle of white wine chilled." A second's pause. "Or would you rather have bourbon or scotch?"

"Scotch, please." I hadn't seen him drink before, but he looked as if he could use a stiff shot of something. He sat on the sofa, leaning forward with elbows on his knees and hands clasped. "Just a little."

Mother went to the cabinet where the sweating wine bottle sat on a silver tray with four stemmed glasses. She opened the cabinet door and placed one of the glasses inside, then brought out a tumbler and a never-opened bottle of scotch. Her slight smile didn't alter, but I realized with a sinking feeling that Luke had already disappointed her, failed a test he didn't know he was taking. She would have expected him to accept what she mentioned first, probably expected him to notice the tray with the wine and glasses.

The conversation began pleasantly enough, with questions about where Luke was living and how he liked working in McLean. We talked about plans for redevelopment of McLean's Central Business District and decided the changes would have no impact on either the clinic or Mother's office building. I watched Luke relax and heard his voice settle into its usual easy rhythm. So far, so good. But the evening stretched ahead like a minefield.

My eyes strayed to my watch and the mantel clock a dozen times before Mother rose at last and suggested we go in to dinner.

Our best gold-rimmed china, seldom used, a crisp new linen tablecloth, a low centerpiece of mixed flowers: it was all perfect, and much more formal than I'd wanted. Silver candlesticks flanked the floral arrangement, but the candles were unlit and unneeded because the room was suffused with the soft golden light of the waning sun.

Michelle appointed herself server for the evening, and she carried dishes in from the kitchen and set them on the table with a flourish. Rosario had prepared boned chicken breasts fragrant with wine and herbs. The sights and aromas of the meal didn't arouse even a trace of appetite in my clenched stomach and dry mouth.

When we'd finished the business of filling plates and wine glasses and passing the bread basket, Mother asked Luke how he came to buy the clinic. They faced each other down the table; Michelle and I sat on either side.

"I had a place over in Maryland, kind of out in the country," he said. "I wanted something bigger and easier for people to get to. And I liked the idea of my specialty practice being part of a full-service clinic. Lucky for me Dr. McCutcheon decided to retire when he did." He grinned at me, on his right. "Lucky in a lot of ways."

I ducked my head, ridiculously self-conscious.

"It must be a relief to the staff," Mother said, "that you haven't let anybody go or made any major changes yet. After the panic the sale caused."

I almost dropped my knife. I fumbled to keep the heavy silver from clanking against the rim of my plate. For God's sake, why did she say that? I opened my mouth to speak but closed it in consternation. What was I going to do, tell my mother to shut up?

It was a moment before Luke turned to me and said, "This is the first I've heard about any panic."

I shrugged. "You know how it is, somebody new taking over. People talk and wonder. But everybody settled down after we got to know you."

He was clearly disturbed, maybe because the staff's worries had escaped his attention, or because I'd discussed this with my Mother but not with him. He frowned at his plate.

"I'm sorry," Mother said. "I shouldn't have brought it up."

The talk stopped dead for a minute and I rushed to fill the gap. "You should see Luke work, Mother. I watched him perform heart surgery on a German shepherd yesterday. A mitral valve replacement. It was amazing."

She nodded. "I'm sure it was. What made you decide to specialize in canine and feline cardiology, Luke?"

He seemed distracted, but he pulled himself back to the conversation. After a sip of water, he said, "I was planning to be a general practice vet, but I worked on a cardiology research project in school and got interested in the field. A lot's happening, new developments and treatments coming along all the time. We can do a lot more now than we could a few years ago.

It's a good feeling to turn things around dramatically, give an animal a chance to live out a normal life span."

"How long did it take to become a specialist?" Michelle asked.

"Three years, after vet college."

With apparent absorption, Michelle asked half a dozen questions about specifics of his cardiology residency, a subject I was certain didn't interest her in the least. All the while, Mother watched him, assessing, taking in every detail. I could tell, in the way his gaze flicked toward her repeatedly, that he was acutely aware of her scrutiny.

After a few minutes Mother smiled and said, "Some people might say you should be using your skill to help humans instead of cats and dogs."

"Mother," I breathed, a faint appeal that she seemed not to hear.

I saw Luke draw back into himself, bar the door, and peer out at her with eyes alert and wary. "Some people can say what they want to." His voice was tight, strained. "I couldn't care less. I've never met a cat or dog that didn't deserve a longer life. I can't say the same for humans."

I gulped my wine.

Mother laughed lightly. "Well, if you're a confirmed misanthrope, it's just as well you've avoided human patients."

The silence following this was more than I could stand. I blurted, "Cats and dogs have been research subjects in a lot of experiments. It's only fair for the species as a whole to get some benefit from the suffering of—"

"Rachel," Mother broke in, her expression bemused. "I agree completely. Why don't we talk about something more pleasant?"

Hot blood rose to my face. I pressed my napkin to my mouth, removing beads of perspiration from my upper lip.

Mother said to Luke, "You're obviously very successful, to be able to purchase a facility like Dr. McCutcheon's clinic."

"I do all right," Luke muttered. He cut a sliver from his chicken but didn't raise it to his mouth.

"I was surprised when Rachel told me how young you are," Mother went on. "I wouldn't have thought someone your age would have the resources for such a big investment."

Slowly Luke laid his knife and fork on his plate. "Dr. Goddard," he said, a faint humorless smile pulling at his lips, "I'm in hock up to my ears, if that's what you want to know. I couldn't have done it if Dr. McCutcheon hadn't financed part of it. But I won't fail, because I know what I'm doing."

Mother's puzzled face said she had no idea why he'd bristled at her comments. "I'm sure you do."

I had to turn this around somehow. It wasn't beyond the point of rescue yet.

While I was casting about for something to say, Michelle spoke up. "It must be easier to manage without a family to support."

Oh, great. Thanks a lot, Mish. I kicked her under the table and was gratified to see her mouth drop open in surprise.

"Maybe so," Luke said, his expression guarded, suspicious.

Mother sipped her wine, set down the glass, and asked, "Have you ever been married, Luke?"

The quick "no" I expected didn't come. I met Luke's troubled eyes, and felt my stomach lurch with shock even before he spoke.

"A long time ago," he said directly to me. "It didn't last long. I'd almost forgotten it ever happened."

"Wow," Michelle said with a little laugh. "That's something. Forgetting you were married."

Luke flushed darkly. I sipped my water, swallowing hard. How long ago could it have been? He was only thirty-six now.

"Any children?" Mother said, her tone so light that she might have been inquiring about a pet or a car.

I made myself look at him, and I saw the shadow cross his face as he waited just a second too long to answer. "No," he said.

I didn't want to imagine what his hesitation had meant. Mother's eyes caught mine and held them with naked concern, with sympathy and distress.

Luke broke the heavy silence. "Did you ever consider getting married again after your husband died?"

I shot a frantic pleading look at Luke, but he was watching Mother.

"No," she said, icing over. "My girls and my work have always been enough."

"It couldn't be easy raising two children alone. How old was your husband when he died?"

Alarmed, unable to think of a single thing to say or do, I waited for Mother's reaction.

Following a pause that seemed interminable, she said, "He was in his early thirties. He was a young lawyer getting established in his career."

The statement had a finality about it that didn't invite further questions. I knew that tone well. I hoped it would stop Luke.

"Rachel told me you specialize in treating phobias," he said. "And you're a master hypnotist. What do you do, hypnotize people and convince them they're not really scared?"

Now he was making me mad, deliberately acting like a jerk with no thought to how it affected me.

"Hypnosis is just one tool among many," Mother said, her voice cool and level. "And I'm sure you don't really believe treating deep-seated fears is that easy. Is everybody ready for dessert?"

For a moment no one spoke. I stared at my plate. I'd eaten almost nothing.

"Thanks, but I'll have to pass," Luke said. He pushed back his chair and stood. "I need to get back to the clinic and check on a surgery patient."

Mother also rose. The two of them regarded each other steadily, Luke's face rigid and Mother's set in a polite smile. "Well, it was very nice meeting you, Luke."

"Thanks for inviting me. Good night." He dropped his napkin on the table and headed for the door.

"Michelle?" Mother said. "Help me clear?"

I would have to see Luke out, say good night to him. As Mother and Michelle began gathering plates, I trailed him to the foyer, where he waited at the door.

"Come stay with me tonight," he whispered.

I shook my head. How could he even suggest it?

"Why not? Are you afraid your mother won't approve?"

"What makes you think I'd go anywhere with you?" I snapped.

"Aw, shit." He raked a hand through his hair. "Rachel, we've got to talk."

"That's the last thing I want to do right now."

He grasped my wrist. "Look at me, for God's sake."

I tugged my arm free. "Just go, Luke."

"All right," he said. "Okay. But we're going to talk about this, when we've got some privacy. Listen—"

He leaned toward me. I turned away, unable to keep pain from breaking through my fragile wall of anger.

"I love you, Rachel. Remember that."

I stepped around him and opened the door. After he was gone I stood in the foyer for a moment, listening to the murmur of Mother's and Michelle's voices from the kitchen.

Everybody's got a secret, I thought. *Everybody's got something to hide.*

Chapter Nine

Mother wouldn't be quick to probe the wound. Having exposed Luke's inadequacies, she'd leave me alone to think about my poor choice. My doubts would do the rest, and she knew it. We'd been through this kind of thing before.

It was Michelle who couldn't contain her curiosity for more than twenty-four hours. The next day, a Sunday, I got out of the house early and stayed gone all day, birdwatching with Damian's three teenage daughters in the woods of Riverbend Park, then wandering around a shopping mall buying shoes and clothes and books I didn't need.

When I returned home laden with shopping bags Michelle and Mother were in the kitchen preparing dinner. A note in Mother's handwriting was tacked to the little bulletin board beside the wall phone: Dr. Campbell called and would like you to call him back. They both watched me jerk the yellow square of paper free of the pushpin and toss it in the trash can, but they didn't comment, asking me instead what I'd bought.

Mother, who enjoyed cooking on the weekends, had prepared one of my favorite dishes, rice with chicken chunks, almonds and raisins, spices and herbs. Michelle complained all through dinner about her school schedule. I was conscious of Mother's sidelong glances, knew she was judging my demeanor and the state of my appetite. I ate more than I wanted, and told her the food was delicious.

Michelle and I cleaned up the dishes, at first in silence. After a few minutes she leaned over the open dishwasher and whispered, even though Mother was upstairs and unable to hear, "What are you going to do about Luke? Are you going to keep seeing him? You didn't know he'd been married, did you? What a rotten way to find out."

"It's no big deal," I said, not looking at her. I dropped flatware into its basket.

"I don't understand why he didn't tell you something that important."

I scraped bits of rice from a plate into the sink before I said, "I haven't known him long. There are lots of things we don't know about each other yet."

"Well, you know him well enough to sleep with him. You have been sleeping with him, haven't you?"

I flipped a wall switch and the garbage disposal roared.

As soon as the noise stopped, she said, "I can't help wondering what else he's hiding."

It took an effort to keep my voice level. "Do you think I'll find out he's a serial killer? An escaped madman?"

"Oh, Rachel, be serious."

"I am being serious." I removed the dishwasher liquid from the under-sink cabinet and squeezed the big yellow bottle. Lemon-scented gelatinous detergent oozed into the cup on the dishwasher door. "Exactly what is it you think he's hiding?"

"I don't know." But her lifted brows, her skeptical eyes, suggested plenty of possibilities.

"Just drop it, will you?" I slammed the dishwasher door and jabbed a button with my index finger. Water hissed into the machine. "I don't want to hear it."

"Why are you getting mad at me?" Her tone was instantly hot, affronted. "I'm not the one who lied to you."

"He didn't lie to—Oh, for God's sake. I'm not going to talk about this."

I walked out.

She followed right behind me, up the hallway toward the stairs. "I don't know what you see in him anyway. He's an arrogant s.o.b. All that talk about dogs and cats being more deserving than people. Who does he think he is? What do you want with somebody like that?"

I stopped and turned so abruptly that she almost collided with me. "I'm asking you for the last time. Drop it."

She took a step back, her expression petulant and defensive. When I ran up the stairs she didn't follow.

<>>><>

Later, I was stretched out on the little couch in my room, trying without much success to concentrate on a veterinary journal, when I heard one soft rap on the door.

"Go away," I muttered under my breath. Aloud, I said, "Come in."

The door opened a few inches and Michelle poked her head in. She dropped my name into the silence between us. "Rachel?"

For a moment I was swept back to childhood nights, my door slowly swinging open in a slant of moonlight and my sister's tiny voice reaching for me in the shadows. *"Rachel? I had a bad dream."* I would lift the covers and she'd crawl in, snuggling close for safety, her bony knees and elbows pressing against me. It was always me she came to when she was scared. I remembered Mother's distressed little smile as she brushed back Michelle's blond wisps one morning and murmured, "Why didn't you come tell Mommy you had a bad dream?" Michelle, perhaps sensing she'd failed Mother somehow, answered in an uncertain whisper, "I just wanted Rachel. Is that okay?"

Now my sister said, "I'm really sorry about all this."

She withdrew and closed the door. I didn't know whether she was talking about her own behavior or Luke's. Certainly not Mother's.

On Monday and Tuesday Luke tried repeatedly to get me alone at the clinic, tried to make me listen to him, but I resisted even though I knew I was behaving with the maturity of a twelve-year-old. I was afraid of what else he might tell me. I was afraid he would leave me feeling stupid as well as betrayed.

He caught up with me at quitting time Tuesday when I was hanging my lab coat in my staff lounge locker. I turned and found him behind me. I tried to step around him, but he grasped my arm and wouldn't let go.

"Isn't it about time you let me explain?"

"Let go of me. You're acting like a bully."

I saw he was tempted to tell me what I was acting like, but instead he said, "I'll let go if you'll promise to listen."

I was close enough to catch the scent of his skin, that wonderful smell that had enveloped me when we made love. Meeting his gaze briefly, I saw nothing but an honest appeal. I nodded, and he released my arm.

"Okay," he said. "First, I'm sorry I didn't tell you about the marriage—"

"Your marriage."

He drew in a breath. "My marriage. I was twenty-three, and it lasted a little over a year, in legal terms, but we only lived together a few months. We were miserable as hell the whole time. It was a mistake from the start, and we both knew it. I haven't seen her since the divorce."

This sounded well-rehearsed. I wondered how many times he'd said it over in his head. Leaning back against my locker for support, I asked, "Did you have—Is there a child?"

He took too long to answer. My stomach clenched into a painful knot as he swiped his hair off his forehead and stared at the floor.

"She—We had a baby." Luke's voice was low and flat. "He was premature and he died when he was a week old." He glanced at me, then away. "The baby was the only reason we got married in the first place. Pure stupidity on my part. I hardly knew the girl."

And you don't know me, I thought. *But you've already told me you love me. Am I another impulsive mistake? Did you tell her you loved her too?*

"Rachel. Say something."

I shook my head. I had nothing to say.

"Aw, come on, Rachel. Are you going to let this wreck everything?" He moved closer.

I stepped aside. "Don't pressure me."

"Oh, man, your mother really did a number on us, didn't she? I've got to admire her technique."

I bristled. "If you think insulting my mother's the way to win me over—"

"You're a different person when you're around her, you know that?"

"I don't know what you're talking about." But I knew well enough.

"She's got you cowed. She's got you under her thumb, and she doesn't want some man coming around threatening her control."

"Now you're insulting me."

He gripped my arm again. "Rachel, I love you, I think we could be happy together—"

"We don't even know each other." I yanked my arm loose. "Just leave me alone."

I bolted, got out of the building and into my car, but I was in too much turmoil to go home, where I would have to face the truth of what he'd said. I drove around side streets for a long time, avoiding rush hour traffic on the main roads, barely noticing where I was. Every few minutes my cell phone bleeped inside my shoulderbag, but I ignored it.

I told myself that if I patched things up with Luke and continued the relationship, he'd force me to choose between him and Mother. I couldn't do that. Mother and Michelle were all I'd ever had, my only family. I wanted Luke desperately, the sight of him and the sound of his voice at work every day tormented me, but my doubts about him and his hostility to Mother would always come between us.

I told myself I couldn't trust him, that he might have other secrets that would hurt and shock me. I didn't know what could be worse, though, than hiding a marriage and child. I was jealous of that nameless, faceless woman who'd been his wife, had his baby. His dead son. His dead marriage. Had he meant to keep it from me forever?

Finally I told myself that I was nothing but a fraud. Deep under the layers of hurt and blame lay a kernel of simple truth: I was grateful that Mother had uncovered an excuse for me to retreat from Luke's intensity, his certainty that we belonged together. He overwhelmed me with all that he wanted to give and expected in return.

But I had no right to hold his secrets against him. God knew I had plenty of secrets of my own.

Chapter Ten

Even as I pored over a book on locks, learning about pins and cylinders and levers, even as I assembled what I imagined to be adequate lock-picking tools, I felt a little sick about what I was planning to do. But that didn't stop me.

If Mother had kept a file on my childhood problems, it might contain all the information she would never willingly give me. The file might be in her office, but I couldn't get into her office. I had to hope it was in her study at home, the off-limits place where I'd never before had reason to trespass.

I shifted my schedule so I'd be free on a Wednesday, Rosario's day off. That morning I left the house before Mother and Michelle, with the explanation that I'd promised to visit several rehabbers and examine the animals they were working with. I did, in fact, drive over to Vienna and examine a blue jay with a broken wing and a litter of orphaned baby rabbits. When I finished, I returned home.

I felt sneaky, pulling into my own driveway just before ten o'clock. I got out and stood by the car for a moment, the sun's heat pressing along my arms and cheeks. A cacophony of bird song rose in the humid, still air, and I concentrated to pick out a Carolina wren and a song sparrow.

I was stalling, with no good reason. No one would be home until Michelle came in around three. I took a deep breath. My heart thudded. *Do it.*

Inside, I sprinted up the stairs and pulled the lock book from under my mattress and the little brown sack of tools from my desk drawer. I thumped back down the steps, grabbed the flashlight from a kitchen drawer, and crossed the hall to Mother's study.

Sunlight glared through the wide windows, flashing off the desktop and the slick-jacketed books that filled a wall of shelves. The scent of lemon polish hung in the air. Overhead I heard the distant roar of an airplane.

Sitting cross-legged on the beige carpet, I opened the lock book to the right section, then shook out the sack's contents. Paper clips. A length of stiff wire cut from a coat hanger. A putty knife. Two flathead screwdrivers, a set of slender miniature screwdrivers, a long metal nail file.

All right. I rose to my knees to study the oak filing cabinets. Four drawers in each cabinet, a lock on every drawer. The book made lockpicking seem easy, and I was certain someone with my manual dexterity could do it even with crude tools.

But faced with the reality of bolts and tight drawers, I fumbled and struggled.

If these were ordinary metal cabinets I might have been able to maneuver them open. But Mother had invested in expensive units with strong locks and drawers that fit perfectly flush. I couldn't get a screwdriver between the cabinet face and a drawer, much less pull a drawer out enough to insert the coat hanger wire behind it and ease back the bolt.

One by one I tried each of my tools in the keyholes. Coat hanger wire, paper clip, mini screwdrivers. With my ear close to the lock I listened for any faint sign that the bolt was yielding.

I was startled by the slap of metal against metal, racketing down the hallway from the front door. I froze. Who? The plop of mail falling through the slot to the foyer floor left me limp with relief.

Swiping at the moisture on my upper lip, I got to my feet, rolled Mother's red leather chair from under the desk and sank into it. What had possessed me to think I could do this quickly and easily? I'd thought it was like surgery, requiring only a knowledge of the parts involved and a deft touch. But I hadn't learned surgery from a book, and I couldn't learn lockpicking by reading about it. Even if I had the right tools, I'd probably have to practice for hours or days before I could do it.

I swiveled to my right. The desk had two file drawers. Expecting resistance, I yanked angrily at one of them. It flew open and banged my right knee, making me yelp. I saw a collection of file folders. With one hand I rubbed my throbbing knee—I'd have a nasty bruise—and with the other I searched the folders. Clippings from psychology journals and newspapers. Drafts of papers Mother was writing.

I swung around and tried the other big drawer. It held only half a dozen folders, all of them containing what appeared to be final drafts of articles.

My disappointment was irrational, since I couldn't expect to find anything sensitive in an unlocked drawer, but knowing that made no difference in how I felt. Idly, certain it was useless, I slid open each of the desk's small side and center drawers. Pencils, pens, index cards, sticky notes, all neatly arranged, a place for everything and everything in its place. I was about to close the center drawer when I caught a glint of metal in a rear corner. I reached back and pulled out a key ring.

Most of the dozen keys had familiar shapes. I recognized them as duplicates that would fit the house locks, Mother's office door, her car's ignition and trunk. But here was something odd: three small, similar keys attached to their own circle of metal, which was in turn clipped to the key ring. As I fingered them, hope jolted to life again.

I tried them first on the desk drawers. None fit. With mounting excitement I inserted each of them into all the file cabinet locks. "Turn," I muttered through clenched teeth. "Open it!"

Nothing happened. The file drawers with their lode of secrets remained shut tight.

"God damn it!" I slammed a foot against one of the cabinets. Then, alarmed, I bent to check for dents or scratches, anything that would give me away. The oak surface was unmarred.

Slapping the keys against my thigh, I turned in a circle. I skimmed bookshelves, focused momentarily on a small print of Escher's strange drawing "Belvedere," in which nothing was what it seemed at first glance. An odd choice for a woman with Mother's refined taste to hang on her wall, but perhaps not odd for a psychologist who sat in this room writing about people with warped perceptions.

I slid open one of the closet's louvered doors and found exactly what I expected on the shelves: packages of laser paper, boxes of stationery, myriad other office supplies. On the floor, pushed back against the wall under the bottom shelf, were four fireproof boxes, three smaller ones lined up in front of a single large one.

I knew Mother kept important documents in these boxes, and I wouldn't find any secrets hidden in them. Still, I got down on my knees, favoring the one that ached, and slid them forward. One was no more than a foot long, a couple were about eighteen inches long and looked like file boxes. The last was close to two feet. They were heavy; the shells of gray space-age plastic had steel liners. All were locked, but maybe I had the keys in my hand.

I tried a key on a medium-sized box. It didn't work. I tried another key. The lock popped open with a satisfying click, and I lifted the lid.

The contents were in perfect order. An expanding file had been set inside the box, and within the labeled divisions were all of our insurance papers, for the house, our three cars, health care, plus records of car and home repairs. I closed the lid, disappointed at finding exactly what I'd expected.

The next box opened on the first try. It was filled to capacity with manila envelopes.

They weren't sealed, just closed with their little gold butterfly clasps. Each was labeled on the outside in my mother's graceful clear handwriting, and contained exactly what she'd written: *Girls' vaccination records, Rachel's report cards, Michelle's report cards*, and so on. She'd kept the minutiae of our progress through school, our grade school drawings and high school essays, the little awards and certificates of accomplishment we'd received along the way. Safe in a box that not even fire could destroy.

I sat back with one of my science fair prize certificates in my hand. Our mother, who considered so little worth saving, had preserved every scrap of her daughters' lives. Suddenly my actions, my doubts, the questions that had swirled in my mind for weeks seemed the worst kind of betrayal.

Then I looked at the other two boxes and my guilt vanished as curiosity took over. I stuffed the science fair certificate into its envelope and put all the envelopes back as I'd found them.

None of the keys fit the largest box. I let it go for the moment and moved on to the smallest one. It opened easily, but inside I found only the key to Mother's safe deposit box and a small green notebook full of account numbers. I closed the lid and locked it.

I ran my fingers across the oblong bulk of the inaccessible box and tried to reason with myself. It wasn't worth any more effort. The odds were it contained nothing but household records.

And yet.

Mother hadn't left the key lying around, any more than she'd left the keys to the file cabinets.

For ten minutes I worked on it, sticking each little key into the lock, trying to twist it, pulling it out and starting over, again and again with no result. Frustration fueled my determination. I'd get the damned thing open if it killed me. If I found a method that worked, it might work on the file cabinets too.

I tried the wire, a paper clip, the nail file. Sometimes I heard a faint click inside the lock, but it didn't open. I ran to the kitchen, rummaged in the drawers for anything I might use, grabbed a corkscrew and a metal skewer. They were also useless. I slammed my fist on the top of the box until pain stopped me.

I sat back and shoved hair off my damp face. A bead of sweat dropped from my chin to the carpet, leaving a dark spot. In spite of the cool air pouring from the overhead vent, my underarms were wet and my blouse clung to the skin between my shoulder blades.

This is nuts, I told myself. *Calm down.*

Then I thought, *A locksmith.*

Hire somebody to enter Mother's private space and break into the cabinets and the box?

No. It was unthinkable.

I shifted the box, judging its weight. I could take it to a locksmith. Obviously I couldn't take the file cabinets, but I was strong enough to get this box out to my car. It would be back in its proper place by the time Mother came home from work. But no, this had to be done before Michelle came home at three. I glanced at my watch: almost noon. I pulled the yellow pages from a bookshelf and hurriedly thumbed through it.

I found a locksmith shop in Arlington, near enough to reach quickly yet far enough afield that Mother wasn't likely to ever use its services. The man who answered the phone said he had to leave for an outside appointment soon but he could make a key if I got the box to him within half an hour. Fifteen minutes later I pulled into the narrow parking strip outside the shop on a commercial stretch of Lee Highway.

I staggered in with the box.

"Hey, whoa," the young locksmith exclaimed. "You shoulda let me do that." He hustled around the counter and lifted the box in muscular arms bristling with curly black hair. The box seemed to become weightless in his grasp.

"Now, let's see what we got here," he said, dropping the box onto the counter with a loud thump. But his attention was still on me. His grin, his appraising look, said I'd made his day just by coming through the door. When he failed to get an answering smile from me, he turned to his task and made a quick examination of the lock.

"Piece of cake. I opened one just like this a couple weeks ago. They don't make these things for security, you know, just fire resistance. About the only thing the lock's good for is keeping the lid on real tight so it won't pop open if a fire heats it up."

Easy for you to say, I thought.

Almost apologetically, he added, "I have to get your ID before I can do this. It's pretty silly, but I gotta have it. I mean, I know the box belongs to you, I'm not saying—"

"That's all right, that's fine," I said, hoping my alarm was well hidden. *Calm down,* I told myself. *This will never get back to Mother.* I showed him my driver's license and waited while he jotted information on a form.

He described in detail what he was going to do, how he would select a key blank that matched the lock type, and little by little grind it to fit. He inserted the blank in the lock, pulled it out and showed me the faint scrapes that told him where to start cutting. I was nearly crazy with impatience, but nodded and smiled and held my tongue. At last, when he got down to the work of making the key, he became absorbed and fell silent.

Too restless to sit in the single orange plastic chair, I surveyed the display of locks on a side wall. Padlocks ranging from minuscule to monstrous, dead bolts, childproof latches, keyless security locks. All the ways to keep people out of places where they didn't belong. I couldn't believe I was here, doing this.

The minutes dragged. I bit my lip to keep from urging the locksmith to hurry. Through the storefront window I watched the traffic start and stop, start and stop in response to the light on the corner. A sharp pain shot through my bruised knee whenever I shifted position.

"Miss? All done."

I turned. The box sat on the counter with its lid thrown back. I caught a tantalizing glimpse of something inside, a smooth blue surface, before he lowered the lid again.

He grinned and held up the shiny new key. "Want some extras in case you lose this one too?"

"No, thanks," I said, not bothering to go along with his good-natured joke. I held out my hand and he dropped the key into my palm. The metal was warm from the cutting. What was that in the box?

I paid the bill in cash so I wouldn't have to wait for my credit card to clear.

The locksmith carried the box to my car. I thanked him and closed the door on his friendly goodbye.

I drove with caution, conscious of the danger my hyper state created. I laughed at the thought of having an accident and afterward trying to explain to Mother why the box was in my car. My gaze strayed to it, sitting beside me like a smug silent passenger with a story that would, in time, come out.

Back in Mother's study, I sat on the floor and opened the box. A photo album. I lifted it and found a second album underneath. And a third.

Pictures locked away in the back of a closet. Why?

Would I find something here to jog my memory? I plopped an album onto the carpet and opened the cover. On the first page was an 8x10 color photo of Mother, young and lovely in a white satin wedding dress, a cloud of veil floating around her head. Her smile was joyous. I'd never seen this picture before. I'd never seen her smile that way.

I turned the page. Now she was joined by a young man with blond hair, dressed in a wedding tuxedo. My father, the man in the picture Mother kept on her dresser. The man whose other pictures I'd supposedly destroyed in my grief.

Confused questions crowded my mind. I searched the pictures for answers.

Leaning close, I looked into my father's eyes and tried to feel a connection. If he'd been a monster, if he'd done unforgivable things to me, some part of me must remember. But he remained a picture, nothing more. It was hard to believe he had anything to do with my life.

I turned to the next page. Snapshots, four to each sheet, probably honeymoon photos. Her, him, the two of them together, in some place with palm trees and a beach. Pages and pages of them smiling, laughing, kissing. Then came a photo of them posed before a house I didn't recognize, white with blue shutters and door. More pictures taken in the yard. My young mother planting a rose bush, standing proudly beside the same bush in flower.

I wandered through the early days of their marriage. The entire first album was filled with photos of the two of them, separately and together. They'd been happy. Their love was palpable in their eyes, their smiles, their touching hands.

Suddenly choked with tears, I closed the book and put it aside. Now I understood, more completely than ever before, what my mother had lost. A whole life, a whole future. Love.

With a kind of dread, I lifted out the next album. I wasn't sure I could look at any more pictures of their brief shattered happiness. But I had to see it through. They were my parents, and this might be the only way I'd ever learn about their life together.

I took a deep breath and turned back the cover.

The two of them sat on a blue sofa, and Mother held a blanket-swaddled infant. The parents smiled down at the baby, whose eyes were squeezed shut. I had the sensation that I was hurtling back into another time. This must be me. Their first-born.

I bent low over the photo to study the baby. I recognized nothing of myself in the child, but that wasn't surprising. Infants seldom resemble the adults they'll become.

Eagerly I flipped the page to more baby photos, many of the child alone, others with the parents, one or both. I soon realized that these weren't pictures of me. The fuzz of hair growing in on the baby's scalp was blond, not red. Her eyes were blue. Michelle.

I turned the pages with increasing puzzlement. Where was I? Why wasn't I in any of the pictures with my little sister and our parents? I looked through to the end without finding myself.

I sat for a few minutes with the third and last album unopened in my lap. Surely this would be the one with pictures of me, pictures of all of us together. If I saw myself with my father, something might shake loose and rise to the surface of my memory.

I found more photos of Mother, Father, Michelle, and dozens of pictures of my sister as she grew from a baby to a toddler to a beautiful little girl of two or three.

I fumbled through the album, faster and faster. Where were the pictures of me? Why were the pictures of Michelle separated this way, all together, with no sign of me?

Swallowing back the sourness that rose in my throat, I forced myself to think. One thing was clear: Mother had lied to me when she said I'd destroyed all the pictures of my father. But had it been a complete lie? Why would she make up something like that? Maybe I'd destroyed the photos that showed me with my father. Yes. That must be what happened. I couldn't imagine what else would explain my absence from these family pictures. As if I hadn't been part of their lives, wasn't one of them.

But why did Mother hide all the pictures of herself and my father? Why pretend they didn't exist? All I could think of was that she was protecting both of us from painful reminders.

I returned to the first page of the album. For a long time I sat staring at my young parents and tiny sister, trying to make sense of it all.

In the dogwood outside the window a mockingbird broke into song, imitating a cardinal. The throaty, mellow notes were pitch-perfect, but I realized absently that the cadence was off, too rushed and insistent. I would never mistake it for the real thing.

Chapter Eleven

When I was twelve and Michelle was nine, Mother bought a telescope so we could all look at the stars and planets and moon together. On a hot clear night, we set the instrument on its wooden tripod in the back yard, and waited for daylight to recede and the universe to come shining out of the darkness.

Mother sat in a wrought iron chair she'd brought down from the patio, and Michelle and I lolled on the grass at her feet. The pink-washed sky faded to black, the birds hushed in the trees around us. Fireflies winked across the lawn. Michelle, giggling, tickled my neck and ears with grass blades until she saw the first bat swoop low, then she squealed and clutched at me, burying her face in my shoulder. We smelled of sweat and citrus insect repellent.

I'd studied every inch of the lunar map in our new astronomy book, and when the brilliant full moon rose above us I patiently guided Michelle's eyes to the Bay of Rainbows, the Sea of Tranquillity, the Lake of Dreams. I pointed out the places where astronauts had walked. All the while, I sneaked glances at Mother on my right. Was she impressed? She smiled and briefly rested a hand on my shoulder. I was thrilled. She thought I was a good, smart girl. She loved me.

Then her gaze shifted to Michelle, and Mother's expression softened, a deep tenderness bloomed in her eyes, and I felt an invisible circle closing them in, shutting me out. Her show of affection for me was like the heat of the moon, an illusion, a glow that gave no warmth.

That night marked my first conscious awareness of what I'd always sensed, that Mother would never love me the way she loved Michelle.

Perhaps now I knew the reason why.

For days after I found the pictures I was nearly mute at home, fearful that I couldn't speak to Mother without exploding into a babble of questions and demands. Before I dug any deeper, I had to work out all possible meanings of what I'd found, and not found, in Mother's study. I needed to fortify myself by imagining the worst I could learn if I pushed for answers.

I was willing to believe that grief over my father's death made me destroy the pictures that showed me with him. But that didn't explain why there were so many photos of my parents and sister together, some of them formal studio portraits, with no sign of another, older daughter. Families didn't do that, they didn't pose for portraits with only one child.

Maybe I wasn't one of them. Maybe I was adopted. The thought pierced me like a sword, but I forced myself to consider it. I'd never seen my birth certificate, a fact that hadn't struck me as odd until now. I'd never needed it, never been asked to produce it. Mother had obtained my first passport when she took Michelle and me to Europe as teenagers, and I'd simply renewed it as an adult. I'd used my passport as proof of identity when I applied for a driver's license. No one, anywhere, had ever asked to see my birth certificate, so I'd given it no thought.

But if I was adopted, why hadn't Mother told me? What possible reason could she have to hide it from me? And when did it happen? After those pictures were taken, when Michelle was about two and I was four or five? Surely I would remember it, if I'd been that old.

This argument made me laugh scornfully at myself. I couldn't remember a damned thing; I was stumbling around in the dark.

Or was I? I reached out and found them lurking at the border of consciousness, a sad-faced woman and an angry man, phantoms

I'd never been able to explain or get rid of. Did Mother know who they were? Was something about my origins so awful that she never wanted me to learn the truth?

Mother could see, of course, that something was wrong. She came to my room one night, sat on my bed, and tried with her soothing quiet voice to coax out a clue to my emotional state.

She talked and I studied her face for similarities to mine.

You're so lucky you got Mother's coloring, Michelle had said many times over the years, as if unaware of her own delicate, fair beauty. I'd always taken it as a given that I looked like Mother. But did I? We both had auburn hair, and dark eyes with thick lashes. Both tall, slender. The curve of my jaw was similar to hers, and my full lower lip. Yes, in some ways I looked like her. It was my father I didn't recognize in myself. I looked like Mother, Michelle looked like our father. That wasn't unusual. Not at all.

"Rachel?" Mother gave my arm a little shake to bring me out of my reverie.

Her eyes were wide, soft with concern. She watched me pull up my knees, smooth down my robe. The novel I'd been trying to read before she came in had fallen from my lap and lay open on the bed beside me.

"I asked if you're still seeing Dr. Campbell," she said.

This was the first time she'd mentioned Luke since the dinner.

"I see him at work every day," I said, avoiding her eyes.

Silence hung between us. She pushed the thin gold band of her watch forward, then back, on her wrist. She still had on the green silk blouse she'd worn to work, and I could see the outlines of her slender arms inside the sleeves. She always wore long sleeves to work, even in hot weather. I wondered if she was reluctant to expose too much of herself to patients.

Finally she said, "That's not what I meant. I can't stop thinking about that night he was here——"

"It doesn't matter to me, Mother," I said quickly.

She looked straight into my eyes, holding me fast, not about to let me off the hook. "It matters to me, because you're my daughter and I care what happens to you. I'm not blind, Rachel. I know you were hurt when you found out he'd been hiding something important from you. I can't forgive him for it."

I almost laughed. This, from the queen of secrets! Feeling shaky and daring, as I always did when I challenged her, I said, "We all have things we don't want to talk about, don't we?"

Only a student of her moods would have seen the slight narrowing of her eyes, the brief dimming of their light.

Ask her, I urged myself. *Ask her if you're adopted. Ask her what the pictures mean.*

The very idea made me shrink back. Tell her I'd hired a locksmith to open the box I'd found inside a closet in her off-limits room? Tell her I thought she was a liar? She would fix me with a sad but forgiving look, and I'd be lost. She'd make me doubt myself, I'd end up convinced I was wrong, crazy, a bad daughter. And my questions would put her on guard; I'd never find out what I wanted to know.

She sighed and let her shoulders slump a bit. "I'm interfering, I know. But I can't help worrying about you. I don't want you to get hurt." She touched my knee, her hand light, the weight heavy. Smiling suddenly, she said, "When children reach adulthood, they have to learn to be patient with their parents, instead of the other way around."

She leaned to brush my cheek with a kiss. I was ashamed that I'd listened for lies beneath her loving words. But when she was gone, and the door shut after her, all the doubts and questions clamored in my mind again.

That night I dreamed of the three of them, a happy little family with only one daughter.

◇◇◇

I talked to myself incessantly, the dialogue always going on at some level, whether I was driving down the street or examining an animal or sitting speechless at the dining table with my mother and sister. How much did I want to find out, what kind of answers could I handle?

Everybody claimed to welcome the truth, they demanded it—honesty is the best policy, I want your honest opinion, tell me the truth!—but the way people behaved showed that even this desire for the truth was a lie. People lied to each other all the time, about small things and great. There was so much in life we couldn't bear to look at straight-on, or simply preferred to leave unacknowledged. Surely a lot of families had secrets that no one wanted to uncover and bring into the light, for fear of hurting and being hurt.

I should leave well enough alone. I should get on with my life. The present, the future. I should.

I couldn't.

I had to know.

I made the call from my bedroom after work, before Mother and Michelle got home. It was mid-afternoon in Minnesota. The courthouse would still be open.

For ten minutes I paced back and forth with the phone in my hand, mentally reciting the reasons why this was a good idea. I would get my birth certificate, it would tell me what I already knew, that I was Michael and Judith Goddard's child, and the question of adoption would be laid to rest without Mother ever knowing it had been raised.

But dread sat on my chest like a stone, and it was only the awareness of time passing that made me act. If I didn't do this now, I might never work up the courage again.

I called long distance information. I waited another minute, eyes squeezed shut, breathing deeply, before I punched in the number I'd been given. After my call was transferred to the right extension, I was talking to a clerk who handled birth records.

"I'm trying to find out—" I cleared my throat. "I need to find out if you have my birth records on file."

"We charge for copies of—"

"I'll do that, I'll send you a check for a copy, but could you just tell me now if you have the record?"

A silence, then a little grunt of puzzlement. "Well, were you born in Hennepin County?"

"Yes, in Minneapolis."

"Then we'll have the record. What's the date and the name?"

I gave her my birthdate and name, spelling Goddard for her.

"Just a second. I'm going to put you on hold."

The line went dead silent, no canned music to distract the mind. Chewing my thumbnail, I stood at a window and looked down at the driveway. Its black surface was dusty and dulled by the heat. Along the far edge, two dozen house sparrows bustled and pecked, probably scooping up ants that I couldn't see.

"Ma'am?"

I snapped to attention. "Yes!"

"I'm sorry, but we don't have any record of that."

For a moment I couldn't take in what she'd said. Then I stammered, "But—but it has to be there. Maybe you looked at the wrong day. It was August—"

"Yes ma'am, I got that right," the clerk said, with the exaggerated patience of someone who dealt daily with the public's inquiries. "I looked at that date, and I checked a few days before and afterwards, and it's not here."

My mind snatched at an explanation. "Maybe the records were destroyed in a fire or something—Could you—"

"No, ma'am. I'm sure these records are complete. Are you sure you were born in Hennepin County? I know you're talking about yourself, but—"

I stopped listening. I pushed the off button and dropped the phone onto the bed. Thinking I was going to be sick, I rose, veered toward my bathroom, and smacked into the door frame.

I groped my way inside and sank onto the edge of the tub. The air felt clotted, unbreathable, and I couldn't pull enough of it into my lungs.

In a while the nausea passed, leaving a knot of pain under my heart. I stood on shaky legs, went to the sink, splashed cold water on my cheeks. Soon I would be expected to go downstairs and eat dinner with my mother and sister.

I raised my eyes to a reflection I didn't recognize. The face in the mirror had the slack stunned look of people who appeared on the evening news after a tornado or hurricane or earthquake had laid waste to their lives.

I touched the cool smooth surface of the glass and whispered, "Who the hell are you?"

Chapter Twelve

The only sound in the room was the faint tick of Theo's marble mantel clock. Outside on the sidewalk, people passed within a few feet of the front windows, but their voices and laughter were muffled, distant. A hot summer Sunday in Georgetown. Crowded sidewalks, traffic-clogged streets. People living their lives. I was on the verge of redefining mine. The answers I needed were locked in my memory, waiting to be freed.

With narrowed eyes, Theo peered at me from his armchair. "Are you afraid, Rachel?"

I shrugged, dropping my gaze to the two Siamese cats crammed onto my lap. "A little. But I'm ready. I'm prepared."

I was terrified. How could I prepare myself for the unknown?

Over a lunch I barely touched, we'd talked about books, my work, the heat and lack of rain, everything except the reason I'd come to see him. I'd known he was watching me, though, for signs that I might not be able to deal with the memories hypnosis dredged up. I put on a show of strength and composure.

"Have you talked with your mother about this?" Theo said. "I don't like keeping it from her."

"Theo—"

He raised a hand. "Very well, I won't mention it again."

I'd seen suspicion in Mother's eyes when I told her I'd be with some rehabber friends that afternoon. She could tell I was lying.

Forget about Mother. You're doing this for yourself. The moment
I formed the thought, a wave of familiar guilt swept over it, as
surely as the tide rolls in to knock down a sand castle.

"Are you going to try regression?" I said. "Taking me back
to a younger age?" The idea scared me.

Theo shook his head. "No, at least not at the beginning.
What I think might work best for you is simple free association.
My greatest concern is that you understand the unreliability of
memory. Even pleasant memories may contain many distor-
tions. And you aren't likely to recover whole memories, with
every detail intact."

"I know."

He smiled. "But perhaps you will be able to fill in some of the
blanks, and what you learn may not be as terrible as you expect."

I drove the two of us to Theo's office on K Street. He wanted to
conduct the session in a professional setting.

The elevator rose through a silent, deserted building and
released us into a sixth floor corridor that smelled of wax. Theo's
four-footed cane thumped along the gleaming blue tile floor.

When I stepped inside the office suite, fusty warm air made
my throat close up. I coughed.

Theo flipped on lights and went straight to the thermostat.
"Eighty degrees!" He twisted the dial. "I cannot believe that
turning up the thermostat for the weekend is cost-efficient in
the least. But I always seem to be overruled in the matter."

Theo shared quarters with another psychiatrist; two doors
opening off the small waiting room bore their nameplates.

I didn't want to be here. I shouldn't be doing this. I took a
step backward, toward the corridor, the elevator, my car.

"Come in, come in," Theo said, pushing open his office door
and waving a hand at me.

I hesitated a second before I followed. Like the man, the
office was congenial and welcoming. Bookshelves overflowed,
the top of the big oak desk held a clutter of journals and books.
An oriental rug, predominantly red and blue, hid most of the

beige carpet. In the wide window a pothos, glossy and riotously healthy, trailed from its pot.

My fear ebbed for a moment. Then I turned and saw the brown leather reclining couch, a classic analyst's couch, against one wall. Down its center the leather was worn nearly white from the contact of human bodies, and I had the sensation that I was seeing a ghost.

"Well, now," Theo said, a hand on the back of his desk chair. "Shall we sit down and talk a bit first?"

I focused on a single strand of black hair in his white beard, and imagined the young Theo trapped inside that arthritic body, sending out tiny and easily overlooked signals that he was still alive.

I pulled myself up short. "I'd like to get right to the point."

His laugh was a pleasant rumble. "In this office, that would be both unusual and refreshing."

When I tried to laugh with him, all that came out was a harsh croak.

I felt him studying me while I studied a red poppy in the rug's design. After a moment he swung his chair around and rolled it toward the couch. "All right then. Why don't we begin?"

What made me think I could go through with this?

"Rachel, would you like to lie down?" Theo said, his voice already assuming that gentle tone associated with hypnosis. He gestured at the couch.

I stepped over to it, looked down at the ghost. Theo sank into his chair, smiled encouragingly and made another sweeping motion, inviting and urging me to submit.

I wanted to run. The thought of stretching out and giving myself over brought a wave of nausea. But I had to do this. I didn't know any other way to free my memories.

I made myself sit down. Instantly dread swooped over me, a smothering cloak. *I can't.* I jumped up.

"Rachel?" Theo said. "Do you need something?"

Sitting again, I let out a short breath. "No, no, I'm just nervous."

"Are you sure—"

"Yes!" The volume of my voice startled me. "Yes, I'm sure," I said more quietly. *I will do this.*

I was conscious of his hesitancy, and was relieved when he seemed to put it aside. "Please lie down, Rachel," he said.

Swinging my legs up, I laid myself out on the couch, ready for dissection. I didn't realize my hands had formed fists at my sides until Theo touched my right wrist, murmuring, "Relax, Rachel. Relax. Take a long deep breath and let it out slowly, very slowly."

His soothing tone was so much like Mother's.

Breathe, deeply in, slowly out. Hands palm-up at my sides, the way Mother taught me. Open. Receptive. But my body remained rigid, caught fast in a web of tension.

"I'd like you to close your eyes," Theo said. "Take another deep breath and let it out slowly."

I closed my eyes. I breathed.

"I want you to continue breathing deeply and slowly as you relax your body. I want you to concentrate on the muscles and nerves of your feet. All the muscles and nerves in your feet are completely relaxed. Completely loose and relaxed."

Let go. Let it happen.

"Concentrate now on the muscles and nerves of your calves and thighs. All the muscles and nerves in your calves and thighs are completely loose and relaxed. Your legs are lying loose and relaxed on the couch."

Warmth spread through my legs as I felt them go limp.

"All the tension is leaving the muscles and nerves of your stomach, your buttocks, your lower back. The muscles and nerves are completely relaxed."

My body sank heavily against the couch.

Theo's voice whispered on. "The muscles and nerves of your fingers, your hands and wrists…your arms…your shoulders…your neck…your scalp…your face…completely loose and relaxed. Your eyelids are very heavy. You will keep your eyes closed until I tell you to wake up."

I was aware of my eyelids fluttering, some part of me testing. My eyes refused to open.

"I want you to imagine that you are floating in a boat in a pool of clear, warm water. You are lying back against soft cushions. The sky is deep blue with puffy white clouds, and a light breeze is blowing around you. The sun is warming your skin. Feel the warmth of the sun on your face and arms."

I drifted, floating, borne up by gently rocking water.

Theo's voice moved closer to my ear. "I'm going to count backward from one hundred to zero. With each number I speak, you will become more and more relaxed, going deeper and deeper. When I reach zero you will be at the deepest level of relaxation. Your mind will be open and free. Don't be afraid. I will always be here with you, and you will always be able to hear me."

He began to count slowly. "One hundred...ninety-nine..."

Resistance flared in me, a sudden leaping flame. *No. It's wrong.*

Theo counted.

Something awful would happen. You won't allow anyone except me—I had to open my eyes. I had to get up. But I couldn't move. My body was lead-heavy, rooted, beyond my direction.

Theo counted.

My skin prickled and burned. *Mother will never forgive me.*

Theo counted.

Images swam up in my mind, the sad-faced woman, the angry man. A gabble of voices.

Take her and leave then, I don't give a damn.

I never said I wanted to leave.

I want my Daddy!

Your father's dead, an accident.

Theo counted.

Mommy! My sister, crying, terrified, rain streaming through her yellow hair, thunder rolling across the sky.

I struggled upward like a swimmer wearing weights, struggled toward air and light. *Oh no, oh no.*

Theo counted.

Mother's face, leaning over me, her voice soft. *I'll take care of you. I love you.*

Had to get away, couldn't let myself remember, couldn't look, couldn't listen.

Theo counted.

Thrashing, fighting, yet not moving at all, I struggled toward the light. *Don't leave me, don't leave me!*

Theo counted.

"No!" I sat bolt upright, eyes open, gasping for breath.

"Rachel!"

His hands reached, mine flailed, beating off his touch. I wobbled to my feet, but my legs wouldn't work, they couldn't hold me up. I sat down heavily.

"Rachel, wake up!" Hands slapped together in my face.

I was instantly aware, clear-eyed, wondering. Theo and I stared at each other. My blood roared in my ears.

"Are you all right?" he said at last.

The room around me came into focus. Cozy, safe. I nodded and whispered, "I think so."

"Well. That's good." He reached to pat my arm.

Beads of sweat clung to his forehead, each as sharply defined as a pearl. I touched my own forehead and my fingertips came away wet.

"Clearly something is at work here that I didn't see," Theo said. Positioning his cane between his knees, he stacked his hands on its handle. "I apologize for this. All I can say in my defense is that I anticipated no problems, because you've been hypnotized successfully in the past."

By Mother. *No one else, you will never allow anyone except me—*

I forced myself to my feet. "I'm sorry. I'm sorry."

"Rachel," Theo said, "please sit down. We need to talk about this. Let me get you some water."

I sat with my hot face in my hands. Theo's footsteps shuffled across the carpet, a door opened, water ran, the door clicked shut.

"Take this, please," he said.

I clutched the white paper cup with both hands. On the water's surface two bubbles burst, one then the other, creating little waves in the tiny pool. Why were people always given water at times of crisis? Was this a crisis?

Theo said, "Do you have any idea why you reacted this way?"

I downed half the water in a cool gulp. "I'm not used to any-body but Mother hypnotizing me." *You will never allow anyone except me—*

"Well, let's leave that for the moment," Theo said. "You seemed to see something that frightened you. Can you tell me what it was?"

"I don't know. Crazy stuff."

"Try to describe this crazy stuff."

I looked at him and blurted, "Theo, was I adopted?"

His white eyebrows shot up. "Adopted? What brought that on?"

"Did Mother ever tell you I was adopted? Did she tell you where I came from?"

"Rachel, Rachel." He reached over and grasped my arm, his crippled fingers surprisingly strong. "What on earth—I know nothing of an adoption. Look at yourself. You are your mother's daughter. Why in the world would you question that?"

"These people in my head! This man and woman, I keep seeing them, I've seen them all my life, I don't know who—And I'm not in the pictures—"

I tried to stand. I wanted to get away. His hand tightened on my arm, pulling me back to the couch. Water sloshed from the paper cup onto the rug, and I moaned in distress at the sight of the wet blotch.

"Never mind that," Theo said. He removed the cup from my fingers and set it on the floor by his chair. "Describe these people you see."

I shook my head. "I can't. They're like shadows. They're not clear. They've never been clear."

"Ah." Theo fell silent.

For a long moment I sat watching the water spot spread darkly through the rug's multicolored fibers.

Theo asked, "Rachel, who is Kathy?"

I jerked my head up. "Kathy? How do you know about Kathy?"

"You spoke her name. You cried out her name. You said, 'Kathy, come back. Kathy, don't leave me.' Who is Kathy?"

I rubbed my arms where chill bumps had risen. The room was much too cool now. I didn't remember saying anything about Kathy. "She was a friend of mine. When I was a kid. That's all."

"She moved away, and you were upset about it?"

I didn't answer. He could take my silence for agreement.

"Why do you think you called her name just now?"

I shook my head mutely.

Kathy. My secret friend. I'd shut her out of my mind for years.

Kathy, why are you crying? She was always melancholy, and I never knew why, only that her heart had been broken somehow and I wanted to make her happy again. She'd been closer to me than anyone in the world. I knew the depth of her sadness and she knew all my hopes and dreams, my secret thoughts. I could trust her never to betray me because she lived only in my imagination.

"Rachel," Theo said, his voice low, coaxing, "we must talk about what happened. It's important."

"I can't. I can't right now. I shouldn't have tried this, it was a stupid idea."

"Perhaps all it means is that hypnosis is not the right approach," Theo said. "I think we can get at your memories in more conventional ways. But it would be very helpful to understand what happened today."

"I can't talk about it, Theo."

He sighed and sat back in his chair.

"You can't tell Mother about this, Theo. Promise me."

"I've already made that promise, Rachel. You know you can trust me."

I stood. "I have to go."

He wanted me to rest and collect myself, but within a few minutes I was driving him home, maneuvering the narrow streets of Georgetown with meticulous care to prove I was calm. I refused his invitation to come in, but said I'd see him again soon.

On the George Washington Parkway, traffic was a hum and a blur around me. I drove automatically, as if my car were linked to those ahead and behind, pulled and pushed along like a toy on a track.

I knocked on the apartment door, tentative raps that gained speed and force until I was banging my fist against the wood. Abruptly the door swung open, making me stumble forward across the threshold with the momentum of my next blow.

Luke caught me in his arms.

Chapter Thirteen

"What's wrong?" Luke said. He pulled me all the way inside and shut the door.

When I opened my mouth nothing but a rasping noise came out. I dropped my shoulderbag on the floor and hurled myself against him.

"Hey!" he said, surprised. But he hesitated for only a second before he enclosed me in his arms. "What's going on? Huh?"

I buried my face in his neck, drawing in the scent of his skin. "I've missed you so much," I whispered. "Don't let me go."

His arms tightened around me. I felt his heart thudding, answering mine. "Oh, God, Rachel," he groaned, his breath warm against my ear. "I want you all the time."

He covered my mouth with his and pushed me against the door, the length of his body pressed to mine. I tasted salt on his lips. Heat flooded through me and all that mattered was our connection, the here-and-now reality of him, my anchor in a whirlpool of fear and confusion.

He drew back for a moment, breathing heavily, his eyes drugged with need as he searched my face. "Are you sure?" he asked, just as he had the first time.

"Yes." I nodded. "Yes."

We undressed each other where we stood, fingers fumbling with buttons and zippers, lips brushing bare skin, his tongue flicking over my nipples. He was stiff in my hand and I would have drawn him into me there against the door, but he stepped away and said hoarsely, "Come to bed."

We fell onto the bed and I clamped my legs around him, thrusting with him in a rough, urgent rhythm. I was aware that I was crying, the tears bathing my face. When I came a ragged moan tore from me, and I sobbed against Luke's shoulder as I felt him shudder and heard the breath catch in his throat.

He rolled onto his side, gasping, and pulled me against him. "Rachel. God, Rachel, I love you."

He held me until my sobs diminished to silent tears. At last I lay quiet, covering my swollen eyes with the back of my hand. I stayed that way for a long time before I lowered my hand and opened my eyes to let the light back in.

Luke's face swam in my tears. He'd pushed himself up on an elbow. I reached to smooth his disheveled hair, then brushed my fingertips over his cheek. His skin was hot and moist with sweat.

"I'm surprised you didn't slam the door in my face," I said.

"I can't see that ever happening." He nudged my chin up and lightly touched his lips to mine. "Okay," he said, "tell me what brought this on. You didn't come here in that kind of frenzy just because we haven't seen each other for a while. What's wrong?"

I pulled away from him, sat up so that I couldn't see his expectant face. "I'm afraid to tell you. You'll think I'm losing my mind."

"Aw, come on." He sat up beside me and tried to look in my eyes, but I averted my head. "Rachel. Give me some credit, okay? You came to me. That says a lot."

I couldn't imagine what words to use. Here in the ordinariness of his apartment, every idea I had about my family seemed too crazy to speak aloud. "Could we get up?" I said. "I feel like I need my clothes on for this."

He laughed. "Okay, go sit down in the living room and I'll make you a cup of tea."

He pulled on his jeans and tee shirt and padded out in his bare feet. I dressed more slowly, dreading what I was about to do and sick at the risk I was taking. I wished I could forget everything else and just go on from here with Luke.

In the living room a mocking swath of sunshine fell across the space where the stack of packing boxes once stood. They were gone at last; Luke had settled in. But the mere thought of the boxes brought back the memory they'd awakened, and it hit me like a glancing blow, leaving me momentarily disoriented.

It was a memory of our move from Minneapolis to McLean, I was suddenly sure of that. I'd cried about it, but that was normal for a child. I'd been leaving behind all that was familiar, and I was still grieving for my father. Michelle had played on the boxes, giggling, unaffected by loss. She was too young to absorb anything more than the excitement of upheaval.

A neat explanation, produced by my rational mind. Why didn't it dispel the alarm and panic the memory stirred?

Stop it. Don't think about it.

I sank onto the couch.

From where I sat I could see Luke moving about in the narrow little kitchen, pulling a mug from a cupboard, standing over the kettle on the range. I concentrated on the fluid movements of his hands, the fringe of sandy hair across his forehead. But as I watched him, a vague mental image of someone else shifted into clear focus. The man I'd dreamed about, seen at the edge of my thoughts, suddenly had firm outlines, a body. Tall and rangy, with a natural grace. So familiar. Not Luke, no, of course not, but so much like him.

I pressed a hand to my forehead. I was grafting something positive onto a nightmare to make it less frightening. I couldn't believe anything my mind spat out.

"Here you go," Luke said, holding out the mug. "With lemon and a scandalous amount of sugar, just the way you like it."

"Thanks." I sipped the tart-sweet tea as he settled beside me.

We sat in silence until I placed the half-empty mug on the coffee table. Then Luke said, "Did something happen today? What got you so upset?"

I shook my head. "You wouldn't understand—I have to go back farther. Tell you all of it."

"All of what?"

I rubbed at my temples. "God, I don't know where to start. I don't understand any of it. It scares me to death. I go around half the time feeling like I'm not quite sane. But I've got to tell somebody, Luke."

"Tell me."

He clasped my hand. The strength and warmth of his grip held me, kept me from floating away in an ether of panic.

I dragged in a deep breath, stared straight ahead, and began. Coaxing me through frequent silences, Luke pulled it out of me bit by bit, a jumble of tangled strands.

I told him about Mother's unspoken rule that my father was never to be discussed, and her distress when the subject was brought up. Her story about me destroying family pictures and my discovery that the pictures still existed—and didn't include me. The dreams, the memory that came back the day Mrs. Coleman brought Maude, and her daughter, to the clinic. The missing birth certificate. My certainty that Mother was hiding something important from me.

"I've tried to imagine everything it could possibly be. I've thought about things that make me sick to my stomach. Things that never would've entered my mind a few weeks ago. Maybe my father abused me, and I repressed the memories, and Mother doesn't want me to recover them. Or maybe I'm adopted, and my origins were so dreadful or shameful that she doesn't want me to find out. Either I'm adopted or she lied to me about when and where I was born." I laughed, a harsh wild sound. "Maybe I never was born. No wonder I'm having trouble remembering things—I don't exist!"

I stopped and sat with my head in my hands. "Now's your chance to go call the men with white coats and butterfly nets."

"I'll hold off on that." Luke's fingers kneaded the back of my neck. "Have you asked your mother about the birth certificate and the pictures?"

"No!" I jerked my head up. "I'd have to tell her I broke into that box, I went behind her back——"

"God damn her!"

His outburst made me flinch.

He jumped up and paced, raking his hair back. "Christ, what a witch. I could wring her neck. All she has to do is tell you the truth, but she's got you scared to death to even ask about it. Nothing is wrong with you. She's the one who's crazy."

I slumped back, covering my face, trying not to cry again.

Just then my cell phone bleeped inside my shoulderbag, which still lay where I'd dropped it on the floor. *Mother,* I thought. It was nearing dinnertime and she'd wonder why I wasn't home.

Luke retrieved the purse and held it out to me. "You going to answer it?" he said when the phone had rung five times and I'd made no move to take the purse from his hand.

"I guess I should," I said reluctantly, hoping the ringing would stop by the time I got the phone out. It didn't.

"Rachel, how are you feeling?" Theo asked. "I've been terribly worried about you since we parted."

I released my breath and allowed my shoulders to relax. "I'm fine, Theo. I'm with a friend. I'll be in touch." I pushed the off button before he could answer.

The phone rang again as I was putting it back in my purse. I sighed. I shouldn't have hung up on Theo so abruptly. But this time it was Mother. At the sound of her voice every inch of my body snapped taut.

"Rachel, I don't like to interrupt whatever you're doing, but I was wondering if you'll be home for dinner."

"No," I said.

She was silent, probably waiting for an explanation. I didn't offer one.

"Rachel, where——"

"I'm with some friends. I'll get something to eat."

"Are you all right? You don't sound like yourself."

No, I didn't. I felt oddly dissociated from my own voice. "I'll see you later, Mother." I switched off the phone. For a moment I sat with it in my hand, once more fighting the urge to cry. I'd never been a crier, and I couldn't get used to these sieges of tears.

When I glanced at Luke, I saw he was watching me closely, a crease cut between his brows. I remembered what he'd said the day we talked in the staff lounge: *You're a different person around her.*

"You didn't want to tell her you were with me," he said now. "No."

"Is it just me she despises," he asked with a sour smile, "or would she do that number on anybody you brought home?"

"She's never thought anybody was good enough for me or Michelle. She puts a lot of emotional energy into worrying about us."

"Trying to protect you from the big bad world."

His tone was sarcastic but what he said was true. I nodded. A feeling had always existed, unspoken, that our little family was somehow damaged and not yet out of danger. We had to huddle together against a threat that was never identified.

What came into my mind then was one of the paintings I'd seen in the Picasso exhibit at the National Gallery. "The Mother." A thin dark-haired woman in motion, head thrust forward; a white-swaddled infant in her arms; an older child, a girl, clutching her hand. The mother was tense with urgency and purpose. Fleeing from something, taking her children to safety. The way Mother had fled with us.

Fled from what?

I got rid of the painting with a shake of my head. "If Mrs. Coleman hadn't brought her little girl with her the day Maude was hurt, none of this would be happening to me."

"It probably would have surfaced some other way," Luke said. "Rachel, you'll never get answers if you don't confront your mother. Whatever the truth is, you've got a right to hear it."

"You don't know—" I broke off, pulling back inside myself, reluctant to go on.

"I don't know what?"

"I haven't told you what happened today. I went to Theo Antanopoulos—I told you about him—"

"I remember. Go on."

"I wanted him to hypnotize me to see if I could get back some memories. And he tried. But when he was putting me under I panicked, I just lost it completely."

Luke rubbed my shoulder. "Why? Were you afraid of what you might remember?"

"Yes, I was. But I'd made up my mind to face it. It was the induction itself that scared me the most." I paused, recalling the rising tide of panic that had overwhelmed me. "I felt like I was doing something terribly wrong. Something I'd been forbidden to do. I think Mother's conditioned me not to let anyone except her hypnotize me."

"What? You mean she's hypnotized you?"

"Lots of times. Michelle too."

"What for?"

"To help me get over my father's death. According to Theo. Then for other things later on. I used to get jittery before important exams at school, but after Mother hypnotized me I'd calm down. Michelle used to be afraid of thunderstorms, and dental work, anything involving a needle in the mouth, but Mother used hypnosis to—"

"Hold on," Luke said. "I want to hear what happened after your father died. You were just a little kid. She was using hypnosis on you?"

"Theo said she used hypnotherapy to help me deal with my father's death." I looked at Luke. "But I didn't deal with it. I forgot it completely. I forgot him."

He stared at me for a long moment, understanding growing in his eyes. "Jesus Christ."

"I heard her voice when I was with Theo. I remembered her telling me never to let anybody else hypnotize me."

My mind circled, closing in on the unspeakable thought. A vulnerable child, a child in pain who longed for comfort and approval. A powerful adult who knew how to burrow deep into the minds of others. So many things I'd never asked about. Things I should have wondered about and didn't. My natural curiosity had been stamped down and silenced. Until now.

Luke was angry, almost shouting, but I barely heard what he said.

Why would Mother do that? To protect me? Or to protect herself? From what?

"Whatever it is," I said, "this thing she doesn't want me to remember, it's important enough to make her—"

"You've got to get away from her," Luke said. "Listen to me." He grasped me by the shoulders. "Stay here with me. No pressure, no decisions, I promise. I just think you ought to get away from your mother."

"I can't." My voice cracked. "Mother's the only one who knows the truth. If I leave she won't forgive me for it. I'll never find out anything if I don't stay close to her." The sudden thought of Michelle sent a shudder through me. "And my sister needs me, whether she knows it or not."

I leaned against him, and he closed his arms tight around me, as if he feared I might evaporate. I felt like a ragged scrap of silk, ripping down the middle.

Chapter Fourteen

"Come on," I said to Michelle. "We haven't done this in such a long time."

She laughed her sweet girlish laugh. "Okay, just let me change my shoes."

I waited out on the patio while she put on athletic shoes that she didn't mind getting dirty on our walk along the creek. She came back smiling eagerly, looking like the little sister I'd dragged along on such walks all through our childhood.

Every step down through the backyard took us farther from the house and our mother. I turned once and wasn't surprised to see her watching us from her study window. She smiled and waved; we smiled and waved back. I would get Michelle down into the woods, where Mother couldn't even see us from her window, and then I could talk to her openly.

The tiny flowers of some creeping weed covered the creek banks in yellow. Above us, tree branches were misty green with emerging new leaves. "Look," I said, pointing up. "A pileated."

The big black-backed woodpecker clung to a tree trunk and gave its loud cackling call, and from perhaps fifty feet away came an answer. Only one pair lived in these woods. In summer we'd see one or two young ones with the parents for a while, but by the following spring they'd be gone, killed by the winter or off to find their own mates and territories.

"I forget sometimes how peaceful it is here," Michelle said. She linked an arm through mine. "Thanks for reminding me. We used to have fun down here, didn't we?"

"We always had fun together," I said. It was silly to miss being ten or eleven years old, but I did, sharply, painfully.

"You taught me so much," Michelle said. "I grew up seeing the world—nature—through your eyes. You've always been in tune with the natural world, but I have to make a conscious effort to connect with it. I wish I could be more like you."

I barked a surprised laugh. "You're kidding."

She stopped, withdrew her arm and stepped back to look at me. "No, I envy you sometimes. You're able to be passionate about things—"

"Hot-headed, Mother would say." I forced a grin.

Michelle went on looking at me, serious, almost contemplative. "Well," she said, "Mother's always believed calm and rational behavior is better than passion. I'm not sure Mother knows what passion is."

Startled to hear her say such a thing, so close to criticism, I was speechless for a moment. Finally I said, picking my way toward the subject I'd brought her here to discuss, "I think all the passion went out of her life when our father died, and she's been trying ever since not to feel anything too deeply."

Michelle nodded. Somewhere nearby a squirrel chattered a warning and a bluejay screamed. "It's sad that she's completely closed off any possibility of falling in love and getting married again," Michelle said. "I guess in a way I'm glad we didn't have to change our lives to fit in a stepfather while we were growing up, but now—"

"She's still young," I said. "Fifty-two's not old. And she's attractive."

We were both silent a moment. Then Michelle said, "She wouldn't like us discussing her this way."

"She can't hear us, Mish."

At the same moment we both glanced back, in the direction of the house. I could just see the roof and chimney through the trees.

I said, "If she's clinging to his memory, if she can't forget him and that's the reason she won't see other men, why do you suppose she never talks about him? Why doesn't she want to make sure his children don't forget him?"

"Oh—" Michelle looked faintly annoyed, as if she'd had an automatic negative reaction to my question. "It's her way of coping."

"To blot him out of our lives? To blot out the first few years of our lives?"

"Rachel," Michelle said, slipping her arm in mine again. "Why are you bringing all this up now? You were talking about Daddy just recently. What—"

I pulled away. "I'd like to remember those years and I'd like to remember our father. I was old enough. I don't understand why I can't remember him clearly. Something's missing, and I want to find it. Don't you ever feel that way?"

She shrugged. "I was too young to remember. We've talked about this before—"

"I tried to have myself hypnotized so I could remember," I blurted.

"Hypnotized?" She looked confused. "By Mother? Why would she—"

"No. Another doctor. But I couldn't go through with it. I panicked during induction."

"Oh, Rachel," she said, touching my arm, concerned. "When? Why didn't you tell me about it?"

I told her now, in as much detail as I could remember.

She sighed. "Mother wouldn't like this if she found out. She'd be hurt that you went to someone else for help."

"Don't tell her," I said. Why had Michelle's first thought been for our mother's feelings?

"I won't," she murmured. Then, curious, studying me, "Did you remember anything—"

"No, I didn't get that far, I told you."

She chewed her bottom lip, an old habit when she was thinking.

I said, "Mother thinks I shouldn't try to remember because I was so traumatized by our father's death. I gather I had some kind of breakdown."

Michelle's eyes widened. "What? She said that?"

I told her what Mother had said about my destroying the pictures. Michelle's expression went from surprise to a kind of concerned acceptance. "I don't remember that at all," she said. "Well, I can see her point. Mother's just looking out for your emotional well-being."

"Oh, for heaven's sake!" I cried, and the loudness of my voice startled a couple of chickadees into angry chitters. "Let me look out for my own emotional well-being. What right does she have to keep our father a mystery to us? What right does she have to tell us what to think and feel and how to act and who to see and—Why do you let her dictate who you'll see, Mish? Why did you let her stop you from seeing Kevin when I know you wanted to?"

She took a couple of steps back, and her face was a cold mask. "I don't know what you're talking about. I made my own decision about Kevin. This is the busiest time of my life, finishing my degree, planning my future, and I don't need the distraction of—"

"She told you to stop seeing him, didn't she? She sat you down when I wasn't around, and talked you into it, just like she's been trying to talk me into breaking it off with Luke."

"That's ridiculous," Michelle said. "You're imagining things. She did no such thing."

"Don't use that voice with me! That patronizing therapist voice. You're my sister, my baby sister, don't talk to me like a stranger."

She spun away, marched raggedly along the path, back toward the house. I caught up and took her arm. She faced me, and I was startled to see tears on her cheeks. "I've seen Kevin a couple of times," she said in a whisper, as if afraid of being overheard even here. "I've been wanting to tell you. But I'm not dating him. It's just been lunch. I made the decision not to date him, I explained to him why." She closed her eyes briefly, pressing a hand to her forehead. "Please don't let Mother find out—"

I took her by the shoulders and looked into her eyes. "Michelle, you're a grown woman. You can see anybody you want to."

She let out a long sigh. "It's just easier if she doesn't know about it." Then she shook her head, making her blonde hair whip around her neck. "Rachel, I wish you'd stop dragging up all this about Daddy. It upsets her, she doesn't want to talk about it. And it's obviously hurting you, it's got you confused and torn. Can't you let it be?"

"Is that what therapists are telling patients these days? You're better off if you let the past be?"

"You're not a patient!"

"No, I'm your flesh and blood, and I deserve at least as much support as you'd give a patient who's trying to understand her past."

She swiped at her cheeks with the back of a hand. "All my patients are going to be children," she said. "They won't have pasts."

I laughed, although I felt like crying. "Well, that's one problem solved."

She sniffled and looked up, beyond me, as she blinked rapidly. "You've got your work," she said. "You've got Luke. You function well, you're not a neurotic crippled by unresolved issues. You should be enjoying the present, not digging around in the past. I'm not going to help you do something that will only hurt Mother."

Before I could answer, she turned and hurried away, toward the house, leaving me feeling as alone as I'd ever felt in my life.

Chapter Fifteen

Friday, the Fourth of July. This day that would end so badly began in a cool mist, the air a white gauze of fog drifting in from the Potomac.

Mother, fussing over preparations for the party she gave each year, peered out through the patio doors and wondered aloud whether it would be cloudy all day. When the fog burned off and sunlight drenched the back lawn, she fretted that the afternoon would be unbearably hot. Then the clouds settled back in to stay and she worried that we might have rain for the first time in three weeks.

Rosario went on with her baking, Michelle and I set up rented tables and chairs on the patio, and none of us bothered to respond to Mother. Rosie and Michelle knew as well as I did that her concern over the weather was more than a convenient focus for free-floating anxiety. Any extreme would force the guests indoors, and Mother didn't want two dozen people roaming her house.

It would have been useless to ask why she did this every year, inviting a group of near-strangers to the house. The July 4 party, a longtime event at the home of Theo and his wife Renee, moved to our house when Renee's battle with cancer began. The arrangement was supposed to be temporary, a favor, until she recovered. But she didn't recover. For some reason Mother felt obliged to continue the annual ritual after Renee's death, even though it was a chore and a strain.

Michelle and I worked silently, unfolding chairs, pushing card tables together in two long rows. She avoided my gaze and shied away every time I brushed against her. Watching her from the corner of my eye, I began to wonder. She was acting secretive, guilty, the way she used to as a kid when she was waiting for some misdeed to be discovered. Candy pilfered from the basketful meant for trick-or-treaters. Christmas gifts unwrapped for a peek, then inexpertly rewrapped. A sister's confidence broken.

Mother gave no sign that Michelle had told her what I was up to, but I wouldn't expect that. Mother would choose the moment to reveal what she knew.

I had another reason to worry—I'd invited Luke to the party without telling Mother. He'd said yes without hesitating, and he was entirely too enthusiastic about showing Mother she hadn't driven him out of my life. For days I'd been trying to make myself tell her he was coming, but now the party was hours away and she still didn't know.

My mother and sister and I floated through the house in our separate bubbles of anxiety, occasionally bouncing off one another.

It was also Michelle's birthday, but our pause at lunchtime to celebrate was only a momentary break in the tension. At the dining room table, when our barely touched sandwiches had been cleared away, Mother presented Michelle with a small oblong package. She smiled as Michelle stripped off the silver ribbon and glossy white wrapping paper, opened a blue velvet box and gasped at an elegantly simple gold bracelet. "It's beautiful, it's perfect!" Michelle cried, and she rose to give Mother a hug and kiss.

My gift, a navy blue leather briefcase with her initials in brass, was something she'd pined for and hinted about, but it was accepted now with a short "Thanks" and a flick of a smile in my general direction.

‹›‹›‹›

I was in jeans and Michelle wore Bermuda shorts, but Mother's idea of informality was black silk slacks and a white short-sleeved blouse. At four o'clock she stood stiff and alert on the patio, waiting for the first guests to arrive. They would all show up because none of them had anywhere else to go, and they'd all arrive precisely on time like patients keeping appointments.

They advanced up the driveway in little chatting groups, dressed in Bermuda shorts and tee-shirts or sun dresses. These people, all psychiatrists and psychologists, were Theo's friends, not Mother's. Many had been his students decades ago and were in the habit of attending Renee's July 4 party.

I worked the drinks table, handing out glasses of chilled white wine and cans of cold beer. Every few seconds I scanned the driveway for Luke. Mother stood next to the table, greeting her guests.

Melinda Morse, a tiny woman with moist bush baby eyes, grasped Mother's hand and said in a whispery voice, "I always appreciate the invitation, Judith. Since Robert died, and with my son living so far away—"

I saw Mother's gaze shift beyond Dr. Morse and lock on something, someone. Luke was rounding the corner of the house onto the patio. Mother looked at me, brows lifted inquiringly.

"I invited him." I handed Dr. Morse a glass of white wine. She murmured her gratitude and crept away into the crowd.

"Well," Mother said, "you're certainly entitled to invite a friend." As Luke approached she put on a brilliant smile. "Hello, Dr. Campbell. I'm glad you could come."

She didn't give him a chance to answer, but exclaimed that she'd forgotten the rest of the appetizers, and vanished into the house. Luke leaned to kiss me lightly and murmured, "Better than being shot on sight."

Michelle didn't bother to put on a show of civility. She returned Luke's greeting with a cold glare, then turned her back on him.

I was still steaming over that when Theo arrived.

"Rachel." He squeezed my hand and studied my face. "How have you been?"

"I'm okay, Theo." I withdrew my hand and cast a quick glance around, making sure Mother wasn't in earshot.

Theo stepped closer, keeping his voice low. "I've felt terribly guilty all week. I know it was my fault. I didn't adequately prepare you. Why don't you come see me this weekend and we can get into some of your issues in more depth."

I located Mother, with a knot of people twenty feet away. But she was watching us with an alert expression. Suddenly I was certain Michelle had betrayed my confidence.

Mindful of her gaze on us, I stepped back from Theo and said, "This is my friend, Luke Campbell."

"Ah." Theo was instantly distracted, his keen dark eyes making a quick assessment of the man before him.

"I've been looking forward to meeting you," Luke said, shaking Theo's hand. "Rachel tells me you're originally from Athens. I spent a week in Greece one summer when I was in college, and I've always wanted to go back."

In seconds they were talking about Theo's family and background.

I left them and followed Michelle into the kitchen. "Did you have to be so rude to Luke?" I said, sliding the patio door shut.

"You know, Mother's a good judge of people." She lifted a big blue bowl of potato salad from the refrigerator and pushed the fridge door shut with her elbow. "You ought to pay more attention to her opinion."

Through the glass doors I saw Luke and Theo at the far end of the patio, Luke with his hands in his jeans pockets, Theo leaning on his cane, gazing out over the flower beds as they chatted. Mother circulated among the other guests, but her head swiveled toward the two of them every few seconds.

"What did you tell Mother?" I said.

"I don't know what you're talking about." Michelle sailed past me with her chin up and the blue bowl in her hands, but her exit was blocked by the closed patio doors. She tried to shift the bowl, cradle it in one arm so she could open a door with her free hand, but the bowl was too big and slippery. She grunted in frustration.

I slid back the door. Her gaze met mine for a second, and in her eyes I thought I saw a glimmer of apprehension.

"God, what a dull bunch of people," Luke whispered when we managed to separate ourselves from the crowd and meet in a corner of the patio.

He'd discovered that a collection of shrinks talked about the same mundane things anybody else would: politics, the break in the heat, the drought that had them watering their lawns and gardens for hours every week.

"And they all want me to diagnose their cats and dogs, sight unseen," he said. "That guy talking to your mother, he spent ten minutes describing some skin problem his Lab's developed, and he got a little huffy when I told him to take the dog to his own vet. What a jerk."

I laughed, watching Max Richter's broad gestures. Every few seconds his large swooping hand landed on some part of Mother, her shoulder or hand or arm. Her smile was fixed and her body rigid against his incursions.

"He's by himself this year," I said. "Usually he brings his latest girlfriend or wife. He's been married four times."

"Jeez." Luke studied Mother and Dr. Richter. "He likes her, he really goes for her, I can tell."

"He's been coming on to her as long as I can remember. Even when he had a wife or girlfriend standing next to him. Maybe he sees her as a challenge. But she's not interested."

"He's lucky. He doesn't realize he's cozying up to a poisonous spider."

I looked down at a potted hibiscus, watched a pollen-gilded bumblebee back out of a red flower, and wondered why I still felt this urge to defend Mother.

<>〈〉<>

Luke and Theo and I sat at one of the improvised long tables and Mother and Michelle sat at the other. Dinner was cold ham and roast beef, potato salad, julienned cold vegetables, and Rosario's meltingly tender butter rolls. Mother would only go so far in carrying on Renee's tradition; she wouldn't set up a messy barbecue on the patio and cook hamburgers and hot dogs.

At our table a long serious debate about the pros and cons of timer-controlled lawn sprinklers gave way to fascination with the idea of heart surgery on cats and dogs. Everyone chewed contentedly and urged Luke to describe myriad unappetizing surgical procedures.

Every time I glanced Mother's way our eyes met. Half of my mind was keeping up with the conversation, while the other half frantically tried to construct plausible answers to Mother's inevitable questions.

As afternoon slid into evening, the sun broke through the clouds and burned red low behind the trees, reaching through the foliage to lay long fingers of pink light across the grass. When the meal was finished, Mother went into the kitchen and emerged a few minutes later bearing aloft a white-frosted cake with lighted candles.

The guests burst into song. *Happy birthday, dear Michelle.*

Perennially delighted by the cake and the attention, Michelle laughed and blew out the candles.

"Born on the Fourth of July?" Luke said.

"Yeah. I forgot to mention it," I murmured.

Why had I always felt this pang, as if the celebration of my sister's birthday denied something to me? It didn't make sense. Certainly I wasn't envious of a song from these people.

With a wry smile, Luke said, "I hope your birthday's livelier than this."

I laughed. "Mine's even quieter, actually. Just the three of us."

"Not this year." He stroked my back. "August 26. You'll have a birthday to remember this time, I guarantee."

I grinned. "I'll look forward to it."

My sister, smiling prettily, laid cake slices on the guests' plates. Rosario had made two cakes to ensure we'd have enough for everybody. Twenty-four years old, Michelle was today. Mature in some ways, still so childlike in many others.

Mother's cherishing gaze never left Michelle's face. However hard I tried, I never brought that look to Mother's eyes, that soft smile to her lips. Some kind of obstacle had always stood between Mother and me, something that made us draw back from one another. For all her show of love and concern and closeness, for all the gentle touches, she withheld herself from me, while her love for my sister overflowed, uncontainable, demanding expression.

<> ><>

"Rachel."

I turned to Dr. Aaron Krislov, distinguished professor of psychology at Georgetown University, a bearded man in blue Bermuda shorts and a yellow Izod shirt that stretched thin over his bulging belly. "Before it gets too dark," he said, "could I wangle a look at your animals?"

Half a dozen others asked to go along. Luke and I led them down through the trees to see four orphaned baby raccoons and a battle-scarred squirrel. Everyone was disappointed to hear they'd missed the hawk.

<><>

When I stepped back onto the patio, I saw Mother and Theo in the kitchen. She stood straight and still, hands clasped, her eyes boring into Theo as she spoke words I couldn't hear. He raised an arm a couple of times in a gesture I recognized as a plea, but she went on talking and didn't allow him to interrupt.

I spun around, searching for Michelle. She sat at a table chatting with Melinda Morse and nibbling the last of her cake.

When I reached her, I squeezed her shoulder hard enough to make her wince. "I want to talk to you."

"Rachel—" She squirmed out of my grasp.

Dr. Morse's big eyes got bigger.

I leaned close and whispered in Michelle's ear, "You little rat. You told her, didn't you?"

Michelle's face went red. The tip of her tongue flicked over her lips, catching a stray crumb at the corner of her mouth. "Not everything," she whispered back.

But enough to do damage, I'd bet. I left Michelle and maneuvered through the crowd to the sliding doors. When I pushed one open, Mother broke off before I could catch anything she was saying. Theo stood with his head bowed, one hand clutching his cane and the other raised to his mouth.

"Rachel," Mother said, "you're interrupting a conversation."

"About me?" I wasn't going to slink away and be a good girl. I shoved the door shut, catching a glimpse beyond it of Luke's puzzled face and behind him Michelle, both of them moving toward the kitchen.

"If you want to berate somebody," I told Mother, "then pick on me. Leave Theo alone."

Her mouth opened and I saw a flash of pure amazement on her face. But her words came out as a gentle reproach. "Rachel, really, what's gotten into you?"

Her tone made me wonder momentarily if I'd misunderstood. But Theo's tear-filled eyes told me I hadn't. "Mother, I don't know what Michelle told you, but Theo was trying to help me."

"And you thought you had to keep it a secret from me." Soft, sad voice and expression. She was infinitely disappointed and hurt by her daughter and her friend.

The door slid open and Luke stepped in, followed closely by Michelle. Mother made a little noise of exasperation. "Dr. Campbell, would you mind letting us have some privacy?"

Luke ignored her, asking me, "What's going on?"

"It's none of your business!" Michelle cried.

"I think I should go," Theo said.

I laid a hand on his arm. "No, please don't."

"I think it's best." He patted my wrist, but his sorrowful gaze was on Mother. "Judith, I would never do anything intentionally to hurt you, and you should be well aware of that after all these years. I was simply trying to help this dear girl."

Mother regarded him icily. He waited through a moment's silence, then said, "If I might use your telephone to call a taxi—"

"I'll drive you home," Luke said.

Theo protested a little, but weakly, before accepting the offer.

Luke took my hand, and I cut him off as he was about to speak. "I'll be fine," I said. "Really I will."

"Call me later. Or come over to my place."

I nodded, and he kissed me lightly. When he stepped away I saw Michelle roll her eyes. Mother's mouth was a thin line.

"Shall we go out the front way?" Theo said, and I realized he didn't feel sufficiently collected to stop and say goodbye to everyone on the patio.

I was left standing in the kitchen with my mother and sister, the two of them side by side, united against me.

"We still have guests," Mother said. "We'll talk about this later."

When Mother decided it was time for guests to go, she could get the idea across firmly without lapsing for a second from her perfect hostess act. She'd move among the men and women on the patio, telling them how much she'd enjoyed seeing them, that she hoped they'd be back next year, and they'd have no choice but to leave.

I waited in the kitchen, scraping leftovers into the garbage disposal, slamming plates and silverware into the dishwasher, trying to decide what I'd say to Mother. I wanted to run away, but I couldn't do that anymore. It was time I stood my ground and got some answers.

Under my defiance I harbored the hope that it would all make sense in the end, that Mother would explain, make me understand.

When the last guest left it was nine o'clock, nearly full dark. In the distance I heard the crack and boom of the fireworks display getting started at Langley High School.

Mother and Michelle gathered the remaining dishes and brought them in. We scraped and rinsed in silence. After we'd stacked the dishwasher for the first of two cycles that would be needed, Mother told Michelle, "You're the birthday girl, you've done enough work. Go on upstairs and relax now. Rachel and I need to talk."

Michelle's eyes widened. "Don't you want me to stay?"

"Please, Michelle." A firm order, not a request.

Michelle was clearly wounded by this exclusion, but Mother let her go without attempting to salve her feelings. I suspected Michelle would stop halfway down the hall and tiptoe back to listen at the door.

Mother and I were alone in the kitchen, facing each other.

"Let's sit down," she said.

All right, I thought. Now. My mouth had gone dry.

For what seemed an endless time, we sat in silence at the little maple table where we always ate breakfast. On the far side of the kitchen water sloshed in the dishwasher. A stream of air from the baseboard vent chilled my ankles.

"Rachel," she said at last.

Her long slender fingers reached toward me. I laid both my hands in my lap. For a moment she left her arm outstretched on the tabletop, then withdrew it and sat back.

"Rachel," she said again, her voice soft. "I'm so worried about you."

"Why?"

"Well," she said, "when I discovered you've been to see Theo as a patient, that you attempted hypnosis—"

"You had no right to jump on Theo about it. Don't you people have any ethics? Don't you have any respect for doctor-patient confidentiality?"

I met her gaze for a second before a jolt of alarm made me look away. I was afraid of her. I was afraid she could reach into my mind with her eyes.

"Rachel, you're my daughter—"

"I'm a grown woman and I'm entitled to my privacy."

A pause, then she spoke with gentle humor. "At the moment you seem more like a defensive teenager."

Stung, I realized she was right. I recognized the old resistance, the stubborn need to be a concrete wall to her velvet-covered battering ram.

When I didn't answer, she went on, "Yes, you are entitled to your privacy. I suppose I'm just a little hurt that you went to Theo for help instead of coming to me."

I could have screamed. I refused to let her do this. After the way she'd played with my mind, she was not going to make me feel like the ungrateful daughter, spitting in the face of her love. My hands clasped to my suddenly throbbing head, I said, "I didn't think you'd—"

"Do you have a headache? Let me get you some ibuprofen." She started to rise.

"I don't want you to get me anything!"

She sat down again. "All right. Why don't you tell me what's put you in such a state? What have you and Theo discussed? You know, Theo's a good friend, but he's not the one to give you information about our family."

"I didn't think I'd ever get it from you. Anything he told me would've been more than you have."

"And what has he told you?" Her voice, her face, her body, were quiet, cool.

My eyes filled with maddening tears. "Why didn't you ever tell us about your family? Why did you keep them such a deep dark secret?"

Behind Mother, Michelle appeared in the doorway. Instead of interrupting as I expected her to, she stopped and waited with me for Mother's answer.

Silence, for what seemed an eternity. She followed a fly's zigzag trek across the tabletop but showed no reaction to the filthy insect's invasion of her kitchen. When she spoke at last, her voice was hollow and remote. "What did Theo tell you about them?"

"Not much of anything. He just said it was bad, you had a terrible family and it was amazing you survived."

With a flick of one hand she drove the fly from the tabletop. It zoomed past my right shoulder. "Then you must see why I don't want to talk about it."

Guilt rattled its cage at the back of my mind. This time I wouldn't turn it loose. "Mother, Michelle and I have a right to

know about our grandparents, and our—our—" Aunts, uncles?
I had no idea. "We have a right to know."

"Be grateful for being spared, Rachel. Some things are too—"
She broke off and shook her head. "Just be grateful for being
spared."

"Spared what?" I said, my voice rising. "Mother, I want to
know. I want to know now."

She leaned toward me, anger flaring in her dark eyes. "All
right, Rachel. What do you want to hear first? Do you want
to hear what my father did to my mother? Breaking her arms,
fracturing her skull, knocking out her teeth. Kicking her in the
ribs. Do you want all the details?"

I couldn't speak. The chill around my ankles spread through
my body.

"You said you wanted to know." Her voice cracked, but she
forced the words out. "Maybe you'd like to hear about the way
my mother killed herself—"

"Oh my God," I whispered.

"She drank a pint of Clorox bleach. It ate through her throat and
esophagus and stomach. She died in agony. I watched her die."

I reached for her hands. "Oh, God, Mother, I'm sorry—"

She snatched her hands away, raised them in a defensive
motion in front of her. Her gaze darted about the room. "Then
he didn't have her around to beat up anymore. He wasn't happy
then. He needed her. So he put a shotgun in his mouth and
blew his brains out. And I was glad. I was glad he was dead and
it was finally over."

She stopped abruptly. I heard my own breath, ragged and
noisy, and in the background the rhythmic sloshing of the dishwasher. Beyond Mother, I saw Michelle, eyes wide and shocked,
both hands clamped over her mouth.

Mother slumped back in her chair, and a mask came down
over her face, smoothing away emotion. She was deathly pale.
"I had a sister," she said, her voice quiet and toneless. "Anna.
She disappeared and never came back. And that's what I did
too, in my own way."

She closed her eyes for a moment, and when she opened them her lashes were wet. "I didn't want to give you and your sister that kind of heritage. What would have been the point?"

I sat numb and cold, groping for the questions I'd wanted to ask, the demands I'd meant to press. My father. The pictures. The missing birth certificate. The things she'd said to me under hypnosis. What was she trying to make me forget?

I blurted, "Mother, was I adopted?"

She stared at me, her dry lips slightly open.

"Mother?" I said. "Was I?"

She let out a little cry that mixed amazement, bewilderment, pain. "Why would you think something like that?"

I couldn't waver now. I couldn't let the familiar grip of guilt stop me. But I was unable to make my voice any louder than hers. "Is it true? Is that why I don't have a birth certificate?"

"Rachel, for God's sake!" Michelle exclaimed. She rushed forward and threw her arms around Mother's shoulders. "Have you gone completely crazy?"

"Mish—"

A groan from Mother cut me off. She pressed both hands to her left chest, closed her eyes, opened them and blinked rapidly. Her breath came in quick gasps.

"Mother?" I said. "Mother!"

I was up and leaning over her, pushing Michelle away. I clamped my fingers on Mother's wrist and refused to let her shake off my hand. For a terrifying second I couldn't feel a pulse, then it came, erratic, weak, beat on top of beat, a pause, a cascade of faint vibrations too rapid to count.

"My God, she's fibrillating. Mish, call 911."

Michelle stood motionless, open-mouthed, blank-faced.

"Do it! Now!" I pushed her toward the wall phone.

She fumbled with the receiver, got the 911 operator, babbled uselessly. Mother protested the fuss even as she gasped for breath. I crossed to Michelle, grabbed the phone and reeled off the information.

When I hung up, Michelle had her arms around Mother. She glared at me over Mother's head. "Just look what you've done. Are you satisfied now?"

I drove behind the ambulance, Michelle flushed and trembling beside me. When I said I was sure Mother would be all right, she snapped, "What do you know? You're nothing but a cat and dog doctor."

I bit back angry words and drove on in silence to Fairfax Hospital. *She will be all right. She will be. I didn't cause this. Dear God, did I cause this?*

As the medics had forced Mother to lie on the gurney, she'd reached for my hand and gripped it weakly in her cold, cold fingers. "You're not adopted," she'd said, the words breathy and urgent. "You're not."

I'd tucked her arm against her side and murmured, "I know, Mother, I know." At that moment I'd believed her.

Nothing was resolved. I'd made my mother ill, and the answers I needed remained out of reach, waiting for some still unimagined question to be asked.

Chapter Sixteen

Michelle and I didn't hear the doctor's report. We heard Mother's version of it, after she'd been moved into a room for overnight observation. We stood on either side of her bed, with a gray curtain separating us from the patient who shared the room. I could hear the unseen woman snoring softly.

"Just minor irregularities," Mother assured us. The head of her bed was raised part way so that she was almost in a sitting position. Her auburn hair fell loose on the pillow, catching the light from the single lamp above the headboard. "It's probably nothing more than stress."

Michelle glowered at me.

Ignoring my sister's look, I said, "It didn't seem minor. Did he find an underlying problem?"

Mother smoothed the blue sheet over her legs. "Well, it's not serious."

"I wish I could go on believing that," Michelle said. "But I'm starting to think it's worse than you ever let me know."

I glanced from her to Mother. "You mean this isn't something new? Why didn't you tell me you had a heart problem?"

"Really, it's nothing to worry about." She waved a dismissive hand.

"Tell me, Mother. Please. When did this start?"

"Oh, a while back. I was feeling something a little—" Her long fingers fluttered over her chest. "—unusual, and I went to

Dr. Beaumont. Of course he immediately sent me to a specialist."
She gave a little laugh: *We know how doctors are, don't we?*

Worry was full-blown in me. Every other concern melted away in the face of this reality. My mother was ill. Something was wrong with her heart. "What did the cardiologist say?"

Her dark eyes met mine. "It's hypertrophic cardiomyopathy—"

"My God." I groped for the chair behind me and dropped into it.

"But it's mild," Mother said. "My medication takes care of it most of the time. I'm hardly aware of a problem."

I gripped the chair's cold metal arms. "How long have you known?"

She hesitated. "About eighteen months."

"Eighteen months!" I jumped up. "Why didn't you tell me?"

"Because I saw absolutely no reason to worry you. You were in Ithaca, you were very busy with your training, and you couldn't have done anything anyway."

"I've been home since Christmas. You could've told me."

"Rachel." The sheets rustled with her movement. Her fingers were cold on my hand. "You're right. I should have."

She held out her arms and I leaned into them gratefully, embracing the slender body that now seemed so frail. "I'm sorry I upset you," I mumbled against her shoulder.

She patted my back. "Let's not think about it anymore."

I drew back and wiped tears from my cheeks. Mother's hand glided over my hair and brushed my cheek.

"Mother." Michelle's voice was too loud in the hushed room. "Did the doctor give you any special orders for when you go home?"

"Oh, the usual. Take it easy, avoid stress."

"And that's what you're going to do," Michelle said. "You should cut back on your practice—"

"No, no, no. That's absolutely not necessary. As long as I keep down the stress level in other areas."

Michelle threw me a barbed glance. I was one of those other areas.

The door swung inward with a whoosh and a stocky young blond woman in blue scrubs appeared. "I'm going to have to ask y'all to leave now," she said. "It's way past visiting hours, and your mother and her roommate both need their rest."

She pursed her lips and raised her eyebrows to emphasize the order before departing.

"Yes, you two go home now," Mother said. "I'll see you both in the morning."

Michelle and I didn't speak during the drive, and once inside the house she went directly to her bedroom. I unloaded the dishwasher and loaded the machine with the rest of the dirty dishes before climbing the stairs too.

◇◇◇

"It doesn't necessarily mean her condition's worsening," Luke said when I called him. "The arrhythmia could be entirely psychogenic."

"You mean it is a reaction to stress." I sat cross-legged on my bed, forehead in palm. "I did bring it on."

"No, I didn't mean that. Stop blaming yourself. That's probably what she wants you to do. Don't fall into the trap."

"Oh, Luke. You make her sound so diabolical."

"Hey, remember you're the one who said she used hypnosis to control you."

"Maybe I'm imagining things. I mean, I was all wound up when Theo was trying to hypnotize me—"

"Rachel, for God's sake! You're finally getting at the truth. Don't start doubting yourself now."

I rubbed the aching muscles at the back of my neck. "I just wish I felt sure I didn't contribute to this heart problem."

"You know better than that, Dr. Goddard. Heart disease doesn't develop overnight in people any more than it does in animals. If you can't trust your own medical knowledge, then trust mine."

He was right. But that didn't take away the guilt.

⟨⟩´⟩⟨⟩

Sleep was a foreign thing, distant and unattainable. The day's events churned through my mind, Mother's wildly skipping heartbeat pulsed against my fingertips. I rose and paced the room. I opened a window and breathed in the heavy humid air, listened to the screech and buzz of nocturnal insects. I flopped on the bed again and kicked the twisted top sheet away.

Despite my anxiety over Mother's illness, my thoughts kept sliding in one direction: her keys were in her purse, and her purse was in her room, unguarded. The file cabinet keys had to be in her purse.

I shifted, turned onto my side. No, I couldn't do it.

Deep silence enveloped the house. Was Michelle asleep?

I slipped out of bed, crept to the door, opened it a crack. Across the hall, no light showed under Michelle's door.

The hallway was so dark that I had to feel my way to Mother's room. Inside, I closed the door quietly, then groped across the room toward the dresser. My searching hand struck the lamp shade. I grabbed and fumbled to keep the lamp from tipping over. After giving my suddenly racing heart a minute to slow down, I switched on the light.

Mother's purse lay on the dresser, a navy blue leather shoulderbag with a gold clasp. I eased the clasp open, slid a hand inside, gripped the keys tightly so they wouldn't jangle when I removed them. Even so, I glanced at the door, afraid I'd somehow given myself away.

My throat was so tight that I was conscious of every dragging breath. I sorted through the dozen keys, able to identify most of them. One looked like the key I'd had made for the box in Mother's study. The two smallest keys, I hoped, would open the file cabinets.

I moved slowly down the stairs, feeling for each step in the dark, and tiptoed along the hall to Mother's study. Behind the closed door, I switched on the ceiling light and was momentarily stunned by the full illumination of my actions. I almost stopped then, but a minute later I was riffling through the manila file folders in one of the cabinet drawers.

Like everything Mother did, the filing system was impeccably organized. Dividers identified cases according to the patients' afflictions: ACROPHOBIA, AGORAPHOBIA, CLAUSTROPHOBIA, and so on. I skimmed the names on the individual folders, glanced inside some, feeling like a peeping tom at the windows of strangers' lives. I began to doubt that I would find a case record about myself among these files, but I kept going out of a compulsion to be thorough.

At very back of the last drawer, I saw a folder with no name on it. I yanked it out.

The folder contained a single sheet of blue note paper with a few lines in a handwriting I didn't recognize. A small memo square, paper-clipped to the sheet, bore Mother's familiar script. I took the folder to the desk and sat down to read. Mother's note said, "Explore the motivations of a woman who is capable of such a thing."

The slightly uneven top and bottom of the note paper made me believe the names of both recipient and sender had been scissored off, and perhaps part of the message too. What remained was:

I want you to know that I have no regrets. I could lie and say I'm sorry it happened because it turned my life upside down, but I'm not sorry. It was wonderful, and it gave me the one beautiful thing I've got left.

"What on earth?" I murmured. I read the letter again, then Mother's one-sentence memo. If the letter had been written to her, why had she attached the note and put both away in a folder as if this were a possible topic for a paper? I had no idea how to interpret any of it, but the words were charged with meaning, weighted with a dark emotion I couldn't name. They chilled me.

Overhead I heard movement, then footsteps in the upstairs hall. Michelle walked like a lumberjack when she was groggy.

The file was back in the cabinet and I was out the door when she called, "Rachel? Where are you?"

"Right here." I moved into the light that now spilled down the stairs.

Michelle stood halfway up the steps, barefoot in a short pink nightgown, hair tangled around her face. "What are you doing in the dark?"

"I couldn't sleep. Have you been awake too?"

She rubbed at her eyes. "I went to sleep and kept dreaming about Mother. I'm so worried. Do you really think she'll be all right?"

She was my little sister again, a scared child coming to me for reassurance. I climbed the steps to meet her, hoping she wouldn't spot Mother's keys in my hand.

"I'm sure she'll be okay," I said. "Go on back to bed."

I took her arm and nudged her up the stairs. We paused at the top.

"Promise me you'll be careful not to upset Mother when she comes home," Michelle said. "She can't take any more stress."

"Oh, God, Mish, let's not stand here and argue in the middle of the night."

My insecure baby sister had vanished. Michelle gave me that level, superior look I hated, her almost-a-therapist expression.

"Rachel, I don't know what's going on in your head. You're starting to scare me." Then she softened, shifting gears again. "I'm willing to listen if you want to talk about it. You know, we used to be able to talk about anything."

I shook my head. "There have always been things we couldn't say."

We held each other's gaze for a long moment. I wondered how well I really knew her. She didn't know me at all. "What do you think about the things she said tonight? About her parents."

Averting her eyes, she said, "If Mother doesn't want to talk about all that, she has a right—"

"But they were our grandparents. And they sound like lunatics. Doesn't that bother you?"

She tilted her chin obstinately. The door to her mind had clanged shut. "It has nothing to do with us."

She would believe that no matter what I said. She was turning away, toward her room. "Mish, what's your first memory of me?" I said. "Of us as a family?"

"Oh, Rachel!" She flapped her arms, then faced me again. "Where did this obsession come from? I can't believe you asked Mother if you were adopted! She gave birth to you, she's loved you all your life. How could you ask her something like that?"

I could take her downstairs, use the key in my hand, make her look at the pictures hidden in Mother's study, the pictures that didn't include me. "You don't understand—"

Her face was hard and cold. "I understand this: you're endangering Mother's health. I want you to stop it. Now. Don't you dare say another word to her about any of it."

She marched to her open bedroom door, stepped into the room and turned to throw me a harsh glance, a further warning. She didn't slam the door, but closed it silently, the way Mother would.

I returned the keys to Mother's purse. Back in my room, I sank into the chair at the dresser. My mirrored image confronted me: messy hair, rumpled gown, eyes hollow and mournful.

My questions had made my mother ill tonight, sent her to the hospital. My probing had touched her very heart, the core of her life. I was an ungrateful child, an unloving daughter.

But I did love her. I loved her and yearned for her approval and embraces and proud looks. I thought of that other box in her study, filled with school records, report cards, my A's preserved along with Michelle's. No one who saw that cache of memories could have said, *She didn't love you, she only loved your sister.*

She wanted me to stop examining my own life, our life as a family. How could I persist after what had happened that night? Mother was the one person who knew all the answers, but now I didn't dare push her to tell me. I didn't want to hurt her, couldn't bear knowing that I'd done something to endanger her.

Mother came home Saturday morning wearing a heart monitor.

"I have to put up with this thing for forty-eight hours," she said, and her exasperation might have made anyone think the monitor was a fifty-pound weight.

The device hanging on a strap around her neck resembled an ordinary cassette recorder-player and was only fractionally larger. A tape connected to five electrodes on her chest recorded her every heartbeat. After she'd worn the monitor for forty-eight hours, the tape would go to a lab for analysis.

I didn't want to leave her, but Mother brushed aside any suggestion of my staying away from work. "Michelle will be here," she said. "I'll be fine. Don't fuss."

But Michelle fussed, and when I came home I saw that Mother had settled happily into being cared for by my sister. I stood on the sidelines, watching Michelle hold Mother's arm as if she were an invalid and walk her into the dining room for dinner. When Mother wanted something from the kitchen, Michelle leapt to her feet to fetch it.

After dinner they went to Mother's bedroom. From the hallway I heard them murmuring beyond the open door. I stood out of sight and listened for a long time to the soft rhythm of their voices, catching only a few clear words now and then.

What am I doing?

Suddenly aware of how ridiculous it was to be eavesdropping on my mother and sister, I strode purposefully past the door, headed for my room. When I glanced at them in passing, I saw Mother on the bed with her legs stretched out and Michelle in a chair drawn close, one of Mother's hands caught in both of hers.

"Rachel?"

Mother's voice stopped me. I turned back to her doorway.

Smiling, she patted the bed beside her. "Come sit with me."

When I sat down Mother's right hand slid into mine. Her skin was so cold it made me worry that her heart wasn't circulating blood efficiently. "Are you feeling all right?" I asked.

She nodded, looking exhausted but happy. "I feel wonderful, just having the two of you here with me."

<>◇<>

Fuzzy-headed and bone-weary with the need for sleep that wouldn't come, I padded down to the kitchen at 2 a.m. In the glow of the small fluorescent light over the sink, I poured a glass of milk, then forgot to drink it as I stood at the patio doors looking into the night. There was no moon, and beyond the circle of the patio floodlight I saw only flat blackness without a hint of shadows or shapes.

"Can't sleep?"

I jumped. Mother had come into the kitchen silently.

"What are you doing up?" I said.

"Oh, I can't get comfortable with these electrodes stuck to me." The recorder strap crossed her shoulder and chest, and the machine dangled below her left arm. Its lead wire disappeared between the front folds of her white cotton robe. Mother's hair was a mass of tangles, as if she'd been twisting restlessly in bed.

Beside me, she peered into the yard. "Oh, look."

Two young foxes ventured into the light for a second, then trotted back into the dark.

"They're growing up," Mother said. "Going around without their parents."

With both hands she shoved her hair away from her face.

"Remember that bad winter," she said, "when you were thirteen or fourteen, you started putting out the cats' dry food for the foxes?" She laughed. "I couldn't understand why Kate and Sarah were using so much food. I was about to have Dr. McCutcheon run tests on them to see if they both had a metabolic disorder."

"Then I confessed."

Mother laughed again, obviously finding it funny in retrospect. I didn't recall her laughing at the time. She'd given me a lecture about sneakiness. The fox-feeding stopped.

It was absurd, this welling up of resentment over something that happened when I was a child. With a harshness that surprised me, I said, "Mother, you ought to be in bed." I softened my voice. "You need rest more than anything else."

"I know. I'll sleep when I'm tired enough."

She stepped to the switch by the hallway door and flipped it. I blinked in the glare of the ceiling light. I watched her move around the room, straighten a hand towel on the rack behind the sink, push the salt and pepper shakers into perfect alignment on the counter next to the stove. The familiarity of these actions touched and comforted me. She was my mother, not some stranger I had to fear. I needed to believe that.

The tidying up done, she poured a small glass of skim milk and pulled an oblong plastic container from a cupboard.

"Maybe a snack will help me sleep." She popped open the container's flat lid and removed two sheets of graham crackers. Laying them on a saucer she took from another cabinet, she smiled at me and said, "Let's sit down and talk a little."

I carried my milk to the breakfast table and sat across from her. She pushed the saucer holding the crackers toward me, and I snapped off a brown rectangle, scattering a few crumbs on the tabletop. When I dunked the cracker in my milk Mother laughed.

"You've always done that," she said.

"Try it."

She dipped her cracker and took a bite. "Mmm. It's good." She licked a white drop off her lower lip.

The sight of her doing this stirred sweet-sad memories: Mother walking between Michelle and me at Disneyworld, all of us munching on popcorn; Mother at the county fair, wrestling with a huge fluff of pink cotton candy and getting a bit stuck on her nose. Laughter. A mother and her happy children.

She placed the rest of the cracker back on the white saucer. Seeing her face grow solemn, I tensed, waiting.

She was silent a moment, using the side of her hand to brush the cracker crumbs into a tiny brown pile. For some reason I thought she was going to ask me about Luke, why I was seeing him again. I braced for that, and what she actually said caught me off guard.

"Rachel—" She hesitated. "I don't understand why you wanted Theo instead of me to hypnotize you. And I won't ask you to explain. But I know I can help you with your memories more than Theo ever could. As soon as I'm rid of this silly machine, I want you to let me hypnotize you."

Everything in me recoiled. I tried to clamp down on the panic, but it surged through my blood and set my heart racing. If she'd made me forget in the first place, what would she do to me this time?

Unable to meet her eyes, I traced the grain in the wooden tabletop with a remarkably steady finger. "I'm not sure it's a good idea."

"I really believe it would be the best thing for you."

She reached across to close her fingers around mine. Our two hands, so much alike. Her gold wedding ring bit into my knuckle.

"Don't be afraid," she said. "I'll be with you. I won't let it go too far. I'll be in complete control."

I snatched my hand away so quickly that hers was left suspended above the table.

"Let me think it over." I rose, meaning to rinse my glass and tuck it into the dishwasher, but instead I plunked it down hard on the counter.

"Rachel, let's talk—"

"Not now. You need to get some rest."

She sighed, a faint exhalation. "I'll go up in a minute."

I fled down the hall, up the stairs, into the cocoon of my room.

When I slept I entered another world, of shadows and far-off voices. Kathy, my imaginary childhood friend, took me by the hand and led me first into a tangled wood, then across a blazing desert, then down a street to a rain-swept playground where a jungle gym loomed like a skeletal monster, its empty swings creaking in the wind as a child cried somewhere nearby.

Chapter Seventeen

"I miss you," Luke said, his breath against my ear. "How long do we have to wait?"

We were in his office at lunch time, with the door closed. Tucked into a corner, we couldn't be glimpsed even through the window. He pressed his mouth to mine and I wrapped my arms around him, pulling him closer, as close as he could get, not close enough.

A long moment later I broke the kiss, gasping. "Patients," I said.

He nuzzled my neck. "I don't think I've got enough patience to last."

I laughed. "I meant the four-footed type. It's almost time."

Groaning, he stepped back, ran his fingers through his sandy hair and rubbed a hand across his mouth. "How much longer is this going to go on?"

I leaned against the wall and shut my eyes for a second, giving in to the fantasy of going home with him now, this minute, staying in bed with him until we were both exhausted and sated.

Opening my eyes, I met his steady gaze. "She seems to need us home with her every night. I think this episode with her heart really spooked her." I paused. "Last night she said she's updating her will."

"Oh, for God's sake," Luke said, half-laughing, half-amazed. He shook his head. "Rachel—"

"What?" I didn't understand his reaction.

"She's playing on your guilt feelings. She's also trying to keep you away from me, but what really worries me is the way she's twisting your emotions."

I sat on a corner of his desk and rubbed at my eyes. So tired. I'd been awakened over and over during the night by my own dreams. "Don't you think I can see that?"

"Then why are you letting her do it?"

"I think she's genuinely afraid of dying."

"Even when she knows damned well she's not?"

"It doesn't have anything to do with what's rational. She knows something's wrong with her heart, and I think it terrifies her, even if she won't admit it."

"I'm still not convinced she has a real problem. I'd have to see her sonogram and EKG before I'd believe it."

"I talked to her doctor, Luke. He confirmed what she told Michelle and me. It's not life-threatening at this point, but it's real, and her condition has deteriorated in the last few months."

Luke let out a long breath and stood with his hands on his hips, staring at the floor.

Before he could say anything, I went on, "She's got this look in her eyes all the time. I don't know how to describe it. Haunted, maybe. She looks haunted and scared."

"Haunted by what?"

Avoiding his gaze, I rose and moved to the window. In the parking lot an elderly man struggled to keep his black poodle from getting at the cat carrier a young blond woman had just pulled from her car.

I hadn't yet told Luke what Mother revealed about her family—my family—the night she fell ill. Suicides. Insanity. My heritage, my bloodline. I wasn't sure I'd ever want him to know. But if I kept something like that from him, what right did I have to let him get deeply involved with me?

I had to answer his question. What haunted my mother? I turned back to him, shrugging. "My father's death, I guess. She's tried hard to put it out of her mind, and I keep bringing it up."

"Rachel, why are you so ready to blame yourself? Maybe she's worried that you're going to find out what she's hiding from you. Maybe she knows you've uncovered her sick little mind control game—"

"Luke!" I pressed my fingers to my temples. The last thing I needed was a tension headache just as I started afternoon appointments. "I don't want to talk about this now."

"When will we talk about it? I can't even get you alone these days unless I drag you into my office."

"I'm telling you I can't take any more of this right now."

"Okay, okay." He lay a hand along my cheek, his skin warm on mine. "Look, it's you I'm worried about. I don't give a damn about your mother's emotional life, or her health either, for that matter."

Stepping away from his touch, I said, "I think I need to find out more about my father's death. About the accident. I've got a feeling—I don't know, maybe it'll jog my memory."

"How can you find out about it? You don't have any relatives to ask, do you?"

"No. Newspaper stories, maybe."

"Stories more than twenty years—"

A knock on the door, then Megan's high musical voice. "Dr. Campbell? Dr. Goddard? Your two o'clocks are both here."

Day after day passed in a haze of rainless heat. High temperature records were broken, health advisories were issued. Under the relentless sun the air grew murky with pollution and humidity, and weeds along the roads yellowed and died in the dust-dry earth. I moved the sprinklers around the yard according to Mother's instructions, and they swirled and sprayed for hours each morning, keeping her plants alive.

The stifling air of early evening kept us indoors. Unable to putter among her flowers, Mother decided to revive our old habit of reading aloud to each other for an hour after dinner. With an enthusiasm that seemed to baffle Michelle, she compiled a list of possible books, presented it to us at dinner one night, and urged us to contribute our own ideas.

"Mother," Michelle said, "I have work to do in the evenings." She frowned at the list in her hand.

"Oh. Of course." A sudden drawing-back, a quickly hidden hurt. Usually I was the one who caused Mother to react that way. With thumb and index finger she lifted the sheet of white paper from Michelle's hand. "Well, then, Rachel and I could read together. Rachel?"

"Sure. Let me see what you've come up with."

Michelle glanced from Mother to me, a frown etched between her eyes, her mouth puckering into petulance. "I guess I could spare a little time," she said.

"Oh, wonderful!" Mother beamed and reached to squeeze her hand.

So we gathered in the den after dinner, and I sat staring up at the proud-Mother wall while she began reading *Rebecca*. Except for the book choice, I felt like a child again, enclosed in our tight little circle, sheltered from the world of strangers outside.

⟨⟩⟨⟩

Mother never mentioned the terrible memories I'd forced her to talk about on the night of July 4. Instead of withdrawing from me as I'd expected her to, she seemed to need my company more and more. She discussed the news with me, asked my opinion about relocating her office when her lease was up. She talked to me about my job and my rehab animals as if she truly cared.

This closeness was something I'd yearned for all my life, but it came too suddenly, and too late, to feel natural. I gave her my company and attention but kept up my guard, torn between love and concern for my mother and suspicion that she was simply trying to silence my questions.

⟨⟩⟨⟩

My own reflection could mesmerize me. I sat at my dresser and studied my face, picking out this feature and that, proving and disproving, arriving at conclusions only to throw everything into doubt again.

Memories came in snatches or in long threads that stretched thin and refused to expand. A musky perfume floating through darkened rooms. A narrow street where half a dozen squealing children hurled snowballs. A woman who looked like Mother braiding my long red hair while I watched her sorrowful face in a mirror.

One Sunday morning as Mother stood at the living room window in a blaze of sun, I suddenly saw her at another window, in another time, holding a scorched African violet up for examination.

"It died from too much sun," I blurted, remembering the drooping, brown-edged leaves.

Mother's eyebrows went up. "What?"

"That African violet you used to have," I fumbled, sensing the wrongness of what I said but unable to pin it down. "It was in a sunny window, it got too much sun."

"Rachel," she said, with a slight bemused smile, "I've never had African violets."

The picture was still as vivid as the splash of light on the windowsill. But no, it wasn't Mother. It was a woman who looked like her. The woman who'd braided my hair.

"Oh." My voice came out faint, and I made an effort to raise it to a natural level. "I don't know what I was thinking."

I turned away from her sudden scrutiny, and smothered the inexplicable panic that rose in me.

During those long weeks of July, Mother suggested three more times that I let her hypnotize me. She wasn't going to let it drop. It was important to her.

"Why don't you let her do it?" Luke said.

Astonished, I faced him. "Are you serious?"

We were in the National Zoo's Amazonia building, a miniature tropical rainforest where monkeys, birds, and a shy sloth inhabited soaring trees under a glass roof. On our first date in three weeks, Luke had wanted time alone with me in his apartment, but I balked at the intimacy we both craved. It was one more form of pressure, a demand I couldn't handle. Disappointed and baffled, he gave in when I suggested the first thing that came to mind, an outing where we'd be surrounded by a multitude of strangers.

I wanted to unwind away from home, put Mother out of my head. But she was all we talked about on the drive into D.C., and we went on talking about her among the camera-flashing Japanese tourists who crowded the narrow path through the exhibit.

"Yes," Luke said, "I'm ser—" A screech erupted from the scarlet macaw in a nearby tree, making Luke break off and wince. "Yes, I'm serious," he said when the bird fell silent. "I've been reading about hypnosis. If you consciously decide not to go into a trance, nobody can put you under. Right?"

A knot of half a dozen Japanese children squealed and pointed at two black monkeys leaping in the branches overhead. Safely out of reach, the monkeys settled to chewing on apple chunks and returned the children's interest with indifference.

Luke and I edged past the kids and stopped at a railing overlooking the small artificial river.

"What's your point?" I said. "Why would I let her try to hypnotize me, then not let her put me under?"

"Pretend to be hypnotized. Find out what she'll say to you when she thinks you're under her control."

I looked down at catfish three feet long. Their plump yellow-sided bodies floated lazily, their whiskers drifted back like loose hair in a breeze.

"I'm not sure I could do that," I said at last. "I don't know if I'm that good an actress."

The children, impatient for a turn at the rail, jostled us and we walked on.

"Listen," Luke said, his voice low. "What have you been doing all your life but acting, to please her?"

Two feet from my head a white-billed hummingbird hung in the air at a feeder, furiously beating its wings just to stay in one place.

"It seems so bizarre," I said.

"It could tell you a lot."

I didn't answer. We moved along the path, stopped to watch blue and red tanagers flitting among branches at the far end of the exhibit, then left the mini-rainforest through heavy double doors.

The air outside was hotter than that inside, and almost as humid. "I'll bet it's a hundred degrees already," Luke said.

In the Mane Restaurant, a utilitarian cafeteria redeemed by wide windows overlooking a wooded trail, we had a lunch of cheese sandwiches and iced tea. Luke made small talk, giving me time to get back to the subject that I knew occupied his thoughts as much as mine.

"What would it prove?" I said, breaking off a discussion of the weather. "If I did what you suggested."

He glanced at the couples and children around us, then leaned forward across the table and spoke quietly. "It'd prove she's used hypnosis to control your memories."

"It seems so deceitful," I whispered. "Dishonest."

"She's not entitled to honesty. If she's done what you think she has, then what the hell do you owe her?"

I stirred my tea, twirling the straw around and around in the tall paper cup. "I owe her my life, my education, everything I've been able to do."

He sat back in his chair, threw up his hands, attracting startled glances from the young couple at the next table. "Okay. I won't say another word about it."

He picked up his sandwich and started eating methodically. I gazed out the window. How unconnected the murky past seemed to this bright hot day, the sun slanting in across our table, the trees shaking their heads in the breeze.

I lifted my iced tea to my lips, but set it down again without drinking. When I leaned toward him, he sat forward, waiting for me to speak.

"I'd have to be really vigilant," I said. "She might catch on that I'm pretending, or she might be able to put me under whether I want her to or not."

Luke considered this, then sighed. "If you really think you couldn't control it, then you'd better not mess around with it. You don't want her getting into your head like that."

Could I do it? If I pulled it off, I might find out for certain whether Mother was capable of the stunning deviousness I suspected. I might defeat her control once and for all.

I said, "If I do decide to try it, I could tape the whole thing. Hide a tape recorder ahead of time. Then I'd know for sure what she did. What she said to me. I'd have the proof."

Another two weeks went by before I found the courage to tell Mother that, yes, I would like her to hypnotize me and help me recover my early childhood memories.

Chapter Eighteen

What I remembered afterward was Mother knocking softly at my door, then entering and coming to stand behind my chair as I sat at the dresser.

I remembered the light touch of her hands on my shoulders and her affectionate smile in the mirror. "Look at us," she said. "We're more alike every day."

I remembered the feeling of words stifled in my mouth, the choke of unshed tears in my throat. Our images looked back at us. My face, hers, undeniably similar.

She fingered the muscles of my shoulders. "You're so tense. We'll have to do a long relaxation sequence. You're not afraid, are you? I'll be with you all the way."

I couldn't remember whether I answered.

I stretched out on my couch. It was just long enough; my head and feet pressed against its arms. Mother wanted to conduct the hypnosis session in her office, but I'd insisted on doing it here in my room.

As her voice murmured soothing words, I felt myself relaxing into drowsiness almost against my will. Afterward I remembered how terribly sleepy I felt then, and how I fought against giving in and letting myself drift away.

I was vaguely aware of getting into bed some time later, Mother tucking the sheet over my shoulders, saying, "Good night, sweetheart, sleep well."

Then it was morning and I opened my eyes to a slash of sunlight on the carpet by the bed.

<><><>

Luke cornered me at the medications pantry. "Will you tell me what the hell happened?" he whispered.

I took a vial of brownish-yellow liquid from the refrigerator. "I have to get this vaccine ready," I said. "My client's waiting with her cat—"

He caught my arm, made me look at him. "Rachel," he said. "What did she do to you? Why are you suddenly treating me like poison?"

Looking at his boyish, worried face brought a wash of bewildering emotions that I couldn't begin to deal with. I squirmed my arm free. "I don't know what you're talking—"

"Your mother, for God's sake. What did she—"

"Please let me do my work. Please." Turning my attention to the vaccine, I inserted the needle into the vial and drew liquid into the syringe. I was surprised that my hands were so steady when I was shaking to pieces inside.

I felt him studying me. I couldn't meet his eyes. The urge to reach out and touch him was almost overpowering, but something held me back, something stronger than an awareness of where we were. He was too much a part of the turmoil I'd been swept up in lately. He'd prodded me to do things I wouldn't have done otherwise.

He was dangerous. I had to free myself of his influence.

"We're going to talk about this," he said, "and we're going to do it soon. I'm going to find out—"

He stopped when Alison walked by, smiling merrily at us in passing.

I closed the pantry door and stepped away. "My patient's waiting."

<><><>

Days passed. I was crisply efficient at work but drifting the rest of the time. At unguarded moments the longing for Luke surged through me like a current, setting every numbed nerve on fire

again and nearly knocking me off-balance. I stamped down hard
on that unwelcome desire, told myself I was well out of it, that
getting involved with my boss had been a bad idea from the start.
I avoided him at the clinic and refused to talk to him when he
called me at night.

At breakfast and dinner I sat with my mother and sister, and
it seemed to me that Mother was more cheerful than I'd seen her
in weeks. I kept quiet except when Mother spoke to me directly,
then I gave a polite answer to whatever I imagined her question
had been. Her expression told me I didn't always guess right.

Luke grabbed my arm, yanked me into the staff lounge and
slammed the door behind us. I was on my way in to hang up
my white coat before going home. He'd been waiting for me just
inside the room and I hadn't seen him until it was too late.

"You're going to listen to me," he said.

I tried to move away from him. He shoved me back and pinned
me against the wall, his hands gripping my wrist and shoulder.

"Now listen." His face was inches from mine, his breath hot
on my cheek.

I averted my head. I wouldn't let myself look in his eyes.

"Try to remember what happened, Rachel. Try, damn it! You
set up a tape recorder before your mother hypnotized you. You
recorded the whole thing. Don't you remember that?"

I looked at him now. My thoughts were a jumble, but his words
struck a faint chord. "Why?" I said. "Why would I do that?"

I felt his hands loosen. He released me as if I were a squirming animal that had decided to cooperate.

"You wanted to find out what she'd say to you while you were
under," he said. "Remember?"

"No." I tried to slip past him, but he was too quick for me,
and I found myself pressed against the wall again. "Let me go.
What do you think you're doing?"

"I'm going to talk some sense into you if I have to keep you
here all night."

"Let me go!" Using my whole body, I shoved, but all I did was rock him backward for a second. He was stronger than I was.

"You remember the tape recorder, don't you?" he said. "Rachel, look at me, listen to me! You told me you were going to hide it behind some pictures and a stack of books on a table next to the couch. Is it still there? Have you moved it?"

I stopped struggling. The tape recorder. New batteries. New tape. Put it in, test it. *Testing one two three.* Yes. But why?

"Jesus Christ, Rachel. What's she done to you this time?"

His hands relaxed again. Moving cautiously, I slid sideways along the wall a few inches. He didn't stop me.

His eyes were bleak. "Will you look for the recorder? Will you listen to the tape? Maybe then you'll—"

I strode away from him, fumbled with my locker's combination, plucked my shoulderbag off its hook. A moment later I was at the door and out, still wearing my lab coat.

〈〉〈〉〈〉

Somehow I got home safely, without an instant's awareness of the drive. Rosario, finishing up dinner in a kitchen redolent of thyme and basil, spoke a greeting I half-heard and didn't respond to. I climbed the stairs unwillingly, yet unable to stop myself.

I found the recorder on the table, hidden in a stack of books, its microphone behind a picture of Theo and Renee. At the sight of it a chasm seemed to open under my feet, dark and bottomless, nothing solid beneath me.

It came back to me now, with a sharp punch of clarity. What I'd suspected, what I'd set out to prove.

I lifted the little machine from its hiding place. Popping open the lid, I saw the tape had recorded all the way to the end.

I sat on the couch for long minutes, turning the tape over and over in my fingers. I could listen to it or I could throw it away and never face what might be on it.

When I realized it was almost six o'clock and Mother would be home soon, I roused myself and made a decision. I pulled my cell phone from my purse and called Luke at the clinic.

〉〈〉〈〉

I reached his apartment before he did. Although I still had a key, I didn't feel entitled to use it. I waited for him outside his door. When he emerged from the elevator and strode down the hall I watched him with a peculiar detachment, as if this tall lanky man had nothing to do with me.

He stopped when he reached me, his lively eyes scanning for clues to my state of mind. I felt as if I'd left myself at home and sent my empty body on this errand.

Luke's gaze dropped to my hand, which held the tape up between us. "You didn't listen to it yet?"

I shook my head.

He slid a key into the lock and pushed the door open, stepping aside to let me pass.

While he switched on lights, found his cassette player, and brought me a glass of ice water, I sat on the living room sofa clutching the tape. He had to gently pry my fingers loose so he could slide the tape into the player and rewind it.

"You ready?" he said, a finger on the play button.

I nodded.

Our indistinct voices became clearer as Mother and I moved closer to the recorder. Reassuring, almost cheerful, she told me to lie down and relax, she was with me, she would be with me every second, I had nothing to fear. I pictured myself stretched out on the couch, Mother beside me in the chair pulled over from the dresser.

"Take a deep breath and let it out very slowly. Yes, that's right. Breathe deeply, in and out. In and out. You can feel your body beginning to relax. You're beginning to feel peaceful, so peaceful and relaxed."

Her voice murmured on, guiding me through the relaxation process for each part of my body. There was no sound from me.

"Now I'm going to count backward from twenty. With every number I speak, you'll feel yourself going deeper and deeper, until you reach the deepest level."

As I sat beside Luke, listening to Mother count, I began to drift away. Luke shook me hard and I gasped, blinking at his worried face.

"I thought I was losing you for a minute." He'd stopped the tape. "Can you listen to the rest of this? Will you be all right?"

I nodded. "I'm okay. I have to hear it."

He hesitated, doubtful, but after a moment he switched the tape on again.

Mother continued counting backward. When she reached the number one, a brief silence followed. She said, very softly, "Rachel? Can you hear me?"

A faint "Yes" from me.

"You've been very upset and confused, Rachel. Would you like to feel better? Would you like to feel peaceful again, Rachel?"

A pause, then another murmured "Yes."

"You want to be happy. You want to put aside all the thoughts that have made you unhappy. Wouldn't you like to put away all those bad thoughts and never be troubled by them again?"

"Yes."

"Do you want me to help you? No, Rachel, don't sit up, lie down, lie down, that's right. Relax."

A whimper that must have come from me.

"I'm your mother, Rachel. You know that, don't you?"

Silence.

"I'm your mother. Your name is Rachel Goddard and you are my daughter. You know that, don't you?"

Silence.

"Rachel?" Coaxing. "Your name is Rachel Goddard and you're my daughter. You believe that, don't you?"

At last, weakly, "Yes."

"Tell me again. Your name is Rachel Goddard and you're my daughter. Is that right?"

"Yes." Stronger now, definite.

"You love me, don't you?"

"Yes." With no hesitation.

"I've been a good mother to you, haven't I?"

"Yes."

"You want me to be happy, don't you?"

"Yes."

"You want to please me?"

"Yes."

"You don't want to upset me and make me ill, do you?"

A rustling sound, movement.

"Rachel, let your body relax. Lie back, yes, that's right, lie back and relax. Breathe deeply, in and out, in and out. With every breath you feel more and more calm and relaxed. Your whole body is completely relaxed. Completely relaxed."

Her voice was quiet, unhurried, soothing. "Rachel," she said, "I know you want to stay close to Michelle and me. I know you won't let anyone come between us. You want us to be happy together, don't you?"

"Yes."

"I know you love your sister and your mother, and you won't let anyone turn you against us. You won't let Luke Campbell turn you against your mother and sister, will you?"

I said nothing.

"Rachel, does Luke ask questions about our family?"

Still I didn't answer.

"Do you tell him things about our family?"

When I failed to answer again, she said, "I won't be angry if you tell me the truth, sweetheart."

Words burst from me in a strangled childish cry, "You will! You'll be mad at me!"

"No, no, I won't. Don't be upset. I won't be mad at you."

A sound like weeping. A deep sigh from Mother.

"Rachel, you know what you have to do, don't you? You have to protect your family. You can't let an outsider make your family unhappy. You have to protect your family from Luke. Will you do that?"

A ragged sob.

"I know you will. I know you don't want him to come between you and your family. Don't cry, Rachel, don't cry, sweetheart, he's not worth crying over."

After a gulping intake of breath I fell silent.

Mother let a moment pass, then said, "Rachel, thinking about your father is very upsetting to you. You don't want to think about him anymore."

Statements, not questions.

"You know that talking about him upsets me too. When you talk about him you make me remember terrible things. You don't want to upset me. You don't even want to think about him any- more. Do you, Rachel? You want to put him out of your mind, don't you?"

"Yes." A whisper.

"Can I trust you? Will you be a good girl and do what I say?"

"Yes, Mother."

"Promise you'll be good?"

"I promise." A little girl's voice.

"After you wake up, you will do what you promised to do. But you won't remember what we talked about while you were under hypnosis. You will act on it but you won't remember what we talked about. Do you understand?"

"Yes."

"I'm going to count backward from five. As I count you'll become more and more awake, and when I reach the number one you'll open your eyes. You'll be awake but you'll feel sleepy and ready for bed."

She started counting.

I listened to the sounds of Mother putting me to bed as if I were a child, saying good night and sleep well. Then the tape held only silence.

My eyes shifted to the glass next to the tape player and I reached for the water, suddenly feeling a desperate thirst. When I lifted the glass my hand shook so violently that Luke had to steady it while I drank. He placed the glass back on the table and wiped a drop from my chin with a fingertip.

Crumbling, sliding toward an abyss, I let him catch me and pull me into his arms.

"I could kill her," he muttered against my hair. "I swear to God I could kill her."

Chapter Nineteen

Luke sat on the couch and listened, his eyes following me as I prowled the room. When shock had worn off, feeling had flooded back, pushing me to my feet, propelling me into motion.

"How could she do this to me? I always knew she was controlling, but my God, something like this—" I shook my head. "How could she believe she's got the right? Nobody has the right—Oh, God."

I stopped and covered my face until I rid myself of the urge to cry. No more tears. No more.

"If I were still a child, she could claim she's just protecting me." I marched to the window, looked out at the streetlights blinking on along Leesburg Pike, turned and started back across the room.

"But I'm almost twenty-seven years old. She's not protecting me. She's protecting herself." Bewilderment, anger, hurt warred in me. "But from what?"

I pivoted, took a dozen steps, spun around. "Why does she have to control me to protect herself? And why is she afraid of you? She's always been afraid of anybody getting too close to us. I always thought she just wanted to keep us to herself, we were all she had, but she's afraid of anybody getting too close and asking too many questions, that's so clear to me now."

I balled my right hand into a fist and rapped it against my left palm. "She's keeping something from me, and I feel like it's something I already know but I can't get my mind around it—"

Waves of pain, rage, fear knocked me in one direction after another, leaving me exhausted. I sank onto the couch, head in hands, and came to rest at last in a cold, still place deep inside myself.

We sat in silence until Luke asked, "What are you going to do about all this?"

I'd already decided. "First, I'm going to find out what I can about my father's death."

"How?"

"The Library of Congress has old newspapers on file from all over the country. If he died the way she says he did, the Minneapolis paper would've had a story. I can go tomorrow, it's my day off." I glanced at my watch. "God, look at the time. She'll think I'm with you."

As I rose, Luke half-laughed, a sound of consternation rather than amusement. "You are with me. And what the hell does it matter what she thinks?"

I grabbed my purse from the chair where I'd dropped it earlier and swung the strap over my shoulder. "I have to get home."

He jumped up. "You can't be serious."

"I'll talk to you tomorrow."

I started for the door but he blocked my way. "You're not going back to that house. Rachel, the woman's dangerous."

Looking into his dark blue eyes, I felt cracks snaking across the wall of my resolve. I laid a hand along his cheek. "Don't worry about me. She can't do anything to me now."

"I'm not so sure about that. Please don't go."

"I have to. I don't want her to get suspicious yet. I'll let you know what I find out."

I pressed my mouth to his in a quick kiss and left him standing in his doorway.

◇◇◇

That night I looked directly into Mother's eyes and lied so convincingly that she believed my story of an emergency at the clinic without hesitation. She was the one who gave herself away. The apprehension that tensed her body dissolved in an instant and I saw her relax like a taut string unloosed.

By clearing my mind and stamping down on any thought that threatened to intrude, I got through dinner with Mother and Michelle. The next morning I stayed in my room, supposedly sleeping late, until I heard them leave.

Although I'd lived in the Washington area most of my life, I'd never used the Library of Congress. In middle school I'd been inside the Main Reading Room and Great Hall on a class excursion, a midwinter traipse through all the imposing government buildings, led by a teacher determined that we'd be at least as well acquainted with the federal city as tourists were.

I remembered feeling as if I'd entered a different century when I walked into the Jefferson Building, with its soaring ceilings, statuary and mosaics, stained glass and murals. But the Madison Building, which housed the periodicals reading room, was a big white box that sat firmly in the late twentieth century and had none of the Jefferson's beauty and grandeur.

Walking between rectangular marble columns to the door, I warned myself not to expect old newspapers to yield many answers. The story about the accident might not tell me anything new about my father and mother.

But if nothing else, the story would certainly hold one bit of information: names of survivors. Maybe I would find a picture of us all together, the young family whose father had been tragically lost. I would surely be mentioned in the story itself. I needed to see some proof of my place among the Goddards.

When I entered the lobby I stood for a moment letting my startled skin adjust to air that was twenty degrees cooler than outside. I took a deep breath and willed myself to go about this task in my normal methodical way, as if I were researching a fine point of veterinary medicine in order to help a patient.

A uniformed young man looked in my purse as I passed through the metal detector. He directed me down the hall to the periodicals room.

It was as starkly utilitarian as any neighborhood library, with bright fluorescent lighting, pink-gray industrial carpet that needed shampooing, dark paneled walls, and a couple of lackluster dracaena plants by the main desk. It was hard to believe this impersonal place held clues to my family's very personal secrets.

While the desk clerk instructed me on the procedure for obtaining materials, a voice in the back of my mind kept whispering that I should just leave it alone, there was nothing to discover except the source of my mother's heartbreak, something I already knew. The voice was Mother's, silky and persistent, firmly planted and ineradicable. I couldn't shut it up, but I wouldn't listen to it.

The clerk directed me to one of a dozen stations where reading machines were set up, and I sat down to fill out a request slip for microfilm.

I didn't know the date of the accident. But I knew it happened when Michelle was two and I was five, and Mother had said it happened in a snow storm, which could mean anytime from November through February. I requested four months of the Minneapolis Tribune. Retrieval time, the clerk said, could be as long as forty-five minutes.

I sat at my desk and waited. All around me in the hushed room, people were engrossed by the past events appearing before them. The machines made little whirring noises as they moved the microfilm from page to page. Footsteps scuffed on the carpet. Rising and walking around, I saw that some machines could make copies from the microfilm, and I decided I would do that when I found what I wanted.

I pulled tissues from my shoulderbag and wiped my clammy palms and the line of moisture above my lip and wished I had something to read. That struck me as funny—writing, writing everywhere, but not a word to read—and I almost laughed.

I didn't think I could bear the waiting.

After twenty-five minutes a young man with a dark ponytail appeared at my side, rousing me out of formless thoughts. The shallow tray he set on the desk contained four cardboard boxes. "Do you know how to use the machine?" he asked quietly.

I shook my head no. He dragged a chair from an unused desk and sat elbow to elbow with me, instructing me in a monotone, an *I've said this a million times* voice. With the first roll of microfilm in the machine, he stood, moved his chair, and left me.

I sat, momentarily paralyzed. Headlines on the screen blurred into black smudges. *All right,* I told myself. *Do it.*

Taking a deep breath, I began.

The days rolled past. I carefully examined every page, catching my breath each time I came across an auto accident story. The man at the desk to my left kept turning to look at me, and I sensed his irritation with my tiny noises. I forced myself to stay silent.

When I finished the month of November I slipped the roll back into its box with a mixture of disappointment and relief that I hadn't found the story.

December had plenty of news about weather. Minnesota seemed to have snow almost every day. My attention was caught by a photo of two small children building a snowman, and I stared at it, lost in a half-memory. Snow, snowmen, snowballs, a sled. Flying downhill on a blue sled, breathless with the thrill of it, but not alone, someone strong was with me, holding me, protecting me. My father?

The image wouldn't gel. I was left with a piercing sense of loss.

I moved the microfilm forward, skimming over local news that meant nothing to me and national and international stories that meant little more. A politician was in trouble over a woman, a Renoir was stolen in Brooklyn. Violence in Angola and Northern Ireland. Nelson Rockefeller was sworn in as Vice President, to serve with Gerald Ford.

When the three-column photo of mangled vehicles popped into view, I somehow knew instantly that I'd found what I was looking for. The picture and the story it illustrated were at the bottom of the Sunday, December 22, front page under a big headline: *Five Die in Snowstorm Crash.*

Heart racing, I skimmed the beginning of the story for a familiar name, and found it in the second paragraph. Michael J. Goddard Jr. I paused, released the breath I'd been holding, and felt the stare of the man next to me.

I went back to the first line and started reading.

> Three adults and two children died in a four-vehicle accident on W. Lake St. during Saturday afternoon's heavy snowstorm. Police said the accident occurred about 1 p.m. when a car traveling west went out of control and crossed into the oncoming lane, striking a pickup truck head-on. The impact of the collision flipped the truck onto the car behind it, and another car struck the pileup from the rear.

> Dead are Minneapolis attorney Michael J. Goddard, 34, who was driving the first car; his two-year-old daughter, Michelle Theresa; Oscar J. Lund, 47, of St. Cloud, driver of the truck; Joanna Marie Bergman, 36, of Minneapolis, driver of the car struck by the truck; and her daughter, Marcy Linda Bergman, 9.

I read the second paragraph again, then again, but still it made no sense to me. The words separated into individual letters that seemed to spin apart.

I blinked, refocused, and read on.

> Goddard's wife, Judith, 34, was admitted to Mt. Sinai Hospital with multiple fractures and a concussion and was in fair condition Saturday night. The driver of the third car, John A. Peterson, 52, of St. Paul, was released from Mt. Sinai after treatment for minor injuries.

> Witnesses said the Goddard car was moving erratically and may have been speeding before it crossed into the oncoming traffic lane. Police said no alcohol was found in Goddard's blood and they have ruled out intoxication as a cause of the accident.

Goddard was a junior partner in the law firm of Jensen, Dubie, Goddard, and Brown, where his father, Michael J. Goddard Sr., is a founding partner. The younger Goddard attracted widespread attention last year when he won a $10.5 million judgment in a wrongful death suit against chemical fertilizer giant Alco Industries. His wife is a psychologist in private practice in Minneapolis. Michelle Theresa was the couple's only child.

Lund, married with two *continued on page 10, col 1*

My mind refused to absorb what I saw in front of me. Michelle slept in the room across the hall from me, she sat across the table from me at breakfast and dinner. She hadn't died in a car wreck at the age of two.

Michelle Theresa was the couple's only child.

The story wasn't real. I was imagining it. I'd been sitting here waiting too long, anticipating, worrying. I closed my eyes, opened them. The words sat heavy and black on the screen.

I was dreaming, then. I gave my head a rough shake, trying to pull myself out of the nightmare, and was dimly conscious of the man beside me turning his whole body in my direction. His movement released a faint odor of perspiration.

I leaned my face into my hands. A rational explanation had to exist for what I was reading. There was a rational explanation for everything.

With fumbling fingers I pressed a button on the machine, zipping through to page 10 and the rest of the story. I found a picture of the baker Lund with his wife on their twenty-fifth anniversary, and a school photo of little Marcy Linda Bergman, smiling gap-toothed, her dark hair in two long braids tied with ribbon bows. Between them was a studio portrait of my mother and father, the kind of formal posed picture a man keeps on his desk at work. I'd seen this photo before, in one of the albums Mother kept hidden. On Mother's lap was a smiling child, little more than a baby. Pale wispy hair curled over the child's head and onto her cheeks. Her eyes were big in her small face, and full of joy. I read the names under the picture: Michael, Judith, and Michelle Goddard.

Transfixed, I sat for a long time, waiting for the flat grainy image to give back a spark of revelation that never came. I leaned closer and tried to examine the face of the little girl. The picture separated into a field of shaded dots, it wouldn't hold together, wouldn't allow inspection.

When a clerk passed I turned and said in the most ordinary of tones, "Excuse me, could you help me make a copy of something?"

He did it for me. He copied the entire story, complete with pictures, and handed the sheets to me. I thanked him and went back to my desk. I placed the roll of December microfilm back in its box and carried all four rolls to the main desk.

When I emerged from the cool building, the humid hot air slammed into me, making me recoil. I stopped for a moment to get my bearings. I couldn't remember how to get back to Union Station, where I'd parked my car. I walked half a block, past the Capitol on one side of the street and the Cannon and Longworth buildings on the other, before I realized I was going the wrong direction.

I retraced my steps, one hand tight on my shoulderbag strap, the other crushing the copy sheets. After a time that could have been minutes and could have been an hour, I was driving toward the 14th Street Bridge on my way home.

Home. I glanced at the two sheets of paper lying wrinkled and twisted in the seat beside me. Home to Mother and Michelle.

Michelle. My dead sister.

The couple's only child.

I couldn't let myself think about this while I was on the road. I pushed it back, back, until it was a monstrous dark thing looming at the edge of my mind.

I drove in heavy traffic along the George Washington Parkway, my fingers tight around the steering wheel. Just past the Key Bridge I glanced down at the Potomac and saw a blue heron, motionless on a spit off the bank. Farther out, gulls bobbed where surface ripples hinted at the river's undercurrent, and along the far shore the white trunks of sycamore trees gleamed like ghosts in the late day sun.

Chapter Twenty

On Wednesdays Michelle always came home in mid-afternoon and spent the rest of the day working at the computer in her room. She was at her desk when I walked through her open door.

"Hi," she murmured absently. She didn't look up, but kept her eyes fixed on the word-filled computer screen.

I stood over her, my gaze following the curve of her long neck, the plane of her left cheekbone, the fall of her silky hair.

Who was she?

Who was I?

She glanced at me, a frown forming between her brows. "Did you want something?"

The folded copy of the newspaper story was in my right hand. "I need to talk to you."

She gave a little sigh. The computer had already regained her attention. Touching an index finger to a key, she said, "Can it wait till after dinner?"

"This is important, Mish. Maybe the most important conversation we'll ever have."

She laughed and sat back. "My goodness." Then she looked at me more closely, and a mask of wariness and reluctance came down over her face. "Rachel, I don't want to talk about Mother. I don't want to talk about our father. I don't want—"

"Michelle!"

She flinched as if I'd struck her. Telling myself to calm down, I moved away from her, to a window, and watched two squirrels chase each other in a circle on the side lawn below. Mother would be home soon. I couldn't imagine what was coming, what must come.

I turned back to Michelle. "Please hear me out, no matter how crazy it sounds."

"Oh, for heaven's sake—"

"Please. Can't you just listen? Can't you do that much for me?"

She let out a sharp breath and folded her arms. "Okay, I'm listening." Her whole attitude said she didn't want to hear a word I had to say.

"I thought if I could find out everything about the accident that killed—" I hesitated. What should I call him? For now, what Michelle would accept. "The accident that killed our father—"

"I knew it," she said. "You're obsessed, Rachel. It's not healthy."

"You said you'd listen."

She unfolded her arms and lifted her hands briefly in a gesture of surrender.

Taking a deep breath, I started over. "I thought if I found out more about his death, I'd be able to understand all the secrecy. Why Mother won't talk about him."

"You know why. It hurts to dredge up those memories."

I let this pass and hurried on. "So I went to the Library of Congress and looked at issues of the Minneapolis newspaper on microfilm."

"Oh, I don't believe this," she said, shaking her head.

"I found the story." I looked down at the papers I clutched.

"Okay, now are you satisfied? Did it help at all? I'll be really surprised if you say yes."

I met her gaze. Her cold blue eyes regarded me as if I were a nutty stranger who'd accosted her and forced her to listen to gibberish.

I had to make her see. The proof was in my hand. I unfolded the two sheets of paper. "The story wasn't what I expected."

"Oh?" A trace of curiosity.

"Mother was in the car with him."

"Yes, I know."

I stared at her. "You do?"

She nodded. "Mother told me."

Wounded, thrown off track, I groped for words. "She told you, but she wouldn't talk about it with me."

"I don't get hysterical when the subject comes up."

Her superior tone jolted me into anger. She thought she knew everything, but she knew nothing, so cozy in her ignorance.

"Did she tell you a little girl was in the car with them?" I said. "Did she tell you that little girl was killed too?"

I watched the color drain from her face and her mouth open slightly. For a split second I wavered, as the enormity of what I was doing came clear. One step farther, and I would destroy my sister's world. But I had to do this. I had no choice.

"The child's name was Michelle Theresa," I said, "and she was two years old. She died that day, with her father."

I held her gaze, braced for anger, denial, an outburst. But she sat perfectly still, hands limp in her lap, and didn't speak. A wren sang outside the window, a burbling happy sound.

"Mish," I said, stepping closer. "I don't know what it means, about you and me—"

She drew herself up in one long motion and was on her feet facing me, her body a rigid column.

Her voice was low, quiet. "You need help, Rachel. You're not rational anymore."

I shook my head. "Mish, read this—"

I offered the two sheets of paper in my outstretched hand. Her eyes didn't waver from my face.

"Read this." I held the papers up, in her line of vision.

Her sharp slap across the back of my hand caught me by surprise, making me release the sheets. They fluttered to the carpet. I bent to retrieve them. When I straightened her face was contorted with fury.

"We've had enough of this from you," she said. "You're making Mother ill, she's worried half to death about you. You need help, Rachel. If you refuse to get it, we—"

I grabbed her arm and shoved the story in her face, an inch from her eyes. "Read this, for God's sake, read it! They had a daughter named Michelle and she died in that accident, and the story says she was their only child. And I'm not in those pictures, all those pictures Mother's got hidden away, you're in them—that girl is in them—but I'm not—"

With a jerk she freed her arm, then she backed away. "It always comes down to this. You've always been jealous of me. You've never been close to Mother like I am, and you've always resented it."

I groaned. "No. This has nothing to do with—"

"What are you saying? That I'm not even alive, I died in an accident?" Her sudden laughter rose to a shrill note. "That makes a lot of sense, Rachel."

"I don't know what it means," I said. "We have to find out. You have to read this, and we have to find out what it means."

She'd closed herself off from me, put up a wall I couldn't penetrate. Her voice cold and even, she said, "Don't you dare bother Mother with any more of your weird ideas. This obsession is your problem, and you have to stop imposing it on other people. You need help, Rachel. You need to see a psychiatrist."

I didn't believe this. The story was here in my hand, in front of her, and I couldn't make her read it. Even if she did, would she accept it as real, or would she think I'd gone to great lengths to fake it? Yes, that was exactly what she'd think. She'd rather believe I was losing my mind than face the secrets I'd uncovered.

Stepping back, I folded the sheets of paper. I would do this alone. I'd been alone from the beginning. Without speaking again, I turned and walked out of her room.

Sitting on my bed, holding the story, I listened to the small sounds of Mother's arrival, the muffled slam of the car door on the driveway, her voice calling a greeting as she came up the stairs. She exchanged a few words with Michelle, but I couldn't make out what they said.

After a moment she tapped on my door. "Rachel? Come help me get dinner on the table. I picked up something at Sutton Place so we don't have to cook."

"I'll be down in a minute." My voice lifted and carried and sounded perfectly normal.

When she'd had time to change her clothes, I heard her speak to Michelle again before she went back downstairs.

I was not losing my mind. The story in my hands was real, even though I didn't know what it meant.

I rose and stuffed the folded sheets into the right pocket of my slacks. Then, feeling as if I were two separate beings, one sickened with dread and the other strong and sure and moving toward a goal, I went downstairs to Mother.

Chapter Twenty-one

Mother stood at the island counter in the kitchen, lifting cardboard and Styrofoam containers from a large white paper bag. On Rosario's day off, we had to provide our own dinner one way or another.

From the doorway I watched her long slender hands dip into the bag, line up cartons on the counter. She'd loosened her hair and it moved along her shoulders, a gleaming fall of rich dark red.

I didn't know this woman. I couldn't begin to know what she had done and might yet do.

With a glance my way she said, "Would you wash the salad? Just to be on the safe side. You never know about salad bars."

My mind ran in furious circles, trying to find a stopping point, but my hands popped off the lid of the salad container and emptied the lettuce, green pepper slices and cherry tomatoes into a colander. While I washed the salad, Mother lifted a knife from a drawer and began carving the chicken.

"I've decided to start a new fear-of-flying group," she said, "so I'll be tied up with that one night a week, probably starting next week."

I tore a handful of paper towels from the roll above the sink and carried the dripping colander to the island. Standing across from Mother, I watched the long thin knife slice through the chicken breast.

"I can easily fill another group with people on my waiting list, if they're willing," she went on. "They always resist group therapy at first, but I can usually make them see the benefits."

She arranged chicken slices on a white china serving platter. I patted the last drops of water off the salad, then tipped it all into the cut glass bowl she'd placed on the counter.

She laughed. "When they hear what it costs to charter a plane, they're glad enough to be doing it with a group. Why don't you add some mushrooms to the salad? If we have any."

Obediently I searched the refrigerator. When I bent over, the folded papers in my pocket made a crinkling noise. I found a carton of plump white mushrooms in the bottom drawer of the refrigerator and took them back to the island.

After dinner, I thought. I would do it after dinner.

No, I couldn't wait. I couldn't sit through dinner silent, pretending I didn't know what I'd learned that day.

But I couldn't imagine speaking it aloud.

I wiped a mushroom clean with a damp paper towel, then sliced it into the salad with a paring knife. The ripe rich smell of it reminded me of the woods in autumn.

"Did you have a good day?" Mother asked. "Did you do anything special?"

I jerked my head up. *Now. Tell her. Say it.* The words wouldn't come.

She regarded me quizzically for a moment, and seemed about to say something when the front doorbell rang, loud and jarring through a speaker on the kitchen wall.

"Who in the world could that be?" she said.

She laid the long knife on the serving plate and went to answer the door. I stayed behind, gripping the edge of the counter, dragging in breaths with an effort, until the sound of Luke's raised voice reached me and snapped me into action.

I raced down the hall.

He stood on the threshold, hands clenched at his sides. Hot air pushed into the house through the open door.

"Luke," I said, "what—"

"Why didn't you call me? I've been worried sick about you."

He didn't know what he was doing, he'd blundered in at the worst possible time. Frantic, but unable to get my voice above a hoarse whisper, I said, "Don't, Luke. Just leave, please."

"Like hell I will. What's going on?"

Mother slipped an arm around my waist. "Rachel asked you to leave, Dr. Campbell, and I'm asking the same. I don't know what you're after, but you're not welcome in my house."

I pulled away from her, felt her arm tighten for a second before she gave in and let go.

"Good night, Dr. Campbell." She started to close the door in his face.

He slapped a hand against the door to stop it, then pushed past her and into the foyer. He glared down at Mother. "What the hell are you doing to her? What kind of crazy mind control game are you playing?"

"You really are trying my patience," Mother said. "You burst into my home acting like—

"You're fucking with her mind, you goddamn witch!"

"Luke!" I cried. "Stop it!"

"I want you to leave my house this instant," Mother said, opening the door still wider. "Or I'll call the police."

"You're not gonna do this to her anymore," Luke said. He held out a hand. "Rachel, come on. Come home with me."

I looked at his outstretched hand, his pleading eyes, and then at Mother's face, all her fury on the surface, nothing hidden now.

"My daughter's not going anywhere with you," she said. "And I won't have you harassing her this way."

"Rachel," Luke said. He stepped toward me.

I wanted to go with him, get away from Mother, go where I couldn't see her eyes or hear her voice. But I had to face what I'd discovered that day.

"Please leave," I said, trying with my eyes to tell him what I didn't dare say aloud.

He held my gaze for a moment. His face mirrored the struggle I felt inside. When he spoke again his voice was flat, resigned. "Will you call me later and let me know you're all right?"

Before I could answer, Mother said, "Why wouldn't she be all right? She's with her family."

After another long look at me he turned and walked out. Mother quickly shut the door behind him.

She grabbed my arm and steered me down the hall toward the kitchen. "I hope you realize now what a mistake it was to get involved with that man. I don't want you working with him. You can find another job. Just put him out of your mind, don't think about him."

I stopped listening because I was seeing her when we were both much younger, and hearing her calm, relentless voice. *You will not think about those people. Whenever those thoughts come into your head you will push them out, you won't think about those people ever again.*

In the kitchen she picked up the knife, saw the chicken was already carved, laid the knife back on the counter. A flush reddened her cheeks. Her hands trembled when she removed three foil-wrapped potatoes from the carryout bag, stripped off the foil, and placed them in the microwave for reheating.

After punching in the timer setting, she turned to me with a tight little smile. "Well. I was asking how you spent your day."

"I went to the Library of Congress."

Her eyebrows lifted and she half-laughed. "Really? Why?"

Slowly I pulled the two sheets of paper from my pocket. I unfolded them and placed them on the counter. Seeing the words and pictures out in the open, in the bright light of our everyday life, I felt as if I'd stepped into space and was floating free, with nothing to hold on to.

Mother came closer, curious. Her eyes widened, her face went white and a gasp strangled in her throat. She swayed and caught the edge of the counter for support.

"Did you really think I'd never find out?" My tongue felt swollen in my mouth, my voice sounded slow and thick. "Did you think you could control my memory forever?"

She raised her eyes to mine. I told myself she couldn't get inside my mind anymore, I didn't have to fear her. But I backed away until I hit the refrigerator door.

"Who am I?" I said. "Who is Michelle? She's not your daughter any more than I am."

Her voice was a ragged croak. "Don't say that, don't."

She stepped toward me, gaze locked on mine. A gush of pure terror made me wrench my head to the side. *You're fucking with her mind, you goddamn witch.*

"What have you done to us?" I choked out the words. "I remember—I remember—"

She seized me by the shoulders. I struggled to get free, but her fingers dug in, pinning me against the refrigerator.

"You don't remember anything," she said. "You can't."

"I do! I always have—" Memories floated like bubbles to the surface of my mind, distinct and perfectly formed before they burst and dissolved. A house, white with black shutters. A woman calling from a doorway. *Time to come in, girls.*

"Listen to me," Mother said. "Look at me, Rachel. Look at me."

She gripped my chin and tried to force my face forward, but I twisted free, stumbled away from her, put the island counter between us. I heard my breath rasping in my throat.

The microwave timer went off, a long shrill note. I glanced wildly around the kitchen, at the neat chicken slices on the serving plate, the salad in the sparkling bowl, the shining counters and rich oak cabinets. All of it was unreal, it was an illusion and the woman's voice in my head was reality. *Kathy, Stephanie, time for dinner.*

"Stephanie?" I whispered. "Kathy?" I felt time flowing around me like a physical thing, relentless.

Mother's hand shot across the island and seized my wrist. "Stop it," she said. "Don't do this, Rachel."

Stephanie, Kathy, time for dinner. I was Kathy, Michelle was Stephanie. Our mother was calling us. Our real mother.

"Rachel." Mother's fingers tightened, sending a shock of pain through my hand. "Just calm down, calm down, relax, that's what you need to do, relax. Let's go sit down, we'll talk—"

I jerked my arm free, making her fall forward and splay her hands on the counter for balance.

"Stephanie," I whispered. I stood still and for a moment forgot where I was. I saw my little sister in the rain, heard her crying, *Mommy, mommy, where are you?* and me hugging her tight, crooning, *She'll come, she'll be here in a minute, don't be scared.*

"Stephie—Michelle—She was crying, she was afraid of the storm. I told her it'd be all right, but I was scared too—"

A long wail tore from Mother, an animal sound that began as a deep moan and rose to a scream. She clutched her arms about her and doubled over.

I watched her as if from a great distance, and I was untouched by her agony. "You drove up in a car," I said. "You told us our mother sent you to get us, and we got in your car—"

"Oh, God," Mother moaned, "Rachel, please don't. Please stop."

I remembered the way her car had smelled, like new leather. I remembered rain pounding the roof, streaming down the windows, closing us off from the world. I'd been alarmed at first, but I was lulled by this nice stranger's voice, her smile, her attention to us and concern for us.

"But you never took us home."

My eyes saw Mother and myself in this kitchen, but my mind was moving through a house filled with packed boxes, boxes stacked higher than my head. I heard her soothing voice. *It's all right. Sit down and drink your milk and everything will be all right.*

"Michelle—Stephie—she didn't seem to care, she was playing, she was happy, but I kept asking questions—"

Mother shook her head back and forth, back and forth.

"What did you do to me?" I said. "Give me pills to make me docile? Then you hypnotized me. You confused me, you made me doubt who I was, you made me think I was your daughter—"

A savage swing of her arm came nowhere near me but startled me into stumbling backward.

"You've always fought me!" she cried. "Michelle was so good, she knew I loved her, she was grateful, but you fought me every inch of the way."

I barely recognized her twisted tear-wet face. "Why did you do it?" I said. "Why did you take us?"

"You should thank me! I've given you a good life, I've been a good mother. She didn't take care of you, she was always leaving you alone on that playground. You were both so small, anything could have happened to you." Mother dragged in a raspy breath. "Michelle was so frightened, out in the storm—I couldn't bear it."

She covered her face and sobbed. Seeing her broken, knowing I had broken her, I felt a stirring of pity and guilt. I crushed it.

"She was the one you wanted," I said slowly. "Because she looked like your little girl who died in the accident."

"That woman had no right to her!" The words were muffled behind Mother's hands. "She had no right to have her child when mine was dead."

The truth unfolded in my mind, like pages being turned back. "You didn't want me at all. I just happened to be there."

Her hands dropped from her face. Her anguished eyes pleaded. "I've been a good mother to you, haven't I? I do love you, Rachel, I've tried so hard—"

"You've tried hard to control me." I felt cold, and utterly calm. "You tried to make me forget who I was."

"It was for your own good, so you could be happy—"

"But I never forgot. Not completely. Do you know I had an imaginary friend when I was little? A girl named Kathy, who looked like me. She was with me all the time. But she wasn't imaginary. She was me."

Mother moaned, a hand to her mouth. "Oh, good God, I never knew. I had no idea."

A movement behind her caught my attention, and I shifted my gaze to the doorway that led in from the hall. Michelle slumped against the door frame. I could see that she'd heard everything or close to it.

"I'm going to tell Michelle the truth," I said to Mother. "I'll make her believe it somehow."

"No! No, you can't, please, I'm begging you—"

She reached out to me across the counter. I stepped back.

"You'll destroy her!" she cried. "Is that what you want? Don't you love her at all?"

"I love her enough to save her from you. You ought to be locked up! I'll tell her, I'll make her believe—"

"No! I won't let you take her away from me."

Her hands scrabbled on the counter, found the long thin knife she'd used to slice the chicken. Then she was around the counter and coming toward me.

In my surprise I froze for an instant, and she was at me, the knife raised. I threw up both arms to shield myself.

Cold steel sliced through my left forearm. When I jerked away the blade ripped open the back of my hand. Searing pain nearly knocked me off my feet.

Mother raised the knife again.

"Mother!" Michelle screamed. She lunged and threw her arms around Mother from behind.

Mother struggled to break free and get at me again but Michelle held on. "Mother, it's me, it's Michelle, listen to me, stop, please, Mother, please stop."

Abruptly Mother surrendered and went limp in Michelle's arms, her low moan mixing with my sister's sobs. The knife clattered to the floor.

My arm and hand were awash in blood. I fumbled for a dishcloth on the counter and pressed it to my arm. Blood soaked through the cloth in an instant and spilled in large drops to the floor.

With Michelle still holding her from behind, Mother began to weep. Her words came out in gasps. "I wanted my baby back. I just wanted to be happy again."

I met her eyes and saw the full depth of a misery and sorrow I'd only begun to imagine.

"What have I done?" she whispered. "Oh, God, forgive me, forgive me."

Michelle released her and stepped back, wide eyes moving from Mother to me to the blood on the floor. A faint whimper sounded from her gaping mouth.

I watched in stupefied horror as Mother leaned down and scooped up the knife. I flattened my back against the refrigerator, bracing for an attack, but she rushed past me, out of the room, into the hall, and in a second I heard a door slam.

"Mother!" I cried. "Oh, Christ, Mish, stop her!"

Michelle looked back at me dumbly. I spun and ran after Mother, but stopped short when I reached the hall, uncertain where she'd gone. Her study door stood open. The downstairs bathroom door was closed, but it always was. Dripping blood from one hand, I tried the doorknob with the other. Locked.

"Come help me!" I screamed at Michelle. When she walked into the hall, her face slack and dazed, I shoved her at the door. "We have to get it open! She's got a knife!"

Michelle rattled the knob, then turned to me as if for further instructions.

I sprinted to the kitchen, yanked open a drawer and snatched up a table knife. Back in the hall, I jammed the knife into the space between door frame and lock. The simple bolt clicked free. I tossed the knife behind me and pushed open the door.

Mother stood at the sink, the carving knife in her right hand. Blood streamed from her left wrist into the basin. Her eyes seemed to look through me without seeing.

"Mother, give me the knife," I said. "Don't do this."

Urgency overcoming fear, I reached out.

She shrank back against the flowered wallpaper. She raised the knife to her throat and with one brutal motion tore through flesh and artery.

For a second her face took on a surprised expression. Blood pulsed from her throat and splattered her arm, her blue blouse, the wallpaper.

She dropped the knife. Her knees buckled.

I tried to grab her but couldn't support her sagging weight with one arm. We both collapsed to the floor.

Michelle rushed in and sank to her knees beside us. "Mother! Oh my God, Rachel, do something!"

I pressed my hand to the gash in Mother's throat. Blood poured between my fingers. Michelle wailed.

Mother's fingers clawed at the front of my blouse. I peeled her hand away, pushed myself up, staggered to the phone on the kitchen wall. The pain in my arm made me want to howl.

With blood-slick fingers I punched 911. The instant I heard a voice I shouted, "My mother tried to kill herself! She's bleeding to death!"

The woman at the other end started to speak, but I dropped the receiver, let it bounce on its cord and clank against the wall. I ran back to Mother and fell to my knees on the bloody tile.

"Please, please don't die," I begged. "I didn't mean for this to happen. Mother, I love you, please don't die."

Her eyes met mine for an instant before her lids fluttered and closed. Her breathing slowed, her body relaxed. Her face had gone stark white but it was peaceful now, as if she were drifting into deep sleep.

The faint sound of a siren dragged me to my feet. Suddenly weak and dizzy, I had to lean on walls and furniture to get to the front door.

The next minutes were a blur of noise and bustle. One medic worked over Mother, another forced me into a chair while he wrapped my wound. I was drenched with blood. I strained to get to Mother but the medic held me back. He kept asking, *What happened? What happened?* Somewhere in the room my sister was crying.

After Mother had been rolled out, the medic told me to lie down on another stretcher. Luke was back, leaning over me. I reached for him.

He kissed my uninjured hand and laid it back on my chest. A smudge of blood was left behind at the corner of his mouth. "I'll be at the hospital," he said. "I'll come right behind."

In the closed alcohol-reeking ambulance, with the keening siren deafening me to all other sound, I forced myself to turn my head and look at the stretcher next to mine.

The medic bent over her, blocking her upper body from my sight. As I watched, he sat back, shoulders slumping. He remained that way for a moment with his head bowed. Then he shifted and I caught a glimpse of her pale cheek before he drew the blood-soaked sheet up over her face.

Chapter Twenty-two

Wrapped in warmth, I drifted toward wakefulness, my senses switching on one by one. A dry sour taste in my mouth. The smell of disinfectant and alcohol. A murmur of voices nearby. Blinding light that made me squeeze my eyes shut again after one quick blink.

And pain. A deep throb that seemed to pulse toward me from a great distance, washing over me in waves.

"Rachel?" a female voice said.

I opened my eyes again, just a slit, and saw a sharp-featured young woman with black hair.

She peered into my face. "You're in the hospital, Rachel. You had surgery on your arm."

Mother.

The full force of memory hit me. I cried out.

"Just try to lie still," the nurse said. "Just rest."

Mother's dead.

I opened my eyes wide, staring around at half a dozen empty beds, a big central desk with a young woman behind it, a silent television set that flashed images in a corner.

"Would you like to see your fiancé?" the nurse said. "I can't let him stay more than a minute, but he's been waiting all this time and he wants to see you."

Fiancé? Bewildered, I didn't answer.

The nurse moved away, her shoes slapping against the floor.

My left arm felt heavy and stiff. I looked down in faint surprise: my forearm was encased in a cast and my hand was thickly bandaged, the bluish fingers sticking out from layers of white. The source of the pain.

In my mind I saw a flash of steel and Mother's tormented face.

The nurse reappeared with Luke at her side. "We're about to take her upstairs to a room for the night," she told him. "So I can't let you stay long."

He leaned to kiss my cheek and whispered against my ear, "In case you haven't heard, we're engaged. I had to say that to get in to see you."

For a moment the warm, sweet smell of him replaced the sharp hospital odors.

"Mother?" I whispered.

"Shh. Don't think about that now." He stroked hair off my cheek. "I want you to come home with me when they release you. I'll be here first thing in the morning."

Where was my sister? Where was Mother? What had they done with her?

Luke kissed me and was gone. The nurse seemed to be adding something to my IV. As she and another woman rolled my bed down a hallway, I lapsed into sleep again.

<>◇<>

When I woke the next morning Michelle was hanging clothes in a small corner closet. The bed next to mine lay empty, made up.

"Mish?" I said, the word thick and toneless. I pushed hair off my face and rubbed at my eyes, fighting off grogginess. An IV needle was taped to my hand, and with every movement I dragged the long IV tube back and forth over the sheet. It made little slipping sounds.

"You're awake," Michelle announced. She faced me, her body stiff and straight, hands locked before her in a tight grip. "I brought you some clean clothes."

Memory rushed back and I moaned under the assault. "Mother—"

"They're doing all kinds of tests on—on her body." Michelle broke off and ducked her head, but I'd already seen the tears glittering along her lashes. "We have to wait for them to finish before we can schedule the funeral."

"Funeral," I repeated, stunned by the meaning of the word.

"I'll make the arrangements. I'm sure you don't want to be bothered with any of it."

"Mish," I said, "please don't talk to me this way."

She stared past me, toward the window, and was silent for a moment. In the glare of morning sun she looked haggard, exhausted. When she spoke her tone had softened. "You need to rest and get better. You've got some damaged muscle in your arm. You'll be in the cast for three weeks, then you'll need physical therapy, but they say you won't lose mobility."

I nodded, biting my lip. I wished my sister would come to me, put her arms around me.

"I called your friend Damian last night," she said, "and asked him to go get your animals. He did it right away. So you don't have to worry about them."

"Thank you." Where, I wondered, were her strength and clear-headedness coming from? Did she have a reserve that I'd never suspected?

She stepped closer and said, "The police were at the house most of the night."

"The police?"

"They said they have to investigate any violent death. And a knife wound." Her gaze flitted to my arm and away again. "They went over every inch of the kitchen and bathroom."

Alarmed, I struggled to push myself up. "The newspaper story—"

"I took it." Her gaze wandered the room, avoiding my eyes. "They never saw it."

I slumped back against the pillow, breathless, mind racing over all the possible consequences of the police finding the story about Michael and Michelle Goddard's deaths twenty-two years ago.

She looked at me curiously. "Did you want them to see it? Are you going to tell them about—all that?"

"Of course not."

Her shoulders slumped with relief and she bowed her head. Then she straightened again, chin up. "They questioned me for a long time, and they'll be asking you questions too. We have to tell them the same story if we don't want it all to come out. You need to back up what I told them."

This was so bizarre I could hardly take it in. Getting our stories straight. Working out what to say to the cops. Good God. "What did you tell them?"

My sister astonished me with the intricately shaded and detailed mix of truth and fiction she'd concocted for the police. Mother had been suffering from depression. This wasn't surprising, because it ran in her family; both her own parents had committed suicide. Michelle and I couldn't persuade her to go into a clinic for treatment. Mother resisted the idea that she was following the same sad path as her parents, and believed she could work out her problems alone.

On the night before, Mother had been uncommunicative, Michelle told the police. We couldn't coax her to talk. We'd been horrified when she suddenly grabbed the carving knife and started out of the kitchen. I was cut accidentally when I tried to take the knife from her. She locked herself in the bathroom, and by the time we got the door open she'd slashed her wrists. She slit her throat before we could stop her.

When Michelle finished we were both silent for a long time. I looked down at my cast and bandage, remembering the moment when I realized Mother meant to kill me.

From the hallway came a rumble and the faint clink of metal on metal: the breakfast trolley.

"Most of it's true," Michelle said at last. "Will you tell them the same thing?"

I nodded.

"Good." She picked up her purse from a chair as if to leave.

"Did you read the story?" I said.

Her face was closed, cold. "No. I tore it up. I flushed it down the toilet in the restroom outside the ER."

I closed my eyes over burning tears. "Mish," I whispered. "I'm so sorry. Mother—If I hadn't—"

"Don't start," she said. "Just don't start. I don't want to hear how sorry you are."

The door hinge creaked, and a young blond nurse poked her head in. "Luke Campbell's here," she said. "You want him to come on in, or do you want him to wait a little bit?"

"Tell him to go away," Michelle said.

"No!" I said. "Tell him to come in, please."

"You don't need visitors—"

"I'm going home with him, Mish."

"You can't be serious."

Watching her severe expression crumble into hurt and dismay, I wavered, but only for a second. The nurse waited for clear instructions. "Tell him to come in," I said.

"Rachel—" Michelle broke off when Luke appeared in the doorway.

"I'm sorry, Mish." I was deserting her when she needed me most, but there was no other way I could get through the coming days. "I can't go back to the house."

She glared at Luke with a hatred so raw it took my breath away. She spun and rushed out of the room.

Luke came to the bed and closed his arms around me. Too weary to cry, I let sorrow and guilt fill me to overflowing, strangle me, drown me, then I felt it all drain away, leaving me empty and cold.

<><><>

By mid-afternoon a police detective was at Luke's apartment to question me. His name was John Rodriguez and he was about Luke's age, with very short black hair and an intensity and attentiveness that kept him always leaning forward, missing nothing.

I sat on the couch and answered the detective's questions dully, trying to dissociate myself from the words and black out the images they called up, suppressing the urge to scream that rose inside me like a living thing fighting for release.

"Mother was under a lot of stress in the last few weeks," I said. "She'd developed heart disease and we'd all been worried about it."

"Would you say she was depressed?" Rodriguez asked. His dark brown eyes were locked on my face.

"Yes. She wasn't herself. My sister's studying psychology, she can describe Mother's condition better than I can." I shook my head. "I never expected anything like this."

He led me over the events of that night again and again, approaching it from a different angle each time. Hoping to trip me up. My story never altered.

"She wouldn't talk to us. We couldn't get through to her. She grabbed the knife and I tried to get it away from Mother and that's how I got cut. I was so surprised, and it hurt so much, I let go of Mother. She ran into the bathroom. I had to jimmy open the door. She'd already cut her wrists. She was bleeding—"

I stopped to suck in a deep breath. Tears ran down my cheeks, silent, unstoppable. "My sister was still out in the hall, I think. That's when Mother—she cut her throat."

I swiped at my wet face with the back of my hand. Rodriguez watched me for a moment, then scribbled in his little notebook.

"Did you get along with your mother?" His voice was quiet, almost soothing, encouraging confession. So much like Mother's. "You have any differences of opinion? Most mothers and daughters do, don't they? It's only natural."

"We got along."

"Kind of unusual, isn't it, two grown daughters living with their mother?"

"My sister's a student, and I'm just starting out in my work. It made sense for us to live at home. Besides, I missed my family when I was away at school. I was glad to be home again."

"You stand to inherit a good bit, don't you? You and your sister'll be pretty well-off."

What did he think? That we were the female version of the Menendez brothers, butchering our mother for her money?

Yes, I realized with a jolt, that was what he thought. In my fear that revelations about kidnapping and a lifetime of lies would be dragged into the open, I'd forgotten how Mother's death and my injury must look to the police.

I couldn't let him see the turn my thoughts had taken.

"Detective Rodriguez," I said, looking him directly in the eyes and trying to keep my voice level, "if I had the choice between an inheritance and my mother's life, I think on the whole I'd rather have my mother back."

Over the next few days the detective came to see me twice more. I guessed from his attitude that he wasn't satisfied with the story Michelle and I told him, that he sensed something bigger swimming below the surface. A shiver ran through me when I considered what he might learn if he dug into the distant past. But he would need a reason to do that, and I was careful not to give him one. I spoke only of recent events in our lives, and when the detective asked about my father I replied indifferently that I couldn't really remember him.

The reporter on the evening news was tall, blond, perfectly made up. She stood in the street where we had lived, and the camera was angled to show part of the house behind her, as much as could be seen past the tall screen of yews. At the end of the driveway someone had placed a wooden sawhorse with a NO TRESPASSING sign attached.

I sat forward on the couch, listening.

"Inside this home in an exclusive section of McLean, a tragedy unfolded..." The reporter went on mouthing words that disguised her lack of knowledge.

The press was playing up the story for all it was worth—prominent psychologist cuts her own throat while daughters try to wrest the knife from her—but neither Michelle nor I made statements or gave interviews, and without our cooperation little personal information had surfaced. Stories appeared about Mother's practice, filled with statements of dismay and sadness from her colleagues. A couple of neighbors said we'd always seemed like a close family.

I felt a shock each time I saw our names in print and heard them spoken by strangers on the TV news. How ironic it was, I thought, that Mother, so private, hiding so much, was the subject of all this publicity. Yet even in death she concealed the truth. These people who wrote about us and spoke sententiously about our tragedy on television had no idea what a story they were missing.

I heard Luke unlocking the door, coming home from work. I rose and switched off the television set just as a photo of Mother flashed on the screen.

I was conscious of Luke lurking at the very edge of the boundary he'd set for himself, giving me space and privacy and freedom from pressure, but always watching for signs that I needed him. In fits and starts, I told him about the old newspaper story I'd found and what really happened the night Mother died. He nodded, silently agreeing to join Michelle and me in our conspiracy to hide the truth.

He was questioned because he'd come into the house while the medics were on the scene. He told the detective he knew nothing about Dr. Goddard's mental state or her reasons for wanting to take her own life. His first visit to the house that night remained a secret between Luke, myself, and my sister.

On the telephone I asked Michelle to come see me. She coldly refused. Rosario, who brought clothes to me at Luke's apartment two days after Mother's death, told me Michelle was obsessed with erasing all traces of blood from the kitchen and bathroom.

I sat on Luke's bed while Rosario hung my blouses and slacks in the closet.

"I washed the walls," she said. Tears filled her eyes. "I thought I had cleaned them well—"

"Oh, Rosie," I said. "I'm so sorry. You shouldn't have had to do that."

She pressed her lips together and took a moment to compose herself, blinking away the tears. "But your sister wasn't satisfied. Already this morning is a man come, taking off the old, putting up new." Her arms swung up and down in imitation of a paperhanger.

I saw blood-spotted wallpaper and quickly shoved the image out of my mind.

She closed the closet door. "And the floor, the tiles—what is in between?"

"The grout." Blood soaking in, the stain spreading.

"A man come and take it out, dig it out. The kitchen and the bathroom, is all broke up. Two men working same time, walls and the floors, they bump into each other." She shook her head. "I got out of the way."

Her eyes, puffy from tears already shed, filled again. She pressed a hand to her mouth. I rose and went to slip my free arm around her shoulders, and for a moment we leaned into one another, my chin resting on the top of her head.

"She was good to me, your mother," Rosario said, wiping at her nose with a handkerchief she'd pulled from her dress pocket.

I guided her to the bed and we sat down together.

"Your mother was not—" She searched for a word. "—warm, but she was good to me."

She gave up her struggle against tears then. I stayed beside her, silent, while she wept.

<> <> >

Theo, too, came to see me and pour out his sorrow. I wasn't sure I would ever tell him the truth. Maybe someday, when I knew all of it myself. But not now.

I was waiting. Waiting for the police to be finished with me, and for Mother to be laid to rest. When I thought of her, a swell of grief and rage and desperation rose in me, and I had to fight to subdue it and regain my equilibrium. I tried not to consider what I would do next, where my search would take me. Getting through each day took all my strength.

The crime lab found only Mother's and Rosario's fingerprints on the knife. Blood and tissue tests showed that Mother had been taking antidepressants, something I hadn't known. Our lie was closer to the truth than I'd imagined.

The police issued a statement saying that Judith Goddard's death was suicide. The case was closed. Her body was released, and on Monday, five days after she died, we buried her.

Chapter Twenty-three

They sweated in the morning sun, sneaked glances at their wristwatches, and avoided looking at the casket, the grave, or my sister and me. Surely, I thought, they'd rather be in their air-conditioned offices listening to the prattle of neurotics.

About twenty psychiatrists and psychologists showed up for the brief graveside service, the same people who came to the Fourth of July party. Men and women who'd thought they knew Judith Goddard. They stood apart from Michelle and me, crowding together on the opposite side of the grave.

No neighbors had come, and no friends except Theo, who was at my side, his hand coming up now and then to touch my elbow, and Kevin Watters, who stayed close to Michelle. Rosario and her husband, looking unnaturally formal in a black dress and a suit, hovered behind us despite my efforts to coax them forward.

Luke had wanted to come with me, but I told him I was going without him and the finality of my tone stopped any argument. Michelle had said, when she called to give me the time and place of the service, "If that man shows up with you, I'll make sure he regrets it." I wouldn't even let him drive me because I didn't want her to see him.

Blank-faced, clutching a single red rose, my sister stood inches from me, but we didn't touch. We didn't comfort one another. She hadn't yet spoken to me or to Theo.

Her new black suit made her skin look bleached in contrast. I owned nothing black and wore instead a plain navy linen dress Rosario had found in my closet at home. I'd had trouble squeezing my cast through the short sleeve.

My arm ached deep in the ravaged muscle. I'd exhausted my three-day supply of codeine two days before and now I was at the mercy of the pain, but I welcomed it, I fastened on it and let it drive everything else from my mind. I didn't know what I would do when the pain subsided.

The minister, an elderly, stooped man supplied by the funeral home, read from the Bible in a wavering voice. "And God shall wipe away all tears from their eyes; and there shall be no more death, neither sorrow, nor crying, neither shall there be any more pain; for the former things are passed away."

We bowed our heads in prayer when the minister asked us to. The sun's rays pressed on the back of my neck like a red-hot iron. Only once did I let my gaze wander to Mother's coffin, poised on a mechanized lift, and the deep hole beneath it. When the lift whirred into motion I began to shake, and Theo hugged my shoulders, steadying me.

The casket descended. Michelle stepped to the edge of the grave and dropped in the rose. A cardinal as red as the flower perched on a nearby headstone and warbled his rich song.

Together, flanked by Theo and Kevin, my sister and I received the murmured sympathy of the departing mourners. *So sorry…so sorry…so sorry.* Their eyes shifted, sliding past our faces and carefully avoiding any unseemly examination of my injured arm.

I leaned to kiss Rosario's cheek, because she looked as if she needed consolation as much as we did.

At last only Michelle and Kevin, Theo and I were left. Michelle started to walk away without speaking, but Kevin, his fresh young face knotted with emotion, came to me and wrapped me in a gentle bear hug. He stepped back and scrubbed a hand over his chin. "Oh, man, Rachel, I don't know what to say. You tell me what I can do to help, and I'll do it, you just ask."

I spoke quietly so Michelle wouldn't hear. "Help my sister. That's what you can do. Don't let her be alone too much."

He nodded. "You can count on it. I kinda love the girl, you know?"

"She's lucky to have you."

Michelle strode back to us with brisk steps. Theo murmured to Kevin, and the two men moved away to give us privacy.

"I want to sell the house," Michelle said without preamble. "As soon as possible. Our names are on the title, it doesn't have to go through probate. We can put it on the market anytime." She paused. "You don't want it, do you?"

I shook my head.

"Well. Okay then. I'm moving to an apartment as soon as I can find one. There's no point keeping Rosario fulltime after I move out, but she can come in and clean a couple times a week until we find a buyer." Michelle looked around as if taking in the scenery. The hot air stirred and lifted her pale hair from her shoulders. She faced me again. "You'll have to do something about those cages of yours."

I nodded. "I'll take them down."

"Good." She turned away.

"Mish."

She looked back at me, her expression guarded.

"We need to talk. I could go over to the house with you now. I have to pick up some things anyway."

"I'm not going home. I'm going to lunch with Kevin, then I've got a class."

"We have to talk about all this sometime."

"No."

"Don't you even want to know who you are?"

She stepped so close her face was inches from mine. "I do know who I am. And nothing you can say is going to change it."

With her chin high she walked away from me, across the bright green cemetery grass.

Theo tried to talk me out of going to the house, and when he saw that was futile, insisted that I let him come with me. But in the end he took one cab and I took another and we went our separate ways.

〈〉〈〉〈〉

I entered through the front door. The house was utterly silent. I stopped to look into the sun-splashed living room, at the gleaming tables and all the small exquisite things Mother had accumulated. The jade figurines, the decorative plates, the antique marble clock on the mantel. The clock hands had stopped at 8:15. Mother had been the only one who knew how to wind the delicate mechanism properly.

She would never walk through these rooms again. I would never see her or hear her voice again.

I knew that neither Michelle nor Luke would understand my grief, Michelle because she blamed me for destroying our family, Luke because he blamed Mother for robbing me of my identity. But I grieved, for the simple reason that I had loved her. She'd been my mother for twenty-one years, and I had loved and needed her.

With my aching arm pressed to my side, I climbed the stairs. In my room I found my blue canvas luggage lined up at the foot of the bed, along with several empty cardboard boxes. Rosario would pack all my belongings the following day and a mover would collect them and take them to Luke's apartment.

I knelt by the bed, felt under the mattress and drew out the book on locks. Somehow it seemed important that no one find it. I stuffed it into my shoulderbag, then went out to the hallway.

Mother's bedroom door was closed. When I touched the doorknob, I felt the same ripple of apprehension and shame that had gone through me when I'd sneaked in to look at the picture.

I opened the door.

The draperies were drawn and the room was dark and cool. I flipped the light switch. Everything looked as it always had, peach and blue perfection. In the air hung the faint flowery perfume of the sachet Mother used in her closet and drawers.

The picture was gone from her dresser. Only Michelle would have removed it. What did she do with it? I wondered if she'd held it and tried to believe the child was her.

I had to take what I was after and get out of this room. Opening the closet, I tried to ignore the neat row of dresses, the scent of sachet. Mother's purse hung from a hook on the back of the door. The purse contained only a few things, and I found her keys quickly.

Downstairs again, I went straight to Mother's study, without allowing myself so much as a glance at the kitchen. I unlocked the file drawer where I'd found the strange note on the night Mother was hospitalized. I pulled out the sheet of blue paper, leaving behind the folder that had held it. Although I didn't know yet what it meant, I was certain this was a message from the past, a link to the life that waited to be discovered.

...no regrets...the one beautiful thing I've got left.

I read the words over and over until I noticed my hand was trembling. I folded the sheet, slid it into my shoulderbag.

Next I moved to the closet, knelt and opened the box that contained the photo albums. Refusing to let myself dwell on the images, I flipped through one of the books until I found the posed studio portrait of the three of them: mother, father, little daughter. It was the same picture that had accompanied the newspaper account of the accident.

For a moment I considered taking the albums away so Michelle wouldn't stumble unprepared onto the photos of Michael and Judith Goddard and their real daughter. Like me, my sister was running on autopilot right now, and these pictures could bring her crashing to reality. The old urge to protect her, to cushion her fall, rose in me. But the time for that was past. I could not protect her from the truth of our lives.

I laid the album back in the box and closed the lid.

Unable to make myself go up to Mother's room again, I left the keys on the desk. I went out through the front door and walked around to the back yard.

The garden looked impossibly cheerful, neat, normal. Only five days had passed since I was last here, but if I'd found the blossoms shriveled, the foliage dried up, I wouldn't have been surprised. Instead, the dahlias and late roses bloomed on, oblivious to the absence of their owner, and a sweet powdery scent hung in the humid air. Cicadas droned in the trees, but the birds had fallen silent in the midday heat.

I walked down to the edge of the woods, past the line of shrubs to the cages. The doors stood open, and when I approached a dozen sparrows burst out in a flurry of wings.

The sight of the abandoned cages brought hot tears to my eyes. I drew in a long steadying breath. What needed doing here?

Maybe some other rehabber could remove the cages as they were, load them on a truck and take them for his or her own use. But suddenly I was seized by a need to destroy them, to know they simply didn't exist anymore.

I dropped my shoulderbag on the ground and, almost running, returned to the house, entered through the front again, and clomped down the basement stairs and into the laundry room where the toolbox was kept. I grabbed a hammer and crowbar.

Awkwardly cradling them in my unencumbered arm, I carried the tools to the cages. With one hand I set to work prying loose nails, screen, strips of wood. Every movement of my body made my wounds throb, and I was quickly drenched in sweat, but I worked on and on, piling boards on the ground.

At last, when the cages were reduced to rubble, I pushed past the shrubs and staggered onto the sunny lawn, still gripping the crowbar.

The dahlia blossoms in the flower bed before me were bright and jaunty, little jewels lifting their faces to the sun. Life, going on.

I raised my arm high over my head, then brought the crowbar down on the plants, slashing leaves and stems, shattering flowers, raining yellow, red, pink petals onto the pine bark mulch.

I swung again and again, until I had no strength left and fell to my knees, sobbing. I didn't hear or see Luke approach, but when he knelt and folded his arms around me it seemed natural that he was there.

"Let's go home now," he said.

"It's not over yet." My voice was muffled against his shoulder. "I have to find out who I am."

"I know," he said. "I know."

Chapter Twenty-four

Hours later, when we were in his small kitchen preparing dinner, Luke asked what I planned to do next.

"I'm not sure," I said. "I have to be careful. Look what's already happened because of me digging around in the past."

"It's not your fault, Rachel."

"Regardless of whose fault it was, it happened." I leaned against the counter and watched him chop vegetables. The knife sliced through a succulent red bell pepper, down, across, again and again, leaving red stains on the wooden chopping block. With a shiver, I turned away, and busied myself stirring the rotini pasta that was boiling in a pot.

"Maybe you ought to stop now," Luke said. He scraped the pepper slices into a skillet that already held snow peas, mushrooms and olive oil, and turned on the burner under the pan. "Just come back to work when your arm heals, and we'll get on with our lives."

It was something I'd said to myself many times in the last few days. I longed for the things that meant normality. I missed the clinic, the people I worked with, the warm little bodies and wide eyes of my patients. Even the smell of alcohol and antiseptic would be a balm to me now. But I was useless for the moment, unable to efficiently do exams, give injections, perform surgery with only one hand. And when my cast came off, I had to complete my search.

"I'll never have any peace if I don't at least find out who Michelle and I really are."

Luke sighed. "Have you had any luck remembering your real parents' last name?"

I shook my head. "I looked through the phone book yesterday. I was hoping something might ring a bell, but nothing did. I know I was just a kid, but how could I forget my own last name?"

"It's a miracle you can remember anything after what that woman did to you."

"Luke, please," I said wearily.

"Okay, okay. I'm sorry."

"It would have been in the papers. Two little sisters disappearing together." Olive oil sizzled in the skillet. I removed a spatula from a drawer and stirred the vegetables. "If I find the story, I'll find the names."

"Do you remember when it happened?"

"Well, she brought us here the summer after our father—after Michael Goddard died. So it must have happened just before that. When I was five." Realization struck me like a blow. "I don't even know for sure how old I was. How old I am."

We fell silent a moment, as I stirred the vegetables and he tipped the rotini into a colander to drain. Steam rose in a cloud from the pasta.

〈〉〈〉〈〉

August 26. The day Mother had chosen as my birthday. I had no idea why, and suspected it was a random choice. But it had been my birthday for twenty-one years, and when it came round again I woke with the thought, I'm twenty-seven today. It was almost certainly a lie but it still felt like the truth. I lay in bed remembering the year Mother had the weeping cherry tree planted as a gift to me.

Luke had bought concert tickets weeks before—Mary Chapin Carpenter at Wolf Trap—but I couldn't imagine rousing myself to go. Over an ordered-in dinner at home, Luke gave me his gift, an exquisite gold chain necklace made of tiny interlocking hearts. With a wry grin, he said, "I told you this would be a birthday to remember. I had no idea."

Earlier in the day a bouquet of yellow roses—Mother's favorite, never mine—had arrived with a card that said simply, "Happy birthday. Michelle."

I heard daily reports about Michelle from Kevin. She'd moved into his apartment temporarily. He was careful to tell me that she was using the bedroom and he was on the couch. At night he heard her moving about, and when he woke at odd hours he always saw light under the bedroom door. She ate almost nothing. Poor Kevin thought he was witnessing a simple display of grief, and I couldn't tell him how much the girl he loved was concealing.

At our next meeting, Michelle sat two chairs away from me at a conference table in the McLean office of David Waterston, Mother's attorney and executor. Waterston, a lean blond man in his late fifties, sat across from us. Next to him was Annette King, the glossy and severely professional woman he'd found to handle the house sale.

My sister spoke only to the lawyer, never so much as glancing at me for agreement or clarification. I might as well not have been present. She looked even worse than Kevin had led me to expect. Always thin, she'd lost weight noticeably since Mother's death and now approached gauntness. Heavy makeup under her eyes didn't quite hide the dark circles.

I tried not to stare at her, fastening my gaze instead on the table before me. Sunlight cut through the blinds and lay in slashes across the gleaming oak surface. I felt like a fraud, discussing my inheritance from a mother who wasn't my mother. I tried to imagine how the discreet and scrupulous lawyer would react if I sprang the truth on him.

I snapped back to attention when I realized he'd asked me a question.

"Is this arrangement all right with you as well as your sister?" he repeated. "Your mother's secretary handling the closing of her office? She'll disperse the case files of those patients who have found other doctors, and destroy the inactive files."

As if recalling the distant past, I remembered when I thought Mother might have a file about me in her office. But no, she wouldn't have committed such secrets to writing.

"That's fine," I said.

Except for a gift of $10,000 to Rosario, Mother had left her estate of more than a million dollars to Michelle and me, evenly divided. When we became adults she'd put our names on the title to the house so that part of our inheritance wouldn't be delayed when she died. Michelle and I had protested at the time, telling her we refused to think about her death when she was barely fifty. Now her foresight meant we could put the house on the market quickly.

Waterston had taken the real estate agent on a tour of the property the day before. She'd come to this meeting with a suggested price and a long list of things that would have to be done to Mother's perfect house to make it marketable.

Annette King, probably in her forties, had sleek chin-length hair of an unnatural shade of blond and wore a crimson linen suit and lipstick to match. She made me think of a gaudy Christmas ornament. I watched her long fingers dance over the papers and legal pad she'd arranged before her, and wondered if her red-painted nails were real or fake.

"My thinking is that I should hold off showing the property to locals," she said, her voice crisp and impersonal. "I'd like to avoid any pointless showings to people who just want to satisfy their curiosity. And I'd rather not answer a lot of questions. So until people forget, I'll limit showings to buyers coming in from out of the area."

Until people forget. Some people never would, not even strangers to whom we were no more than names in the newspaper and on TV. People who'd never met us probably discussed our messed up lives, speculated about us. They would remember.

Ms. King tapped a nail on her legal pad. "As you've requested, I'll arrange the repainting and so on, and handle all the contractual matters. You won't have to be involved except to approve the final price once we've got an offer." She ran the tip of her tongue along her brilliant red lower lip. "But before we can get started, we do need to have an empty house."

Her eyes darted from me to Michelle and back again.

"What do you want us to do?" I asked Waterston.

He sat forward, adjusted his tie and cleared his throat. "The house is yours now, but the contents are part of the estate. If you like, we can schedule an estate sale as soon as we have permission from the probate judge. In the meantime, everything in the house has to be catalogued and removed to storage. But if you want to keep everything—"

"I don't want any of it," I said.

A short silence followed, and I realized how harsh and abrupt I'd sounded. I glanced at Michelle. Tears stood in her eyes. I leaned toward her over the chair that separated us. "Mish," I said softly. "Keep whatever you want. I'm not interested in the money from the sale."

She turned to look at me for the first time, and as she did a tear spilled down each cheek. She started to speak, but her breath caught on a sob.

"Oh, Mish." I rose and went to her side, awkwardly leaning to embrace her with my free arm.

She pressed her face into my shoulder, and I felt the wetness of her tears on my blouse.

"We'll get through this," I said. "We'll get all this done and behind us."

The real estate agent gathered her papers, slapping them together briskly. "I'll be in touch," she said. "And you can call me anytime, of course, if you have questions."

As she bustled out, Waterston also rose. "I'll let you two have a few minutes to talk," he said. He closed the door softly behind him.

I sat in the chair next to Michelle and reached for her hand. Her skin felt icy. "Mish," I said, "how have you been?"

"I miss her so much. I can't believe she's dead." With a low moan Michelle began to cry, rocking back and forth in her chair.

Tears poured down her face and spotted the front of her blue dress. I waited silently.

When her sobs subsided, she turned beseeching eyes on me and said, "She was a good mother to us, wasn't she? I mean—She gave us so much—"

"Yes, she did." I took my sister's hand again. Her fingers tightened around mine. "If I could turn back time, if I could make all this go away, believe me, I would."

She looked down at our clasped hands. Her voice was a whisper. "She was trying to kill you. She would've killed you if I hadn't stopped her. I didn't imagine that, did I?"

"No, you didn't imagine it."

When she raised her eyes to mine again, I saw that she'd begun to accept the truth, or what she knew of it. But I also saw anguish on her face and in every tense line of her body. How much more could I ask her to accept?

"I've been wanting to talk to you," I said, "about what to do next. I want to try to find out who we really—"

"No!" She shot to her feet, rocking her chair backward. "You can't, you have to let it drop."

I stood and reached out to her. She stepped away from me.

"I just want to know," I said. "I need to know."

"Is this his idea? Is he pushing you to do this?"

"Who are you talking about, Mish?"

"Luke! He just wants to come between us, he's determined to keep us apart—"

"Luke has nothing to do with this. He's not coming between us."

"Then why are you with him instead of me?" She wailed the words like a heartbroken child.

I held out my arm and this time she came to me, wrapping her own arms around me and burying her face in my shoulder.

"Nobody will ever come between us," I said. "I have to stay with Luke, but anytime you need me, just call or come to me. I love you so much, Mish. I always will."

‹ › ‹ › ‹ ›

When I sat once more in the periodicals room of the Library of Congress, looking at newspapers on microfilm, I began to doubt my memory again. I'd been so sure the abduction happened during warm weather, but I worked my way through June, July, August, scouring every page, examining even the smallest articles, and found nothing. I requested the April, May and September issues.

Nothing appeared in the April papers. I was near the end of May, pausing to rub my throbbing temples, when I spotted the one-paragraph item in a regional news roundup column. Two Young Sisters Disappear from St. Cloud Playground.

I held my breath while I read it. Catherine and Stephanie Dawson, ages five and three, vanished while their mother was in a nearby shop. In St. Cloud, not Minneapolis.

I sat back, covering my face with my hands, unable to stop the tears. Catherine and Stephanie. I fumbled a tissue from my purse and wiped my face, not caring what people at the surrounding desks thought. I read the little item over and over.

We were the daughters of John and Barbara Dawson. I could see them, still not sharply defined but clearer than they'd ever been. My real mother was slender and had shoulder-length hair that might be auburn, like mine. My father was tall and lanky. I wasn't sure, but I thought he was blond. That must be where Michelle got her coloring.

I rushed to the circulation desk and asked the clerk if the library had back issues of the St. Cloud papers. He flipped through a little box of cards. His casual, "Nope, sorry," was like a punch in the stomach.

But I had the names. It was a beginning. I made a copy of the little story that would lead me back to my real parents. Then I made another copy of the story about Michael Goddard's accident. It was a part of the puzzle. Someday soon I might have all the pieces, and the complete picture would come clear. I didn't know yet whether I would go any farther than that.

⟨⟩⟨⟩⟨⟩

"Are you sure you want to do this by yourself?" Luke said.

I was packing a suitcase. The cast had been taken off my arm that day and the muscles protested at being put to use again, so I folded blouses and slacks mostly with one hand. The doctor wanted me to start physical therapy at once, but I'd told him it would have to wait. I had something to take care of first.

"Let me go with you," Luke said. "I'll cancel my appointments for a week——"

"No," I said firmly. "I'll be fine."

I didn't feel fine. Dread of the unknown threatened to paralyze me every time I stopped to think about what I was doing.

Luke came up behind me and wrapped his arms around me, kissing my cheek. "Just come back to me."

I felt a wash of tenderness for him, and gratitude for his steadying presence in my life. I turned and embraced him. "Oh, I'll be back. You can't get rid of me that easily."

Chapter Twenty-five

I had a plan. I had a script written in my head, and I rehearsed it all the way to Minneapolis on the plane. Driving north to St. Cloud in a rental car, I spoke my lines aloud again and again, until I began to worry that they'd sound phony and stiff because they were over-rehearsed.

I walked into police headquarters with a notebook and a tape recorder in the big canvas bag slung over my shoulder. The recorder had been a last-minute thought, tucked into my bag just before I left Luke's apartment that morning. It would make me more believable, and it would catch any bits of information that emotion prevented me from absorbing.

The receptionist at the front desk, a middle-aged woman with ruddy cheeks and flyaway blond hair, was eager to help. She made a couple of phone calls, telling invisible strangers about my interest in a twenty-one-year-old case. When she replaced the receiver she was beaming with accomplishment.

"Guess what?" she said. "The detective that headed up that case, he's still in the department. You can get the whole story straight from the horse's mouth. Soon as he gets in. He's out on an interview, but it won't be long. Want some coffee while you wait?"

The man who investigated our disappearance. Fear and doubt seized me. I couldn't pull this off. I would give myself away the moment I met him.

I turned abruptly.

The startled receptionist said, "Is something wrong?"

I faced her again, shook my head, smiled. "No, no," I said. "I'll pass on the coffee, but I'd love a cup of water."

Almost an hour went by. I sat on a hard wooden bench inside the front door, next to a metal container of sand bristling with cigarette butts. The place reeked of stale smoke. No one else came in, and between occasional phone calls the receptionist chattered about Princess Diana, the subject of a book she was reading in idle moments.

"I blame that husband of hers for everything," the woman said, shaking her head. "If he hadn't been carrying on with that old girlfriend of his, I bet him and Diana would still be married to this day, and she'd be alive and those two boys would have the kind of home they deserve."

Now and then, even as she seemed consumed by details of the royals' lives, the woman's gaze slipped down to the raw scar on the back of my left hand. But she didn't ask about it. Her glances made me acutely conscious of the far worse scar that was hidden by the sleeve of my blouse. The silk fabric felt like sandpaper scraping across it.

At last a tall gray-haired man walked through the front door. "Detective Steckling!" the woman exclaimed. "This young lady's been waiting for you. She wants to talk to you about the Dawson sisters."

I stood and shook his hand, aware that my palm was moist. "I'm Rachel Campbell." The name tasted strange on my tongue but came out smoothly.

"Jack Steckling." He narrowed his blue eyes, looking down at me. He was ruggedly handsome, square-jawed, with broad shoulders that gave an impression of strength. "You got some information about the Dawson girls?"

"Oh, no," I said. Telling myself to stay calm, I went into my spiel. "I'm looking for information. I'm a Ph.D. candidate in psychology at the University of Maryland, and I'm writing my dissertation on the families of abducted children. This is one of the few cases I've heard of where two children in the same family disappeared. I'm visiting some relatives in St. Paul, so I thought I'd drive up here and see what I could find out."

He nodded. "Yeah, sure. I remember that case like it was yesterday. Come on back, let me see if I can help you out."

Walking with him down a narrow fluorescent lit corridor, I had a peculiar sensation, as if I were floating on water, moving without touching down. I could barely take in the knowledge that the man beside me, although I'd never seen him before, had once been part of my life and I'd been part of his. He'd looked for my sister and me and never found us. He remembered us as if it had happened yesterday. But he didn't see Catherine Dawson in my face. The thought left me feeling obscurely bereft, yet simultaneously relieved.

We entered a room that must have been twenty feet long but seemed small, crowded, crammed full, with most of the perimeter taken up by filing cabinets, a newspaper-laden table, and six desks spaced out at right angles to the side walls. On a table by the windows a coffee maker poured a stream of fresh coffee into a glass pot. The rich aroma made my mouth water.

Only two desks were occupied, by a young man talking on a phone and an older man reading a newspaper. Steckling sank into a padded rolling chair and motioned for me to take the straight-backed wooden chair next to his desk. With movements polished smooth by long habit, he reached inside his jacket, withdrew a large and heavy-looking pistol, and slid it into a desk drawer. A pungent odor of oil rose from the gun and hung in the air, competing with the coffee, even after the drawer was closed.

"So," he said, "what kind of information are you after?"

In spite of my careful rehearsal, I wasn't ready for this. My heart hammering in my chest, I reached down to my bag, which I'd set on the floor, and pulled out the pad, a pen and the recorder. "Do you mind if I tape this?"

"No problem. Go ahead." After he made room by pushing aside his phone, I laid the recorder on the desktop and switched it on. He was looking at my hands, studying the scar, but he didn't say anything. Would a detective's first reaction to the sight be a suspicion of violence?

I asked, "Did you work on the Dawson sisters case from the beginning?"

He leaned back, fingers knitted together over his stomach. The gold wedding band on his left hand was old, badly scratched. "Yeah. First call came to me." His eyes lost focus as he looked into the past. "I'll never forget it. She was screaming in the phone."

"She?" *Keep it cool, impersonal.*

"The mother. Barbara. Screaming her girls were gone. I had trouble calming her down enough to tell me where it happened."

The grip of panic tightened around my chest. I didn't know if I could go through with this.

Screaming her girls were gone.

"The way she told it," Steckling said, "she left the girls on the playground and just went up the street to a shop for a minute. When she got back they were gone."

"She left them alone on the playground?" I heard Mother's voice: *She didn't take care of you. Anything could have happened.*

"Yeah. Seems crazy, doesn't it? But she was in the habit, never gave it a second thought. She said they'd always been okay, and she claimed she never was gone more than a few minutes. Used to go in the shops up on the next block, then come back for the girls."

"Are you saying—" I stopped to clear my throat. "Was she a bad mother?"

"I wouldn't say bad. Just careless." He paused. "But all it took was a little carelessness."

I fussed with the recorder, moving it a few inches closer to him, to give myself an excuse not to look him in the face. Across the room one of the other policemen rose and walked to the door.

"Did anybody see what happened?" I said.

Steckling shook his head. "We had witnesses that saw them in the playground that day, but nobody saw them leave. You see, there was a thunderstorm, and everybody on the playground, the mothers and their kids, they ran for cover when it started."

Everybody went away and left us alone. "Didn't anybody try to get Catherine and Stephanie out of the rain?"

"A couple women said they worried about them, but they figured the mother would come get them pretty quick."

"Why didn't she? Did she say?"

"Oh, she came after them. But it was too late. As best we could figure it, there was about a five-minute window between the time the other mothers and their kids left, and the time Barbara Dawson got back to the playground. Somebody snatched them in those five minutes."

"What did she do then? The mother."

"She figured they'd gone looking for her. So she went back up the block, ran around in the rain, looked in all the stores and the diner. Then she thought maybe they'd headed home—they only lived about four blocks from the playground. So she went home. They weren't there, so she started going around the neighborhood, knocking on doors, asking if anybody'd seen them."

"Wasting time," I murmured.

"Wasting a lot of time." He grunted in disgust. "She didn't call us for three solid hours."

And by then we were in Minneapolis in Mother's packed-up house.

"Did you search outside the St. Cloud area?" I asked.

"We put out a statewide bulletin. Got press coverage. Kept looking, checking out leads. That's about all we can do in cases like this."

Cases like this. He had no idea. "Did anybody ever call and say they'd seen—" I stopped, horrified that I'd been on the verge of saying *seen us*. I finished, "—the girls?"

He barked a humorless laugh. "Oh, yeah. This kind of thing, you end up wading through a blue million dead-end tips, looking for one that means something. Everybody was seeing them everywhere. Once the story got picked up by out-of-state papers, we started hearing from people in Wisconsin, Michigan, even Canada."

The wrong direction. "How long did you look for them?"

"Hell, I guess I'm still looking for them."

My pen slipped from my hand and landed on the carpet without a sound. I leaned to retrieve it. "Why? After all these years?"

"It just eats away at me, that I never could find them, couldn't close the case. Most of the time, a kid disappears, you find him, one way or another. He runs away, he comes back. The father grabs him to get back at the wife after a divorce, and you catch up with them. Or you find the kid dead somewhere. You get some closure. This case, though, we never had a clue. They just vanished into thin air, like the saying goes. I know they're dead, but I'd like to prove it."

His breath came out in a long sigh as he sat forward. "You want to see some of the newspaper stories?"

"Yes, please, thank you."

He was already on his feet. "That stuff's in another room. Sit tight, I'll be back in a minute."

It was much longer than a minute, long enough for me to start feeling disconnected again, to start wondering if any of this was really happening and whether I wanted to go on with it. The other policeman—it was the younger one, a tall blond—left the room and I was alone.

Steckling came back with a bulging file folder. When he plopped it onto his desk a musty odor rose from it.

"This is just part of it." He sat down. "The whole case file's about ten jackets this thick, mostly tips and dead ends and stuff that doesn't mean anything." He opened the folder. "Here's the first story."

He slid a large clipping across the desktop.

My childhood face, and my sister's, smiled back at me. We leaned together, arms around each other, her hair light, mine dark. We wore pants and tee shirts. The caption read *Catherine and Stephanie Dawson in a photo taken last week.*

I didn't realize how long I'd been staring at the picture until Steckling said, "A real tragedy, huh?"

"Yes." My voice was a dry rasp. "It's a tragedy."

He placed more clippings in front of me. In another picture a couple clung to one another, their faces distorted by crying. *Barbara and John Dawson plead for the return of their daughters.*

The mother—it was so hard, even now, to think of her as *my* mother—had the dark hair I recalled, but John Dawson's hair wasn't the pale blond I'd expected, the hair my sister had inherited. It looked light brown, or sandy, like Luke's.

I touched the faces with a fingertip. Vague images swam into my mind. I'd pushed open a door in my memory, just a crack. I watched him yank dresses from her hands, from a half-filled suitcase, and slap the hangers back over the closet rod. Clink, clink. Metal on metal.

"You said you wanted to know about the effect on the parents?"

Steckling's voice brought me back to the present. The memory dissolved.

"Yes." I pushed the clipping aside, out of my line of vision. "I thought I might like to talk to them."

"Well, I'm afraid you can't talk to him because he's dead."

The shock was swift, deep, and left me momentarily speechless.

Steckling went on, "He killed himself a couple years after the girls disappeared."

"Oh my God," I breathed.

The detective nodded. "It never was officially ruled a suicide, but I always thought it was. Shot himself in the head while he was cleaning his hunting rifle. This guy was a hunter since he was a kid, he knew guns, he knew gun safety. That wasn't any accident. But the insurance company couldn't prove suicide, so they had to pay for accidental death."

I licked my dry lips. "But why did he do it? Was it grief?"

"More like a guilty conscience, if you ask me."

"A guilty conscience? Over what?"

"My theory was, he took the girls and killed them."

"You're not serious." The words came out on a burst of astonished laughter.

Steckling started to speak, changed his mind, then changed it again. He leaned forward, elbows on the desk. "I'll tell you something we never did make public. This is confidential, you understand? But if you're going to talk to the mother, you probably ought to know about it."

He meant what he'd said. He thought our father killed us. But it was absurd, it was crazy. Caught up in these thoughts, I wasn't braced for what he said next.

"John Dawson wasn't the younger girl's real father."

I stared at him.

"That came out when I questioned them. We always start with the family, any time we get a crime like this, and no witnesses. Dawson just broke down and spit it out, said he wasn't Stephanie's father. He left Barbara for a while when he first found out. Then they got back together on condition they'd move to a new town and start fresh. They came to St. Cloud when Stephanie was a few months old. Dawson sold insurance, he got a transfer to the St. Cloud office."

"Who—" My voice was so weak I barely heard it myself. I took a breath and started over. "Who was Stephanie's real father?"

Steckling shrugged. "That, I never could get out of them. I really leaned on them, I even threatened to charge them for withholding evidence, but it didn't do a damn bit of good. Dawson swore he didn't even know for sure who it was, and Barbara said it was somebody who was long gone."

I gave my head a slight shake, trying to clear it. I had to be careful what I said, had to avoid questions that betrayed too much knowledge. "What made you think John Dawson was capable of murdering both girls?"

"Stranger things have happened, I'll tell you. A man finds out his wife's been carrying on an affair with another man, had a kid by him, he broods about it, starts thinking maybe the other one's not his either. Hell, who knows? Maybe she wasn't."

A clutch of pain deep inside almost made me cry out a protest. Maintaining a calm, interested expression took all my self-control. "Did he tell you he thought neither girl was his?"

"No, but that's no proof he didn't think it. And even if he believed Cathy was his, he could've killed her too just to get back at his wife. People that do things like that, sometimes their motives are pretty twisted. Of course, he claimed he loved them both, and he swore he never treated Stephanie any different. But if you ask me, that'd be damned hard for a man to do under the circumstances, treat her like she was his."

"You never found any evidence against him," I said, and wished I'd made it sound like a question instead of a flat statement of fact.

"No. We watched him real close, but he was careful. He never led us anywhere."

Because there was nowhere to lead you. "How did they act after the disappearance? What was it like for them?"

"Well, Barbara, the mother, she blamed herself for leaving them on the playground."

"They were so young," I murmured. Did I really remember her walking away, leaving us behind, or had my imagination supplied the desolating picture? "To be left alone like that."

Steckling sighed. "Well, she wouldn't have won any mother of the year awards, that's for sure. What I think—well, what I know—is Barbara Dawson was depressed, real bad depression, over a lot of things. Look what happened to her. An affair, a baby that wasn't her husband's, a breakup with the baby's father, a separation from her husband, leaving a job she liked, moving from the Twin Cities up here where she didn't know anybody. She was pretty low, she admitted it."

"So depressed that she neglected her children."

"I think she took pretty good care of them most of the time. But I guess she needed to get away from them for a few minutes now and then. So she left them where she thought they'd be okay and she went off by herself. Just careless, like I said."

A careless moment that changed so many lives.

"How did John Dawson behave afterward?"

"Oh, he was really determined to punish his wife. Kept telling her it was her fault, she couldn't be trusted. He said that right in front of me more than once. The more I heard, the more convinced I was that he did it himself, to hurt Barbara. It was brutal, some of the things he said to her."

I recalled, with exquisite precision, the sensation of smothering when I pulled my pillow tight over my head to block out their quarreling voices in the next room.

Sour bile rose to burn my throat. I swallowed. "Couldn't he account for himself, where he was when they disappeared?"

"He always claimed he was working in his office all afternoon, up to when his wife called him—she called him before she called us—but the only other person he worked with was a secretary, and she was on vacation. So, no alibi."

What would this man say if I told him the truth? *My father didn't kill anyone. Look at me. I'm right here in front of you, and my sister is sitting in a classroom in Washington.* He wouldn't believe me. He might be very hard to convince.

I said, "How would you have identified the girls if you'd found them?"

"Decomposed bodies, you mean? Well, we had up-to-date dental records. General descriptions, hair color. Hair lasts a long time, even when there's nothing else left but a skeleton. We lifted fingerprints from their room, but that wouldn't do much good unless we'd found the bodies early enough—" He broke off with a shrug.

I looked down at my hands. Fingerprints. The never-changing stamp of identity. I could prove who I was whenever I was ready.

"What happened to Barbara after John Dawson's death?"

"It took her a while to pull herself together," Steckling said. "She was still in pretty rough shape when her husband died. It was tough on her. But she put her life back together."

"How do you mean?"

"She sold the house here, moved back to Minneapolis and—"

"Minneapolis?" I said sharply.

"Yeah. She got a job at the same place she'd worked at before."

"Where was that?" I poised my pencil over my pad, realizing I had yet to write anything down.

"A law firm. One of those big ones with a dozen names. I don't remember—Let me look here." He turned to the front of the thick folder, where a sheet of paper was stapled to the inside of the cover. "Here it is. Jensen, Dubie, Goddard, and Brown. Well, I guess that's not a dozen names, it just seems like it."

My hand reached reflexively for my bag, where I carried the accident story that gave Michael Goddard's place of employment. Jensen, Dubie, Goddard, and Brown.

I drew my hand back to my lap, anchored my fingers around the notepad. "She worked there."

"Yeah, she was a legal secretary. Good one too, I guess, to work in a firm like that. She told me she was going back to work for one of the senior partners. He'd had three or four secretaries since she left and hadn't been satisfied with any of them."

"Is she still living in Minneapolis?"

He nodded. "Far as I know. She kept in touch for a long time, called regularly. She had this idea the girls might somehow find their way back home, and she wouldn't be here for them. Well, I knew they were dead, I was always sure of that, but I'd talk to her, listen to her. She always wanted me to know what was going on with her."

"What was going on?"

"She got married again after a few years. Had two more kids, one right after the other. She was getting close to forty, and she said she wanted to hurry before it was too late."

In all my imaginings, I hadn't considered the possibility that my sister and I had been replaced, that our mother had another family now. She hadn't simply waited for us to return.

"How old are they?" I said. "The children."

"Teenagers, fourteen, fifteen. A girl and a boy."

My half-sister, half-brother. "Do you know their names?"

Steckling narrowed his eyes at me. "You ought to talk to Barbara about all that, see if she wants to get into it. Call her first, ask her if she's willing to talk to you. I wouldn't go knocking on her door without being invited." He smiled, and suddenly looked a decade younger. "But you don't strike me as somebody who'd do that anyway."

My answering smile was automatic. "No, I wouldn't."

Then he said, "Caroline and Mark, that's their names. The girl's the older one. The boy's named after his father. Mark Junior."

"What's their last name?"

"Olsson." He spelled it, then laughed. "Easy to remember. A million of them in Minnesota."

I produced another smile.

"You'll be careful how you approach Barbara, won't you?" he said. "She's always been pretty willing to talk about it, but this business about her husband not being Stephanie's father—"

"I'll be careful." I added what I thought he wanted to hear. "I won't let her know that you told me. If she doesn't bring it up, I won't either."

"I'll give you her home number." He reached into his shirt pocket for a small notepad, consulted the sheet stapled inside the folder on the desk, jotted her name and number. He tore the page from the pad and held it out, with no idea of what he was giving me.

My fingers closed round it.

"You want copies of these newspaper stories?" he said.

"Yes, thank you."

While a clerk did the copying, Steckling brought us coffee in Styrofoam cups, and we chatted about the weather differences between the Washington area and Minnesota. A couple of times I noticed him looking at my scar, but he never asked about it.

Chapter Twenty-six

For a long time I sat behind the wheel of the rental car in the lot next to police headquarters, watching the late afternoon sunlight slowly recede along the rows of vehicles. The folder full of newspaper articles peeked from underneath my bag on the passenger seat, both luring and repelling me.

I wanted to devour every word, follow my parents through the days after my sister and I disappeared into Judith Goddard's life. Yet I wondered how much more of their anguish I could bear to learn about and share. The things I'd heard from Steckling left me feeling battered and threatened. A few steps farther and the quicksand of the past would be sucking at my feet.

I could stop this now. Go home to Luke. To my sister.

I dismissed the thought as soon as it formed. I was here, so close. I had to go on. I reached into my bag and pulled out the St. Cloud map I'd bought at the Twin Cities airport.

The street we'd lived on at the time of the abduction was three or four miles from police headquarters. I drove toward it. Now and then some detail jumped out at me from the ordinary streets—a dry cleaner's sign, a grocery store parking lot, an ancient gnarled oak tree—and I had the sensation that I was driving through the landscape of a half-remembered dream.

When I saw our house, I knew it. It was different, yet the same. A siding-covered house in a middle-class neighborhood, on a narrow lot of maybe a quarter acre. Smaller than my vague memory of it, but then I'd been seeing it through the distorted lens of a child's perception.

The house was still white, the shutters still black, but now the door was bright red. Someone had cared enough to bring the small front lawn to perfection, a smooth unbroken green in contrast to the half-bald yard I remembered playing on. Low dahlias bloomed in beds along the walk leading to the door. The clear bright colors made me think of Mother's gardens, and the blossoms I'd hacked to bits.

I parked at the curb across the street and sat there until a group of children in a nearby yard noticed me. When I glanced at them, I saw small bodies pulling closer together, suspicious eyes trained on me. They'd been taught to be wary of strangers.

I searched up and down the surrounding streets, first close in, then farther and farther away, my frustration growing. The playground was gone. Something had replaced it, but I couldn't be sure if it was the small fire station that looked relatively new or the block of townhouses with scrawny trees lined up in front.

I told myself it didn't matter. Seeing the playground again wasn't necessary. Yet I felt as if I'd lost a vital piece of the puzzle that was my life. Strangers had obliterated the very spot where my universe altered in an instant.

Reluctantly abandoning the search, I stopped at a fast food restaurant and went in for a cup of coffee. The hot greasy smell of fried chicken made me realize I hadn't eaten since breakfast, when Luke badgered me into finishing a bowl of cereal and a glass of juice.

Luke. How far away he seemed.

I ordered a chicken breast and a salad to go with my coffee and sat down to eat, marveling that appetite persisted in the face of calamity.

There was no point in rushing back to Minneapolis. I needed time to absorb what I'd discovered and decide what to do next. As dusk faded to night, I checked into a motel. I took a long steamy shower and pulled on my comfortably familiar terry cloth robe.

I stood at the window for a while and watched the trucks and cars that rolled past on the highway, their long beams piercing the dark and just as quickly vanishing into it again. No one, not even Luke, knew where I was.

When I felt I was ready, I drew the curtains closed. I pulled the chair from the room's small desk, sat next to the bed and opened the folder I'd placed there. I arranged the newspaper clippings in order of their dates, gradually covering the surface of the pale green bedspread.

I picked up the stories one by one and followed my parents on their odyssey through a landscape where all that was right and normal had taken on terrifying forms. Tearful pleas. Neighbors questioned. A man on the next block with a history of molesting girls, briefly under suspicion, cleared when his alibi was confirmed. Hints, then blunt statements that John Dawson was a suspect.

I lingered over the only story that was about my sister and me rather than the distress of the adults around us. Cathy and Stephanie Dawson had been inseparable. Cathy, so young herself, watched over her little sister. They were good girls, sweet and bright and lively children.

Two weeks before the abduction, Stephanie had turned three. She'd had a small party and received a bike with training wheels. Cathy's fifth birthday came four days after the girls disappeared. Her gifts remained unopened on a closet shelf.

Mother had given my sister a second birthday celebration that first year we were with her, while my real birthday was ignored and the celebration put off for months. Some memory of that had stayed with me, causing ripples of vague resentment and a sense of loss.

When I'd read all the clippings, I dug into my bag for the photocopied story about the Goddards' accident and the note on blue paper I'd taken from Mother's study. I smoothed the three sheets of paper and laid them on the bed in their proper place, at the beginning, first the note, then the accident report.

I believed I knew most of the story now. I could put it together in a way Detective Steckling never could, because he would always be missing a vital piece.

Barbara Dawson had an affair with Michael Goddard when they worked at the same law firm, he a young partner, she a secretary. She became pregnant. Her husband found out about the affair and left her.

Why hadn't she gone to Michael, why hadn't they begun a life together? Because he was already married to Judith, who was also pregnant with his child. Perhaps he rejected Barbara's claim on him, made it clear she and her child would never be part of his life.

Judith didn't know about the affair and Michael's other baby. Not yet.

John Dawson resumed his life with Barbara and the two girls, one his and one not, on condition that they move away from Minneapolis. Distraught over the hopelessness of her relationship with Michael, Barbara agreed. When she was alone with John and the girls in a new place, no work to occupy her, she became more depressed, less attentive to her children. And to her husband. The voices in my memory, the shouts, the sobbed pleas, were a legacy of their unhappiness.

I could only guess how Judith had learned about Barbara and the baby. Perhaps Barbara was unable to stay away from the man she still loved, perhaps she called him—or wrote to him.

Through all the following years, Judith had kept this single sheet of note paper, the message it bore disguised and made unintelligible to anyone who didn't know the story behind it.

I want you to know that I have no regrets. I could lie and say I'm sorry it happened because it turned my life upside down, but I'm not sorry. It was wonderful, and it gave me the one beautiful thing I've got left.

Mother's own note was still paper-clipped to it: *Explore the motivations of a woman who is capable of such a thing.*

She might have found the letter in his belongings after his death, but I had a feeling she'd found it before.

I picked up the story about the accident that killed Michael and his daughter Michelle. Witnesses said the Goddard car was moving erratically and might have been speeding before it crossed into the oncoming traffic lane.

An argument in the car? Judith unable to contain her fury at his betrayal? Michael unable to keep control of the car as he tried to defend himself, explain himself?

What had those last moments been like for the little girl, Michelle? Had she heard her parents screaming at each other, her mother raking the air with bitter accusations?

I held the paper under the bedside lamp and studied the child's smiling face, so like my sister's, and considered our entangled lives. This girl and my sister shared a father, a young man who'd been too attractive and charming for anyone's good. The girl and I shared a sister. But the lost child had no blood kinship with me.

What followed the accident? Judith knew Barbara had a living child fathered by Michael. That knowledge ignited a smoldering desire for revenge.

For the first time I willingly remembered the night Mother died. I closed my eyes, saw her tormented face, heard the ragged voice, the words tumbling out, words that made sense to me now. *That woman had no right to her! She had no right to have her child when mine was dead.*

After recovering from her injuries, Judith had driven to St. Cloud, found the Dawsons without revealing herself. Perhaps she watched us many times, always focusing on my sister. How it must have wounded her to see a little girl so much like her own, with the same glowing blond hair, the blue eyes of Michael Goddard. Alive. All her years stretching out ahead. For an instant all I felt was pity for Judith Goddard in her grief.

I remembered that last day on the playground. Thunder rumbled across the sky. Mothers hustled their children away. A woman with a long dark ponytail who had a little boy by the hand said she was sure our mom would be back in a minute.

And I, being strong and brave for my little sister, said yes, we'd be all right, Mommy would be here to get us.

Then we were alone and the storm broke, sudden and ferocious. My sister clung to me and screamed. *Mommy! Where's*

Mommy? I put my arms around her and tried to comfort her, while we stood in the deserted playground with the rain streaming over us and the trees thrashing above.

A woman with an umbrella appeared out of nowhere. "Your mother sent me, come on, get out of the rain!"

To my child's mind, the word *mother* was all that mattered. I didn't know who this woman was, but our mother had sent her, and she sheltered us with her big umbrella, protected us from the terrifying storm.

The inside of her car smelled of new leather.

When had I started to feel afraid? The woman told us she'd promised to take care of us for a while because our mother had something important to do. She stopped somewhere and bought chocolate milkshakes for us, and we drank silently, greedily. Our parents never let us have anything sugary.

Sitting in the motel outside St. Cloud, I could taste the rich sweetness of my milkshake and feel the cold liquid spilling from the straw onto my tongue. I didn't know how much time had passed before I'd awakened in a house where stacks of big brown boxes lined the walls.

I remembered my own confusion and alarm and my sister's happy acceptance of the stranger's attention. I couldn't recall the trip east, the first weeks or months in our new home. Vivid, coherent memories didn't begin until well after that, in the second or third year of school. I was Rachel Goddard then. My sister's name was Michelle. Judith Goddard was my mother.

She must have sedated me in the beginning, and she must have hypnotized me repeatedly to muddy my memories. I was a child, and my world had vanished. I believed what I could see and touch. I answered to the name I was called.

Yet somehow I'd clung to scraps of my other life. My memories were amorphous, and I doubted my own mind, telling myself I had an overactive imagination. But I held onto my real self by inventing Kathy. My imaginary friend was me, Cathy, Catherine, kept alive in the only way I could do it.

My sister hungered for the kind of attention Judith gave her. She'd needed little persuasion to become Mother's adored child. Her memories of our real parents probably faded rapidly, with some assistance from hypnosis.

I was the troublesome one, haunted all my life by faces and voices and images that made no sense to me, and always feeling left out of the love between Mother and my sister. Stephanie Dawson was the one Mother wanted, the one she could make into another Michelle Goddard. I was an innocent bystander, caught up in it all.

How could she have believed she'd never be found out? Had there come a time, after grief's sharp edges dulled and she was rational again, when she'd looked at what she'd done and known she would be discovered someday? Everything depended on her control of my memories and curiosity. For twenty-one years it had worked. I could only imagine her desperation when she realized I was breaking free of her.

I rubbed the back of my neck, stiff and painful with tension, and rose to pace between the bed and desk. Under my bare feet the short green carpet felt rough and unyielding. The room smelled of lemon polish, as our house always had after Rosario's energetic attacks on the furniture.

Mother had given us a good life, in so many ways. We'd been cared for, catered to, encouraged, supported. We were the center of her existence. No professional duty was more important than our piano recitals, class plays, parent-teacher conferences. She took us everywhere from art galleries to amusement parks. She had no private life that didn't include us.

But she wasn't our mother. She abducted us from a playground and took us halfway across the country and twisted our minds and lied to us and cut us off from our family. Her actions had led directly to my real father's suicide. She might have played a part in the deaths of her own husband and child, months before the abduction. In the end her crime had driven her to turn a knife on me, and then herself.

So much loss, such a horrifying waste. I wished I could hate her, with a sharp cleansing wrath. I wished I could crush the pity I felt for this woman who tried to fill her empty heart and life with her husband's other child.

⟨⟩⟨⟩⟨⟩

I called Luke and talked for an hour, telling him everything I'd learned and put together.

"What now?" he asked when I finished.

"I'm going to see her."

"Oh, God, Rachel, I hate the thought of you going through this alone. Why don't I fly out? Tomorrow's Saturday, I don't have to worry about appointments—"

"No, don't. I need to do this by myself." But I had to smile at his protectiveness. "Thanks for wanting to help, but I'll be fine."

"Promise you'll come back to me soon?"

"I'll come back to you soon."

"I love you," he said. "Whoever you are."

I laughed, even though tears had sprung to my eyes. "I love you too," I said for the first time, and meant it.

⟨⟩⟨⟩⟨⟩

I wouldn't think about how I was going to tell her who I was. I wouldn't think about my sister's part in this, or about our other sister and brother, our grandparents and aunts and uncles, a whole large family that I sensed lurking in the background of my memory. All I cared about now was seeing the woman who had given birth to me.

My fingers shook as I put through the call to the number Steckling had given me. A woman's husky voice answered on the second ring, and I was momentarily unable to speak.

"Hello?" she said again.

Somehow I got the words out. "May I speak to Barbara Olsson, please?"

"Speaking."

"This—" I cleared my throat. "My name is Rachel Campbell—"

"Oh, right." Her voice lifted, became warm and friendly. "Jack Steckling called and said you'd be getting in touch. I'd be glad to talk to you. When do you want to come over?"

My throat threatened to close off speech. The voice that came out sounded high and very young, not like my own. "Tomorrow morning? Around eleven? Would that be okay?"

"Sure. Fine. I'll give you directions. Got a pencil and paper?"

A minute later I put down the receiver, leaned my face into my hands and let the tears come.

Chapter Twenty-seven

I thought I wouldn't sleep, but I did, heavily and blessedly free of dreams. When I woke to the buzz of my travel alarm, I didn't know at first where I was. I lay staring at the sliver of dawn between the curtains, remembering.

Today I would see my real mother for the first time in twenty-one years.

I had two houses to find when I got to Minneapolis. The first was in a neighborhood where homes were far enough apart to allow privacy, and each had an attached garage and a large lawn. Mature oaks and maples, already changing into their gaudy fall costumes, lined the broad streets with orange, gold and green. The house that had belonged to Michael and Judith Goddard at the time of his death was white with dark blue roof shingles, colonial blue front door and shutters.

It looked familiar only because I'd seen it in the photos hidden in Mother's study. I doubted I'd ever had a fully conscious look at the exterior during the time—how long? a day or two at the most?—before Judith took us east.

I remembered being wrapped in a big soft robe, and seeing stacks of boxes, little else.

The door opened and a middle-aged man in tee shirt and chinos ambled out, yawning and rubbing at his unshaven face, to pluck the rolled newspaper from the driveway. He glanced at me where I'd stopped in the middle of the quiet street. I drove on. It was Saturday, and all along the block papers still lay on driveways and lawns, draperies were still drawn against the morning sun.

Barbara Dawson, now Barbara Olsson, lived several miles away, in a smaller two-story house with faded green shutters. Mounds of marigolds and blue petunias bloomed profusely in flower beds skirting the foundation shrubs.

An old blue car and a red mini-van sat on the asphalt driveway. Who else was at home? Oh, God, would I have to encounter the whole family?

I parked across the street and sat taking deep breaths. My heart would not slow down. It was almost eleven, the time we'd agreed on, but I couldn't make myself get out and walk across the street. And I couldn't drive away. Paralyzed by indecision, I sat watching the house.

After a few minutes a boy drove up the street in a battered green car, pulled to a stop in front of the house and tooted his horn. In response the front door opened and a teenage girl bounded out, long red hair swinging around her face and shimmering in the sun. She wore jeans and a yellow sweatshirt, and had a big blue canvas bag slung over one shoulder.

Caroline? My other sister.

She turned and looked back at the door, throwing up her arms in a gesture that could only mean impatience.

I shifted my gaze to the doorway, and gasped as a shock went through me. For a moment I thought I was seeing Mother, Judith, standing there. The woman, wearing black slacks and a blue blouse, was tall and slender. Straight auburn hair fell to her shoulders. She looked like Judith. And she looked like me.

She would recognize me. She would see my face and know me in an instant. Any choices I had would vanish as everything spun out of control. I gripped the steering wheel with one hand, fumbling the keys back into the ignition with the other.

Then I let my hands drop. Of course she wouldn't recognize me. She wouldn't know anything unless I told her. I'd come this far. I couldn't leave now.

She talked to her teenage daughter, using the same gesture the girl had, hands flung out, palms up, fingers splayed. Something made the girl laugh, run to the door and plant a quick kiss on her mother's cheek.

I watched them, spellbound. Barbara Dawson Olsson smiled at her daughter, waved to her retreating back. My attention turned to the girl again. I tried to absorb every detail of her appearance and demeanor as she moved to the car with a bouncy step, flung open the passenger door, jumped into the seat beside the boy and greeted him with a flash of a grin. A happy girl, filled with the simple joy of being alive on a bright September morning.

What would she think of me, a dead half-sister suddenly claiming a place in her life?

After the girl and boy drove away, I looked back at the house and saw Barbara still in the doorway, watching me. Over the distance, our eyes met.

Now. It was time, whether I was ready or not. Fighting down panic, I opened the car door and stepped out. She expected a stranger. I would be that stranger. I would play the part until I knew enough to make a decision.

As I crossed the street, my bag slung over my shoulder just as Caroline had carried hers, Barbara came forward onto the lawn. She was smiling.

"Are you Rachel?" she asked in the husky voice I'd heard on the phone last night. She offered a hand.

"Yes, I'm Rachel Campbell." My voice rose a note higher than normal. "Thank you for letting me come."

I reached out and touched my mother, slipped my hand into hers, felt a gentle warm pressure before she broke the contact. A wash of regret made me realize I'd expected to feel an immediate connection. But she was just a middle-aged woman, no one I knew.

Up close I could never have mistaken her for Judith. Her face, beginning its surrender to the downward tug of age, was fuller, without Judith's high cheekbones, and her eyes were a clear blue. But there were striking similarities between the two women's coloring and lithe figures. Obviously Michael Goddard had liked this type.

A shadow suddenly dimmed her eyes, and I felt the clutch of alarm. *She does recognize me.* Then she brightened again and widened her smile.

"Another redhead," she said. "Did you see my daughter leaving just now? Red hair runs in our family. My grandfather, my father, my brothers and me."

I could only smile and nod. In my mind rose a vague image of a man with red hair who hoisted both my sister and me onto his knees, so that our feet dangled together. Our grandfather, an uncle?

Thrown off-balance by this slice of memory, I barely heard Barbara's remarks about the beautiful autumn weather, the warm sunshine. I followed her up two broad concrete steps, across a black rubber welcome mat, and into the house.

"Have a seat," she said. "I just made a fresh pot of coffee for us. I'll be right back."

She vanished through a doorway, leaving me in a living room with periwinkle blue walls and carpet. The fireplace, its mantel painted white to match the rest of the woodwork, was the focal point, with the flowered chintz sofa and chairs angled in front of it. A pleasant but bland space, utterly lacking the individuality and elegance of Judith's living room.

I shook my head. *Don't think about Mother.*

Listening, I tried to determine whether anyone else was in the house. The only sounds I heard were faint clinks, no doubt Barbara gathering things in the kitchen. We were probably alone, thank God.

I studied the framed photographs that crowded the mantel. Caroline with a flute in her hands. A blond boy who must be Mark, my half-brother, holding a soccer ball and wearing a tee shirt with Little Devils printed on it. In other pictures they posed in dress-up clothes, or romped in deep snow with a mixed breed dog that resembled an Irish setter. At the end of the row of photos sat a large one of Barbara herself with a blond man, arm in arm, smiling.

This was her second life. Where in these captured moments of family happiness did Michelle and I belong?

I was startled by Barbara's sudden presence at my side, a touch on my elbow and a drift of floral perfume.

"That's my husband Mark with me," she said, nodding at the photo. "On our last anniversary. And that's Mark Junior." She gestured at the boy with the soccer ball. "I'd introduce you, but they're both off fishing with some of my husband's buddies. That's our daughter Caroline, you saw her."

My smile felt stiff. "You have a beautiful family."

"Oh, don't I?" she said, laughing with pleasure. "I'm so blessed. I thank God every day."

A cold fear traveled down my spine and lodged in the pit of my stomach, a dread of revealing myself and seeing not joy but consternation in my mother's face.

Maintaining an outward calm that had nothing to do with what I felt, I sat on the sofa as she indicated. She settled into a chair across from me. On the table between us she'd placed a painted wooden tray with a glass coffee pot and two mugs.

"Cream and sugar?" She lifted the coffee pot, filled a mug. "Just black?" She handed me the cup. "Tell me about this paper you're writing."

Avoiding her eyes, I gave her my rehearsed story.

She nodded and asked several questions. Like Steckling, she kept glancing at my scarred hand but didn't mention it.

To cut her questions short, I said, "Would you mind if I use a tape recorder?"

"No, of course not."

I removed it from my bag.

I set the recorder on the table, at the same time watching her pour cream from a tiny blue pitcher into her coffee mug. Her fingers were long and slender, the nails painted red. I could feel my real mother's hands working with my hair, weaving long strands into a braid. But the memory refused to mesh with the reality of the stranger across from me.

With a spark of alarm I realized she was studying my face, her eyes slightly narrowed. I said quickly, "Thanks again for seeing me. It can't be pleasant to talk about all this."

"I don't mind," she said, dropping her gaze to her cup. A barely visible wisp of steam danced above the coffee. "It's easier now than it used to be."

I sipped strong black coffee from my own mug, using the moment to renew my courage. "What were your little girls like?"

Her smile was soft, wistful. "They were great kids. Smart, both of them. Cathy was a real tomboy, but Stephie was turning out to be a little lady. She was very feminine, even at that age." Barbara stared into space and murmured, "Great kids."

"It must have been devastating to lose both of them at the same time." I needed to hear her say how much she'd missed us, how much she still loved us, that we were irreplaceable.

All she said was, "Yes. It was." She sipped her coffee.

I waited, but she said nothing more. "Detective Steckling told me a little about how it happened—"

"I can just imagine what he told you," she broke in. She leaned forward and plopped her mug onto the tray. Milky brown liquid slopped out and splashed the side of the coffee pot. "That's one reason I wanted to talk to you, to set the record straight after you heard the police version."

"Oh? How do you mean?"

"What happened to my girls happened because the world's full of loonies, just waiting for the chance to do something crazy. Their father had nothing to do with it, I can tell you that for damn sure."

She gave her head an angry shake. The shining auburn hair slid against her cheeks.

"I appreciate how hard Jack Steckling worked on this case," she said. "I know he was just doing his job. But he was wrong, putting so much pressure on my husband. John loved our girls more than anything in the world. We had a happy family."

A string of angry words popped like gunfire in my memory. *He doesn't want you...Hate you!...Slut...Hate you, hate you, hate you!* Then the voices faded and I saw my father smiling down at me. I'd felt safe with my hand in his, walking down a sunny street, escaping briefly from the misery of our home. Barbara Olsson couldn't possibly believe what she said. She was giving me the version invented for strangers.

Groping among my jumbled emotions and roiling thoughts, I tried to find the right response, the logical next question for an outsider to ask. "Was your husband's death an accident, or..." I trailed off, leaving the rest for her to fill in.

She gripped the chair arms, her body rigid. "I guess Steckling told you it was suicide. Well, it wasn't. You can ask the insurance company. They sure as hell wouldn't have paid out a claim if it was suicide. The police said he felt guilty because he hurt the girls, but that's just crazy. I don't believe for one minute he had anything to do with it. But it's convenient for the police to blame him, so they don't have to admit they never caught the person that did it."

I knew I was venturing onto dangerous ground, but I couldn't stop myself from asking, "Do you have any idea who could have taken them? Maybe somebody with a grudge against you?"

"No. I'm sure it was a stranger." She drew a deep breath and let it out, then ran both hands up under her heavy hair and lifted it off her collar. "God knows the police investigated everybody that ever came into contact with the girls. Relatives, neighbors, friends. People started hating us for it. But it wasn't anybody we knew. I never thought it was. Some nut saw two pretty little girls, and he took them. Just took them."

Memory threatened to overwhelm me, claim my mind and senses. I couldn't let it. I had to stay in control. "You must have thought a lot about what might have happened to them."

"Oh, God," she said, and brought a hand up to her mouth.

With a wrench of guilt I watched tears fill her eyes. I had brought her to the brink of crying, forced her back into the midst of that agony.

"I had nightmares for years," she said after a moment. "I imagined every horrible thing that could have happened." She expelled a sharp breath. "It was like poison in my head, I couldn't get rid of it for a minute. It didn't get better till I had Caroline. I had to put all my energy into taking care of her."

So you shut us out of your mind and moved on.

Even as I was thinking this, she said, "You don't forget two children, though. You don't ever stop thinking about them."

I waited through a moment of silence, then made myself ask, "Do you think they're still alive?"

"Oh, no. No, I don't. They were probably murdered pretty soon after they were taken. I hope so, anyway. I mean I hope they didn't suffer long. Steckling thinks their bodies'll be found someday. Their skeletons. And the police might be able to tell how they died."

As I listened to her I almost believed it was possible, that our childhood bodies were in fact buried in some remote spot, waiting to be discovered.

"I've accepted that they're dead," she went on, "but you know, every now and then I'll see a pretty girl who's about the right age, and I'll think, *That could be Stephanie,* or *That could be Cathy.*" With a fingertip she wiped a single tear from under her right eye. Then she gave a choked little laugh. "I even thought that when I saw you. My Cathy could've grown up to look a little like you."

Her eyes met mine for a moment before I averted my gaze. From the street I heard the shouts of children, free from school on a Saturday morning.

Tell her. She has a right to know. Tell her now. I pushed myself to the verge of spilling it out, but pulled back when she spoke again.

"I really hope their bodies aren't ever found. I don't want to know how they died. I want to remember them the way they were. Happy and laughing all the time. I just want to remember all the good times our little family had together."

She believed what she was saying. *No,* I wanted to protest. *It wasn't like that.* We'd been sad and scared, we'd lived in a house of cutting words and anguished silences. I knew the truth. I remembered.

I pushed the question out of my mouth. "Do you feel guilty about what happened?"

"Guilty?" She gave a harsh laugh. "Oh, plenty of people tried to make me feel like it was all my fault. And I did feel guilty for a while. It's only natural. But the only person that's guilty is the one that took my daughters." Her expression hardened with hatred. "I'd like to find the monster that did it and make them suffer. There's no punishment bad enough."

I saw Mother lying in her own blood on the bathroom floor, my hand over the gash in her throat, blood spurting through my fingers. Hadn't that been punishment enough?

A telephone rang in another room. Barbara started. "Oh. Excuse me. I'll be right back."

I nodded, the image of Judith Goddard's last moments still in my mind. Yes, her crime was monstrous, indefensible. Why then did I want to defend her, to deny that she was wholly to blame? Barbara Dawson and Michael Goddard's infidelity had destroyed Judith's world and John Dawson's world. And it was Barbara, careless and selfish, who'd left my sister and me alone on that playground to be stolen and who now seemed unable to acknowledge any responsibility.

My gaze traveled along the row of photos on the mantel. What would happen to all of us if the whole wretched story came out? Once Barbara and her family knew, it couldn't be kept secret. Sooner or later it would be big news, a morbidly fascinating human drama that would capture the imaginations of strangers. *People Magazine* and *Vanity Fair* reporters would show up at our doors. Someone would write a true crime book about us. Our lives, even Mark's and Caroline's, would be exposed and picked over.

Judith would be painted as a madwoman, and if Michelle and I insisted that in many ways she had given us a good life, we'd be pitied as warped, brainwashed, too damaged by trauma to know what we were saying.

And what would become of my sister? Michelle, Stephanie. She was only starting the journey that I'd begun months before. She would have no desire to see Barbara Olsson, I was sure of that, and she wasn't strong enough yet to face the truth about her role at the center of this tragedy.

The fragrance of perfume wafted into the room. "That was my husband," Barbara said as she sat down. "Calling from the fishing lodge. He always gets worried when he knows I'm going to be talking about Cathy and Stephie."

"Oh?"

"Yeah, he hates the publicity, he thinks it's bad for our kids. And he's right. They hate it too, it really upsets them. I promised them I wouldn't do any more interviews, but you're not the press, this isn't going to be public." She sighed. "I think this'll be the last time I talk about it, though. It's time to let it be."

"Thank you for seeing me, Mrs. Olsson." I switched off the recorder and stuffed it into my bag. "I really have to leave if I'm going to catch my flight. "

She rose with me. "I hope I've been some help with your paper."

"Oh, you have. More than I can tell you."

"Well, then. It was nice meeting you. Have a good flight."

With a quick smile I left her, strode briskly down the driveway and across the street. When I was in the car, she waved at me from the steps. I waved back, then sat watching as she disappeared inside and the door closed.

It was over. I thought of little Kristin Coleman as I'd seen her months before on that rainy day, crying because her dog was hurt and her mother had vanished. It seemed pointless now to wonder what our lives would have been like if that child's tears hadn't brought a buried memory to the surface. It had happened. Mother was dead, and I'd found the truth I was searching for. It would end here.

Judith had lived behind a fragile mask, dependent on my damaged memory to keep her secret. Now my knowledge would act as guardian.

I turned the key in the ignition. I would drive to the airport, get on the next available flight, and go home to Luke and to a shattered sister who needed me.

I wasn't Cathy Dawson anymore, and never would be again.
I was Rachel.
Judith Goddard's daughter.

To receive a free catalog of Poisoned Pen Press titles, please contact us in one of the following ways:

Phone: 1-800-421-3976
Facsimile: 1-480-949-1707
E-mail: info@poisonedpenpress.com
Website: www.poisonedpenpress.com

Poisoned Pen Press
6962 E. First Ave. Ste. 103
Scottsdale, AZ 85251

CPSIA information can be obtained at www.ICGtesting.com
Printed in the USA
BVOW010926281112

306720BV00004B/22/P